T0145969

The Sign of Silence

The Sign of Silence

William Le Queux

MINT EDITIONS

The Sign of Silence was first published in 1915.

This edition published by Mint Editions 2021.

ISBN 9781513280851 | E-ISBN 9781513285870

Published by Mint Editions®

 MINT
EDITIONS

minteditionbooks.com

Publishing Director: Jennifer Newens
Design & Production: Rachel Lopez Metzger
Project Manager: Micaela Clark
Typesetting: Westchester Publishing Services

Contents

I

Introduces a Gentleman

T hen it's an entire mystery?"

"Yes, Phrida."

"But it's astounding! It really seems so utterly impossible," declared my well-beloved, amazed at what I had just related.

"I've simply stated hard facts."

"But there's been nothing about this affair in the papers."

"For certain reasons the authorities are not exactly anxious for any publicity. It is a very puzzling problem, and they do not care to own themselves baffled," I replied.

"Really, it's the most extraordinary story of London life that I've ever heard," Phrida Shand declared, leaning forward in her chair, clasping her small white hands as, with her elbows upon the *table-à-deux*, she looked at me with her wondrous dark eyes across the bowl of red tulips between us.

We were lunching together at the Berkeley, in Piccadilly, one January day last year, and had just arrived at the dessert.

"The whole thing is quite bewildering, Teddy—an utter enigma," she exclaimed in a low, rather strained voice, her pretty, pointed chin resting upon the back of her hand as she gazed upon me from beneath those long, curved lashes.

"I quite agree," was my answer. "The police are mystified, and so am I. Sir Digby Kemsley is my friend, you know."

"I remember," she said. "You once introduced me—at the opening of the Motor Show at Olympia, I believe. A very brilliant and famous man, isn't he?"

"Rather! A famous engineer. He made the new railway across the Andes, and possesses huge rubber interests in Peru. His name, both in Seina and Valparaiso, is one to conjure with," was my reply; "but—"

"But what?" queried my well-beloved.

"Well, there's one fact which greatly increases the mystery—a fact which is yet to be told."

"What's that?" she asked eagerly.

I hesitated.

"Well, I've been making inquiries this morning," I replied with some reluctance, "and I learn to my blank amazement that there is no such person as my friend."

"No such person!" she echoed, staring at me, her lips parted. Being seated in a corner, no one could overhear our conversation. "I don't follow you!"

"Well, Sir Digby died somewhere in South America about a year ago," was my quiet response.

"What? Was your friend a fraud, eh?"

"Apparently so. And yet, if he was, he must have been a man of marvellous cunning and subterfuge," I said. "He was most popular at the club, known at the Ritz and the Savoy, and other places about town."

"He struck me as a man of great refinement—a gentleman, in fact," Phrida said. "I recollect him perfectly: tall, rather thin, with a pointed, grey beard, a long, oval face, and thinnish, grey hair. A very lithe, erect man, whose polite, elegant manner was that of a diplomat, and in whose dark eyes was an expression of constant merriment and good humour. He spoke with a slight accent—Scotch, isn't it?"

"Exactly. You remember him perfectly, dear. A most excellent description," I said; "and that same description has been circulated this morning to every police office throughout the United Kingdom, as well as to the prefectures of police in all the European capitals. All the ports are being watched, as it is expected he may make his way abroad."

"But what do the authorities suspect?" asked Phrida, with a serious look.

"Ah, that's just it! They haven't yet decided what to suspect."

I looked across at her and thought, though slightly more pale than usual, she had never appeared more charming.

Sweet-faced, slim, with a soft, sibilant voice, and dainty to her finger-tips, she did not look more than nineteen, though her age was twenty-four. How shall I describe her save to say that her oval, well-defined features were perfect, her dark, arched brows gave piquancy to a countenance that was remarked wherever she went, a merry face, with a touch of impudence in her smile—the face of an essentially London girl.

Only daughter of my father's late partner, James Shand, we had been friends from childhood, and our friendship had, three years ago, blossomed into a deep and mutual affection. Born and bred in Kensington, she cared little for country life. She loved her London,

WILLIAM LE QUEUX

its throbbing streets, its life and movement, its concerts, its bright restaurants, and, most of all, its theatres—for she was an ardent playgoer.

My father, Edward Royle, was head of the firm of well-known chemical manufacturers, Messrs. Royle and Shand, whose works were a feature of the river landscape close to Greenwich, and whose offices were in St. Mary Axe. He had died two years before, pre-deceasing his partner by a year. The business—a big one, for we were the largest chemical manufacturers in England—had been left solely in my hands. Shand's widow still lived with Phrida in Cromwell Road, drawing from it an income of seven thousand pounds yearly.

As for myself, I was a bachelor, aged thirty-two, and if golf be a vice I was greatly addicted to it. I occupied a cosy set of chambers, half-way up Albemarle Street, and am thankful to say that in consequence of my father's business acumen, my balance at my bankers was increasing annually. At the works at Greenwich nearly two thousand hands were employed, and it had always been the firm's proud boast that they laboured under the most healthy conditions possible to secure in the manufacture of chemicals.

My father, upon his deathbed, had held my hand and expressed to me his profoundest satisfaction at my engagement with the daughter of his partner, and almost with his last breath had pronounced a blessing upon our union.

Yes, I loved Phrida—loved her with all my heart and all my soul. She was mine—mine for ever.

Yet, as I sat at that little table in the white-enamelled restaurant gazing at her across the bowl of tulips, I felt a strange, a very curious misgiving, an extraordinary misty suspicion, for which I could not in the least account.

I experienced a strange intuition of doubt and vague uncertainty.

The facts we had just been discussing were, to say the least, amazing.

Only the Metropolitan Police and myself were aware of the astounding discovery which had been made that morning—a discovery of which the ever-vigilant London evening newspapers had as yet no inkling.

The affair was being carefully hushed up. In certain quarters—high official quarters, I believe—a flutter of excitement had been caused at noon, when it had become known that a mystery had occurred, one which at the outset New Scotland Yard had acknowledged itself utterly without a clue.

About the affair there was nothing usual, nothing commonplace. The murder mysteries of London always form exciting reading, for it is surely the easiest work of the practised journalist to put forward from day to day fresh clues and exciting propositions.

The present case, however, was an entirely fresh and unheard-of mystery, one such as London had never before known.

In the whole annals of Scotland Yard no case presenting such unusual features had previously been reported.

"Have you no theory as to what really occurred?" Phrida asked slowly, after a very long and pensive silence.

"None whatever, dear," I replied.

What theory could I form? Aye, what indeed?

In order that the exact truth should be made entirely plain to the reader and the mystery viewed in all its phases, it will be best for me to briefly record the main facts prior to entering upon any detail.

The following were the circumstances exactly as I knew them.

At twenty-five minutes to ten on the previous night—the night of January the sixth—I was at home in Albemarle Street, writing letters. Haines, my man, had gone out, and I was alone, when the telephone bell rang. Taking up the receiver I heard the cheery voice of Sir Digby Kemsley asking what I was doing. My prompt reply was that I was staying at home that night, whereupon his voice changed and he asked me in great earnestness to come over to his flat in Harrington Gardens, South Kensington, at eleven o'clock.

"And look here," he added in a confidential tone, "the outside door will be closed at half-past ten and the porter off duty. I'll go down just before eleven and leave the door ajar. Don't let anyone see you come in. Be extremely careful. I have reasons I'll explain afterwards."

"Right," I replied, and shut off.

His request seemed just a little curious. It struck me that he perhaps wished to consult with me over some private matter, as he had done once before. Therefore, just before eleven I hailed a taxi in Piccadilly and drove westward past Gloucester Road Station, and into the quiet, eminently select neighbourhood where my friend lived.

At eleven o'clock Harrington Gardens—that long thoroughfare of big rather gloomy houses, most of them residences of City merchants, or town houses or flats of people who have seats in the country—was as silent as the grave, and my taxi awoke its echoes until, about half way up, I stopped the man, alighted, and paid him off.

Then, after walking a couple of hundred yards, I found the door ajar and slipped into the hall unobserved.

Ascending the wide carpeted steps to the second floor, the door of the flat was opened noiselessly by the owner himself, and a few seconds later I found myself seated before a big fire in his snug sitting-room.

My friend's face was grey and entirely changed, yet his manner was still as polished, cheery, and buoyant as ever.

The flat—quite a small one, though very expensive as he had once remarked to me—was furnished throughout with elegance and taste. Upon its walls everywhere hung curios and savage arms, which he had brought from various parts of the world. The drawing-room was furnished entirely in Arab style, with cedar-wood screens, semi-circular arches, low, soft divans and silken rugs, which he had bought in Egypt, while, in contrast, the little den in which we were sitting at that moment was panelled in white with an old-rose carpet, rendering it essentially bright and modern.

The tall, grey-bearded, elegant man handed me a box of Perfectos Finos, from which we selected, and then, throwing myself into a chair, I slowly lit up.

His back was turned from me at the moment, as he leaned over the writing-table apparently gathering up some papers which he did not desire that I should see. He was facing a circular mirror on the wall, and in it I could see his countenance reflected. The expression upon his face—cold, cynical, sinister—startled me. He placed the papers in a drawer and locked it with a key upon his chain.

"Well?" I asked. "Why all this confounded mystery, Digby?"

He turned upon me quickly, his long face usually so full of merriment, grey and drawn. I saw instantly that something very serious was amiss.

"I—I want to ask your advice, Royle," he replied in a hard voice scarce above a whisper. Walking to the pretty rug of old-rose and pale green silk spread before the fire he stood upon it, facing me. "And—well, truth to tell, I don't want it to be known that you've been here to-night, old fellow."

"Why?"

"For certain private reasons—very strong reasons."

"As you wish, my dear chap," was my response, as I drew at his perfect cigar.

Then he looked me straight in the face and said: "My motive in asking you here to-night, Royle, is to beg of you to extend your valued friendship to me at a moment which is the greatest crisis of my career. The fact is, I've played the game of life falsely, and the truth must out, unless—unless you will consent to save me."

"I don't follow you," I said, staring at him. "What in heaven's name do you mean?"

"My dear boy, I'll put my cards down on the table at once," he said in a slow, deep tone. "Let's see—we've known each other for nearly a year. You have been my best friend, entirely devoted to my interests—a staunch friend, better than whom no man could ever desire. In return I've lied to you, led you to believe that I am what I am not. Why? Because—well, I suppose I'm no different to any other man—or woman for the matter of that—I have a skeleton in my cupboard—a grim skeleton, my dear Royle. One which I've always striven to hide—until to-night," he added with emotion.

"But that hardly interferes with our friendship, does it? We all of us have our private affairs, both of business and of heart," I said.

"The heart," he echoed bitterly. "Ah! yes—the heart. You, my dear boy, are a man of the world. You understand life. You are never narrow-minded—eh?" he asked, advancing a step nearer to me.

"I hope not," I said. "At any rate, I've always been your friend, ever since our first meeting on the steamer on the Lake of Garda, last February."

The eminent engineer rolled his cigar between his fingers, and calmly contemplated it in silence.

Then, quite abruptly, he exclaimed:

"Royle, my present misfortune is due to a woman."

"Ah!" I sighed. "A woman! Always a woman in such cases! Well?"

"Mind you, I don't blame her in the least," he went on quickly, "I—I was hot-tempered, and I miscalculated her power. We quarrelled, and—and she, though so young, refined and pretty, has arisen to crush me."

"Anyone I know?"

"No. I think not," was his slow reply, his dark eyes gazing full into mine as he still stood astride upon the hearthrug.

Then he fidgeted uneasily, stroked his well-clipped grey beard with his strong, bronzed hand, and strode across the room and back again.

"Look here, Royle," he exclaimed at last. "You're my friend, so I may as well speak straight out. Will you help me?"

"Certainly—if I can."

"I'm in a hole—a confounded hole. I've been worried ever since I got back from Egypt just before Christmas. Only you can save me."

"Me! Why?"

"I want you to remain my friend; to still believe in me, when—well—when I've gone under," he answered brokenly, his brows contracting as he spoke.

"I don't understand you."

"Then I'll speak more plainly. To-night is the last time we shall meet. I've played the game, I tell you—and I've lost!"

"You seem horribly hipped about something to-night, my dear fellow!" I exclaimed in wonder at his strange words. In all my circle of friends no man was more level-headed than Sir Digby Kemsley.

"Yes, I'm not quite myself. Perhaps you wouldn't be, Royle, in the same circumstances." Halting, he stood erect with his hands clasped behind his back. Even then, at that moment of despair, he presented the fine figure of a man in his well-cut dinner clothes and the single ruby in his piqué shirt-front. "I want to entrust a secret to you—a great secret," he went on a few seconds later. "I tell you that to-night is the last occasion we shall ever meet, but I beg—may I implore you to judge me with leniency, to form no unjust conclusions, and when you remember me to regard my memory as that of a man who was not a rogue, but a victim of untoward circumstances."

"Really, my dear fellow," I said, "you speak in enigmas. What do you mean—you intend what?"

"That matters nothing to you, Royle," was his hoarse reply. "I merely ask for your continued friendship. I ask that you will treat my successor here in the exact manner in which you have treated me—that you will become his firm friend—and that you will perform for me one great and most important service."

"Your successor! Who will succeed you? You have no son!"

"No, I have no male relation whatever," he replied. "But we were speaking of the favour I am begging of you to perform for me. On the fourteenth of January I shall not be here, but it is highly necessary that on that evening, at eight o'clock, a secret message should be delivered into the hands of a certain lady—a message from myself. Will you do it?"

"Certainly. Are you going abroad again?"

"I—well, I can hardly tell. I may be dead by then—who knows?" And he smiled grimly.

He returned to his writing-table, unlocked a drawer, and took therefrom a letter which was carefully sealed with black wax.

"Now, listen," he said, holding the letter in his fingers; "on the night of the fourteenth, just at eight o'clock precisely, go to the Piccadilly tube station, stand at the telephone box numbered four on the Haymarket side, when a lady in black will approach you and ask news of me. In response you will give her this note. But there is a further condition: you may be watched and recognised, therefore be extremely careful that you are not followed on that day, and, above all, adopt some effective disguise. Go there dressed as a working-man, I would suggest."

"That request, Kemsley, is certainly a very queer one," I remarked. "Is she *the* lady?"

He smiled, and I took that as an affirmative.

"You say she'll be dressed in black. Lots of ladies dress in black. I might mistake her."

"Not very likely. I forgot to tell you that she will wear a small spray of mimosa."

"Ah, that shows originality," I remarked. "Mimosa is not often worn on the person."

"It will serve as a distinguishing mark." Then, after a pause, he added, handing me the letter: "There is one further request I want to make—or, at least, I want you to give me your promise, Royle. I ask you to make a solemn vow to me that if any suspicion arises within your mind, that you will believe nothing without absolute and decisive proof. I mean that you will not misjudge her."

"I certainly will not."

"Your hand upon it?"

I put forth my hand and, gripping his warmly, gave him my word of honour.

"I hope you will never regret this, Royle," he said in an earnest tone.

"We are friends," I remarked simply.

"And I trust, Royle, you will never regret the responsibility which you have accepted on my behalf," he said in a deep, hard voice—the voice of a desperate man. "Remember to treat my successor exactly as you have treated me. Be his best friend, as he will be yours. You will be astonished, amazed, mystified, no doubt, at the events which must, alas! inevitably occur. But it is not my fault, Royle, believe me," he declared with solemn emphasis. "It is, alas! my misfortune!"

II

The Scent

A fter giving me the letter, and receiving my assurance that it would be safely delivered, Sir Digby's spirits seemed somewhat to revive. He chatted in his old, good-humoured style, drank a whisky and soda, and, just before one o'clock, let me out, urging me to descend the stairs noiselessly lest the hall-porter should know that he had had a visitor.

Time after time I had questioned him regarding his strange reference to his successor, but to all my queries he was entirely dumb. He had, I recollected, never been the same since his return from a flying visit to Egypt.

"The future will, no doubt, astound you, but I know, Royle, that you are a man of honour and of your word, and that you will keep your promise at all hazards," was all he would reply.

The secrecy with which I had entered and left caused me considerable curiosity. Kemsley was one of those free, bluff, open-hearted, open-handed, men. He was never secretive, never elusive. I could only account for his curious, mystifying actions by the fact that the reputation of a woman was at stake—that he was acting for her protection.

And I was to meet that woman face to face in eight days' time!

As I walked towards Gloucester Road Station—where I hoped to find a taxi—all was silence. At that hour the streets of South Kensington are as deserted as a graveyard, and as I bent towards the cutting wind from the east, I wondered who could be the mysterious woman who had broken up my dear friend's future plans. Yet he bore her no malice. Some men's temperaments are really curious.

Beneath a street-lamp I paused and looked at the superscription upon the envelope. It ran:

"For E. P. K."

The initial K! Was the lady Digby's wife? That was the suspicion which at once fell upon me, and by which I became convinced.

At half-past one o'clock I let myself into my own flat in Albemarle Street. The faithful Haines, who had been a marine wardroom servant in the navy before entering my employ, was awaiting me.

"The telephone bell rang ten minutes ago, sir," he said. "Sir Digby Kemsley wishes to speak to you."

"Very well!" I replied. "You can go to bed."

The man placed my tray with whisky and soda upon the little table near my chair, as was his habit, and, wishing me good-night, retired.

I went to the telephone, and asked for Digby's number.

After a few seconds a voice, which at first I failed to recognise, replied to mine:

"I say, Royle; I'm so sorry to disturb you, old chap, but could you possibly come back here at once?"

"What?" I asked, very surprised. "Is it so very important? Can't it wait till to-morrow?"

"No, unfortunately it can't. It's most imperative that I should see you. Something has happened. Do come!" he begged. "But don't attract attention—you understand!"

"Something happened!" I echoed. "What?"

"That woman. Come at once—do, there's a good fellow. Will you— for my sake and hers?"

The mention of the woman decided me, so I replied "All right!" and hung up the receiver.

Within half an hour I alighted in Courtfield Gardens and walked up Harrington Gardens to the door of my friend's house, which I saw was already ajar in anticipation of my arrival.

Closing the door noiselessly, in order not to attract the attention of the alert porter who lived in the basement, I crept up the carpeted stairs to the door of the flat, which I found also ajar.

Having closed the door, I slipped into the hall and made my way to the warm, cosy room I had left earlier that night.

The door was closed, and without ceremony I turned the handle.

I threw it open laughingly in order to surprise my friend, but next instant halted in amazement upon the threshold.

I stood there breathless, staring in speechless wonder, and drawing back.

"I'm really very sorry!" I exclaimed. "I thought Sir Digby was here!"

The man who had risen from his chair and bowed when I opened the door was about the same build, but, apparently, a trifle younger. He had iron-grey hair and a pointed beard, but his face was more triangular, with higher cheek-bones, and eyes more brilliant and deeper set.

His thin countenance relaxed into a pleasant smile as he replied in a calm, suave voice:

"I am Sir Digby Kemsley, and you—I believe—are Mr. Edward Royle—my friend—my very intimate friend—are you not?"

"You!" I gasped, staring at him.

And then, for several seconds I failed to articulate any further words. The imposture was so utterly barefaced.

"You are not Sir Digby Kemsley," I went on angrily at last. "What trick is this?"

"No trick whatever, my dear Royle," was the man's quiet reply as he stood upon the hearthrug in the same position in which my friend had stood an hour before. "I tell you that my name is Kemsley—Sir Digby Kemsley."

"Then you assert that this flat is yours?"

"Most certainly I do."

"Bosh! How can you expect me to believe such a transparent tale?" I cried impatiently. "Where is my friend?"

"I am your friend, my dear Royle!" he laughed.

"You're not."

"But did you not, only an hour ago, promise him to treat his successor in the same manner in which you had treated himself?" the man asked very slowly, his high, deep-set eyes fixed upon me with a crafty, almost snake-like expression, an expression that was distinctly one of evil.

"True, I did," was my quick reply. "But I never bargained for this attempted imposture."

"I tell you it is no imposture!" declared the man before me. "You will, perhaps, understand later. Have a cigar," and he took up Digby's box and handed it to me.

I declined very abruptly, and without much politeness, I fear.

I was surveying the man who, with such astounding impudence, was attempting to impose upon me a false identity. There was something curiously striking in his appearance, but what it was I could not exactly determine. His speech was soft and educated, in a slightly higher pitch than my friend's; his hands white and carefully manicured, yet, as he stood, I noted that his left shoulder was slightly higher than the other, that his dress clothes ill-fitted him in consequence; that in his shirt-front were two rare, orange-coloured gems such as I had never seen before, and, further, that when I caught him side face, it much resembled Digby's, so aquiline as to present an almost birdlike appearance.

"Look here!" I exclaimed in anger a few moments later. "Why have you called me over here? When you spoke to me your voice struck me as peculiar, but I put it down to the distortion of sound on the telephone."

"I wanted to see if you recognised my other self," he answered with a smile.

"At this late hour? Couldn't you have postponed your ghastly joke till the morning?" I asked.

"Joke!" he echoed, his face suddenly pale and serious. "This is no joke, Royle, but a very serious matter. The most serious that can occur in any man's life."

"Well, what is it? Tell me the truth."

"You shall know that later."

"Where is Sir Digby?"

"Here! I am Sir Digby, I tell you."

"I mean my friend."

"I am your friend," was the man's response, as he turned away towards the writing-table. "The friend you first met on the Lake of Garda."

"Now, why all this secrecy?" I asked. "I was first called here and warned not to show myself, and, on arrival, find you here."

"And who else did you expect to find?" he asked with a faint smile.

"I expected to find my friend."

"But I am your friend," he asserted. "You promised me only an hour ago that you would treat my successor exactly as you treated me. And," he added, "I am my own successor!"

I stood much puzzled.

There were certain features in his countenance that were much like Digby's, and certain tones in his voice that were the same. His hands seemed the same, too, and yet he was not Digby himself.

"How can I believe you if you refuse to be frank and open with me?" I asked.

"You promised me, Royle, and a good deal depends upon your promise," he replied, looking me squarely in the face. "Perhaps even your own future."

"My future!" I echoed. "What has that to do with you, pray?" I demanded angrily.

"More than you imagine," was his low response, his eyes fixed upon mine.

"Well, all I know is that you are endeavouring to make me believe that you are what you are not. Some evil purpose is, no doubt, behind it all. But such an endeavour is an insult to my intelligence," I declared.

The man laughed a low, harsh laugh and turned away.

"I demand to know where my friend is!" I cried, stepping after him across the room, and facing him again.

"My dear Royle," he replied, in that curious, high-pitched voice, yet with a calm, irritating demeanour. "Haven't I already told you I am your friend?"

"It's a lie! You are not Sir Digby!" I cried angrily. "I shall inform the police that I've found you usurping his place and name, and leave them to solve the mystery."

"Act just as you think fit, my dear old fellow," he laughed. "Perhaps the police might discover more than you yourself would care for them to know."

His words caused me to ponder. At what could he be hinting?

He saw my hesitancy, and with a sudden movement placed his face close to me, saying:

"My dear fellow look—look into my countenance, you surely can penetrate my disguise. It cannot be so very perfect, surely."

I looked, but turned from him in disgust.

"No. Stop this infernal fooling!" I cried. "I've never seen you before in my life."

He burst out laughing—laughed heartily, and with genuine amusement.

His attitude held me in surprise.

"You refuse to be my friend, Royle—but I desire to be yours, if you will allow me," he said.

"I can have no friend whom I cannot trust," I repeated.

"Naturally. But I hope you will soon learn to trust me," was his quiet retort. "I called you back to-night in order to see if you—my most intimate friend—would recognise me. But you do not. I am, therefore, safe—safe to go forth and perform a certain mission which it is imperative that I should perform."

"You are fooling me," I declared.

For a second he looked straight and unflinchingly into my eyes, then with a sudden movement he drew the left cuff of his dress shirt up to the elbow and held out his forearm for me to gaze upon.

I looked.

Then I stood dumbfounded, for half-way up the forearm, on the inside, was the cicatrice of an old knife wound which long ago, he had told me, had been made by an Indian in South America who had attempted to kill him, and whom he had shot in self-defence.

"You believe me now?" he asked, in a voice scarce above a whisper.

"Of course," I said. "Pardon me, Digby—but this change in your personality is marvellous—almost superhuman!"

"So I've been told before," he replied lightly.

"But, really, didn't you penetrate it?" he asked, resuming his normal voice.

"No. I certainly did not," I answered, and helping myself to a drink, swallowed it.

"Well?" I went on. "What does this mean?"

"At present I can't exactly tell you what I intend doing," he replied. "To-night I wanted to test you, and have done so. It's late now," he added, glancing at the clock, which showed it to be half-past two o'clock in the morning. "Come in to-morrow at ten, will you?" he asked. "I want to discuss the future with you very seriously. I have something to say which concerns your own future, and which also closely concerns a friend of yours. So come in your own interests, Royle—now don't fail, I beg of you!"

"But can't you tell me to-night," I asked.

"Not until I know something of what my own movements are to be," he replied. "I cannot know before to-morrow," he replied with a mysterious air. "So if you wish to be forewarned of an impending peril, come and see me and I will then explain. We shall, no doubt, be on closer terms to-morrow. *Au revoir*," and he took my hand warmly and then let me out.

The rather narrow, ill-lit staircase, the outer door of which had been shut for hours, was close and stuffy, but as I descended the second flight and was about to pass along the hall to the door, I distinctly heard a movement in the shadow where, on my left, the hall continued along to the door of the ground-floor flat.

I peered over the banisters, but in the darkness could distinguish nothing.

That somebody was lurking there I instantly felt assured, and next moment the truth became revealed by two facts.

The first was a light, almost imperceptible noise, the jingle of a woman's bangles, and, secondly, the faint odour of some subtle perfume, a sweet, intoxicating scent such as my nostrils had never greeted before.

For the moment I felt surprise, but as the hidden lady was apparently standing outside the ground-floor flat—perhaps awaiting admittance—I felt it to be no concern of mine, and proceeding, opened the outer door and passed outside, closing it quietly after me.

An unusually sweet perfume one can seldom forget. Even out in the keen night air that delightful odour seemed to cling to my memory—the latest creation of the Rue de la Paix, I supposed.

Well, I duly returned home to Albemarle Street once again, utterly mystified.

What did it all mean? Why had Digby adopted such a marvellous disguise? What did he mean by saying that he wished to stand my friend and safeguard me from impending evil?

Yes, it was all a mystery—but surely not so great a mystery as that which was to follow. Ah! had I but suspected the astounding truth how very differently would I have acted!

Filled with curiosity regarding Digby's strange forebodings, I alighted from a taxi in Harrington Gardens at a quarter to eleven that same morning, but on entering found the uniformed hall-porter in a great state of excitement and alarm.

"Oh, sir!" he cried breathlessly, advancing towards me. "You're a friend of Sir Digby's sir. The police are upstairs. Something extraordinary has happened."

"The police!" I gasped. "Why, what's happened?"

"Well, sir. As his man left the day before yesterday, my wife went up to Sir Digby's flat as usual this morning about eight, and put him his early cup of tea outside his door. But when she went in again she found he had not taken it into his room. She believed him to be asleep, so not till ten o'clock did she go into the sitting-room to draw up the blinds, when, to her horror, she found a young lady, a perfect stranger, lying stretched on the floor there! She rushed down and told me, and I went up. I found that Sir Digby's bed hadn't been slept in, and that though the poor girl was unconscious, she was still breathing. So I at once called in the constable on point duty at the corner of Collingham Road, and he 'phoned to the police station."

"But the girl—is she dead?" I inquired quickly.

"I don't know, sir. You'd better go upstairs. There's an inspector, two plain-clothes men, and a doctor up there."

He took me up in the lift, and a few moments later I stood beside Digby's bed, whereon the men had laid the inanimate form of a well-dressed girl whom I judged to be about twenty-two, whose dark hair, unbound, lay in disorder upon the pillow. The face, white as marble, was handsome and clean cut, but upon it, alas! was the ashen hue of death, the pale lips slightly parted as though in a half-sarcastic smile.

The doctor was bending over her making his examination.

I looked upon her for a moment, but it was a countenance which I had never seen before. Digby had many lady friends, but I had never seen her among them. She was a perfect stranger.

Her gown was of dark blue serge, smartly made, and beneath her coat she wore a cream silk blouse with deep sailor collar open at the neck, and a soft flowing bow of turquoise blue. This, however, had been disarranged by the doctor in opening her blouse to listen to her breathing, and I saw that upon it was a small crimson stain.

Yes, she was remarkably good-looking, without a doubt.

When I announced myself as an intimate friend of Sir Digby Kemsley, the inspector at once took me into the adjoining room and began to eagerly question me.

With him I was perfectly frank; but I said nothing regarding my second visit there in the night.

My gravest concern was the whereabouts of my friend.

"This is a very curious case, Mr. Royle," declared the inspector. "The C.I.D. men have established one fact—that another woman was with the stranger here in the early hours of this morning. This hair-comb"—and he showed me a small side-comb of dark green horn—"was found close beside her on the floor. Also a couple of hair-pins, which are different to those in the dead woman's hair. There was a struggle, no doubt, and the woman got away. In the poor girl's hair are two tortoiseshell side-combs."

"But what is her injury?" I asked breathlessly.

"She's been stabbed," he replied. "Let's go back."

Together we re-entered the room, but as we did so we saw that the doctor had now left the bedside, and was speaking earnestly with the two detectives.

"Well, doctor?" asked the inspector in a low voice.

"She's quite dead—murder, without a doubt," was his reply. "The girl was struck beneath the left breast—a small punctured wound, but fatal!"

WILLIAM LE QUEUX

"The woman who left this hair-comb behind knows something about the affair evidently," exclaimed the inspector. "We must first discover Sir Digby Kemsley. He seems to have been here up until eleven o'clock last night. Then he mysteriously disappeared, and the stranger entered unseen, two very curious and suspicious circumstances. I wonder who the poor girl was?"

The two detectives were discussing the affair in low voices. Here was a complete and very remarkable mystery, which, from the first, the police told me they intended to keep to themselves, and not allow a syllable of it to leak out to the public through the newspapers.

A woman had been there!

Did there not exist vividly in my recollection that strange encounter in the darkness of the stairs? The jingle of the golden bangles, and the sweet odour of that delicious perfume?

But I said nothing. I intended that the police should prosecute their inquiries, find my friend, and establish the identity of the mysterious girl who had met with such an untimely end presumably at the hands of that woman who had been lurking in the darkness awaiting my departure.

Truly it was a mystery, a most remarkable problem among the many which occur each week amid the amazing labyrinth of humanity which we term London life.

Sir Digby Kemsley had disappeared. Where?

Half an hour after noon I had left Harrington Gardens utterly bewildered, and returned to Albemarle Street, and at half-past one met Phrida at the Berkeley, where, as I have already described, we lunched together.

I had revealed to her everything under seal of the secrecy placed upon me by the police—everything save that suspicion I had had in the darkness, and the suspicion the police also held—the suspicion of a woman.

Relation of the curious affair seemed to have unnerved her. She had become paler and was fidgeting with her serviette. Loving me so devotedly, she seemed to entertain vague and ridiculous fears regarding my own personal safety.

"It was very foolish and hazardous of you to have returned there at that hour, dear," she declared with sweet solicitation, as she drew on her white gloves preparatory to leaving the restaurant, for I had already paid the bill and drained my liqueur-glass.

"I don't see why," I said. "Whatever could have happened to me, when—"

My sentence remained unfinished.

I held my breath. The colour must have left my cheeks, I know.

My well-beloved had at that moment opened her handbag and taken out her wisp of lace handkerchief.

My nostrils were instantly filled with that same sweet, subtle perfume which I so vividly recollected, the identical perfume of the woman concealed in that dark passage-way!

Her bangles, two thin gold ones, jingled as she moved—that same sound which had come up to me from the blackness. I sat like a statue, staring at her amazed, aghast, like a man in a dream.

III

Describes the Trysting-Place

I drove Phrida back to Cromwell Road in a taxi.

As I sat beside her, that sweet irritating perfume filled my senses, almost intoxicating me. For some time I remained silent; then, unable to longer restrain my curiosity, I exclaimed with a calm, irresponsible air, though with great difficulty of self-restraint:

"What awfully nice perfume you have, dearest! Surely it's new, isn't it? I never remember smelling it before!"

"Quite new, and rather delicious, don't you think? My cousin Arthur brought it from Paris a few days ago. I only opened the bottle last night. Mother declared it to be the sweetest she's ever smelt. It's so very strong that one single drop is sufficient."

"What do they call it?"

"Parfait d'Amour. Lauzan, in the Placé Vendôme, makes it. It's quite new, and not yet on the market, Arthur said. He got it—a sample bottle—from a friend of his in the perfume trade."

Not on the market! Those words of hers condemned her. Little did she dream that I had smelt that same sweet, subtle odour as I descended the stairs from Sir Digby's flat. She, no doubt, had recognised my silhouette in the half darkness, yet nevertheless she felt herself quite safe, knowing that I had not seen her.

Why had she been lurking there?

A black cloud of suspicion fell upon me. She kept up a desultory conversation as we went along Piccadilly in the dreary gloom of that dull January afternoon, but I only replied in monosyllables, until at length she remarked:

"Really, Teddy, you're not thinking of a word I'm saying. I suppose your mind is centred upon your friend—the man who has turned out to be an impostor."

The conclusion of that sentence and its tone showed a distinct antagonism.

It was true that the man whom I had known as Sir Digby Kemsley— the man who for years past had been so popular among a really good set in London—was according to the police an impostor.

The detective-inspector had told me so. From the flat in Harrington Gardens the men of the Criminal Investigation Department had rung up New Scotland Yard to make their report, and about noon, while I was resting at home in Albemarle Street, I was told over the telephone that my whilom friend was not the man I had believed him to be.

As I had listened to the inspector's voice, I heard him say:

"There's another complication of this affair, Mr. Royle. Your friend could not have been Sir Digby Kemsley, for that gentleman died suddenly a year ago, at Huacho, in Peru. There was some mystery about his death, it seems, for it was reported by the British Consul at Lima. Inspector Edwards, of the C.I. Department, will call upon you this afternoon. What time could you conveniently be at home?"

I named five o'clock, and that appointment I intended, at all hazards, to keep.

The big, heavily-furnished drawing-room in Cromwell Road was dark and sombre as I stood with Phrida, who, bright and happy, pulled off her gloves and declared to her mother—that charming, sedate, grey-haired, but wonderfully preserved, woman—that she had had such "a jolly lunch."

"I saw the Redmaynes there, mother," she was saying. "Mr. Redmayne has asked us to lunch with them at the Carlton next Tuesday. Can we go?"

"I think so, dear," was her mother's reply. "I'll look at my engagements."

"Oh, do let's go! Ida is coming home from her trip to the West Indies. I do want to see her so much."

Strange it was that my well-beloved, in face of that amazing mystery, preserved such an extraordinary, nay, an astounding, calm. I was thinking of the little side-comb of green horn, for I had seen her wearing a pair exactly similar!

Standing by I watched her pale sweet countenance, full of speechless wonder.

After the first moment of suspense she had found herself treading firm ground, and now, feeling herself perfectly secure, she had assumed a perfectly frank and confident attitude.

Yet the perfume still arose to my nostrils—the sweet, subtle scent which had condemned her.

I briefly related to Mrs. Shand my amazing adventures of the previous night, my eyes furtively upon Phrida's countenance the while. Strangely enough, she betrayed no guilty knowledge, but fell to discussing the mystery with ease and common-sense calm.

"What I can't really make out is how your friend could have had the audacity to pose as Sir Digby Kemsley, well knowing that the real person was alive," she remarked.

"The police have discovered that Sir Digby died in Peru last January," I said.

"While your friend was in London?"

"Certainly. My friend—I shall still call him Sir Digby, for I have known him by no other name—has not been abroad since last July, when he went on business to Moscow."

"How very extraordinary," remarked Mrs. Shand. "Your friend must surely have had some object in posing as the dead man."

"But he posed as a man who was still alive!" I exclaimed.

"Until, perhaps, he was found out," observed Phrida shrewdly. "Then he bolted."

I glanced at her quickly. Did those words betray any knowledge of the truth, I wondered.

"Apparently there was some mystery surrounding the death of Sir Digby at Huacho," I remarked. "The British Consul in Lima made a report upon it to the Foreign Office, who, in turn, handed it to Scotland Yard. I wonder what it was."

"When you know, we shall be better able to judge the matter and to form some theory," Phrida said, crossing the room and re-arranging the big bowl of daffodils in the window.

I remained about an hour, and then, amazed at the calmness of my well-beloved, I returned to my rooms.

In impatience I waited till a quarter past five, when Haines ushered in a tall, well-dressed, clean-shaven man, wearing a dark grey overcoat and white slip beneath his waistcoat, and who introduced himself as Inspector Charles Edwards.

"I've called, Mr. Royle, in order to make some further inquiries regarding this person you have known as Sir Digby Kemsley," he said when he had seated himself. "A very curious affair happened last night. I've been down to Harrington Gardens, and have had a look around there myself. Many features of the affair are unique."

"Yes," I agreed. "It is curious—very curious."

"I have a copy of your statement regarding your visit to the house during the night," said the official, who was one of the Council of Seven at the Yard, looking up at me suddenly from the cigarette he was about to light. "Have you any suspicion who killed the young lady?"

"How can I have—except that my friend—"

"Is missing—eh?"

"Exactly."

"But now, tell me all about this friend whom you knew as Sir Digby Kemsley. How did you first become acquainted with him?"

"I met him on a steamer on the Lake of Garda this last summer," was my reply. "I was staying at Riva, the little town at the north end of the lake, over the Austrian frontier, and one day took the steamer down to Gardone, in Italy. We sat next each other at lunch on board, and, owing to a chance conversation, became friends."

"What did he tell you?"

"Well, only that he was travelling for his health. He mentioned that he had been a great deal in South America, and was then over in Europe for a holiday. Indeed, on the first day we met, he did not even mention his name, and I quite forgot to ask for it. In travelling one meets so many people who are only of brief passing interest. It was not until a week later, when I found him staying in the same hotel as myself, the Cavour, in Milan, I learnt from the hall-porter that he was Sir Digby Kemsley, the great engineer. We travelled to Florence together, and stayed at the Baglioni, but one morning when I came down I found a hurried note awaiting me. From the hall-porter I learned that a gentleman had arrived in the middle of the night, and Sir Digby, after an excited controversy, left with him for London. In the note he gave me his address in Harrington Gardens, and asked me not to fail to call on my return to town."

"Curious to have a visitor in the middle of the night," remarked the detective reflectively.

"I thought so at the time, but, knowing him to be a man of wide business interests, concluded that it was someone who had brought him an urgent message," I replied. "Well, the rest is quickly told. On my return home I sought him out, with the result that we became great friends."

"You had no suspicion that he was an impostor?"

"None whatever. He seemed well known in London," I replied. "Besides, if he was not the real Sir Digby, how is it possible that he could have so completely deceived his friends! Why, he has visited the offices of Colliers, the great railway contractors in Westminster—the firm who constructed the railway in Peru. I recollect calling there with him in a taxi one day."

Edwards smiled.

"He probably did that to impress you, sir," he replied. "They may have known him as somebody else. Or he simply went in and made an inquiry. He's evidently a very clever person."

Personally, I could not see how my friend could possibly have posed as Sir Digby Kemsley if he were not, even though Edwards pointed out that the real Sir Digby had only been in London a fortnight for the past nine years.

Still, on viewing the whole situation, I confess inclination towards the belief that my friend was, notwithstanding the allegations, the real Sir Digby.

And yet those strange words of his, spoken in such confidence on the previous night, recurred to me. There was mystery somewhere—a far more obscure mystery even than what was apparent at that moment.

"Tell me what is known concerning Sir Digby's death in Peru," I asked.

"From the report furnished to us at the Yard it seems that one day last August, while the gentleman in question was riding upon a trolley on the Cerro de Pasco railway, the conveyance was accidentally overturned into a river, and he was badly injured in the spine. A friend of his, a somewhat mysterious Englishman named Cane, brought him down to the hospital at Lima, and after two months there, he becoming convalescent, was conveyed for fresh air to Huacho, on the sea. Here he lived with Cane in a small bungalow in a somewhat retired spot, until on one night in February last year something occurred—but exactly what, nobody is able to tell. Sir Digby was found by his Peruvian servant dead from snake-bite. Cane evinced the greatest distress and horror until, of a sudden, a second man-servant declared that he had heard his master cry out in terror as he lay helpless in his bed. He heard him shriek: 'You—you blackguard, Cane—take the thing away! Ah! God! You've—you've killed me!' Cane denied it, and proved that he was at a friend's house playing cards at the hour when the servant heard his master shout for help. Next day, however, he disappeared. Our Consul in Lima took up the matter, and in due course a full report of the affair was forwarded to the Yard, together with a very detailed description of the man wanted. This we sent around the world, but up to to-day without result."

"Then the man Cane was apparently responsible for the death of the invalid," I remarked.

"I think so—without a doubt."

"But who was the invalid? Was he the real Sir Digby?"

"Aye, that's the question," said Edwards, thrusting his hands into his trouser pockets. For some moments we both sat staring blankly into the fire.

"Among the papers sent to us," he said very slowly at last, "was this. Read it, and tell me your opinion."

And then he took from his pocket-book and handed me a half-sheet of thin foreign notepaper, which had been closely written upon on both sides. It was apparently a sheet from a letter, for there was no beginning and no ending.

The handwriting was educated, though small and crabbed, and the ink brown and half-faded, perhaps because of its exposure to a tropical climate. It had been written by a man, without a doubt.

"That," said Edwards, "was found in a pocket-book belonging to Cane, which, in his hasty flight, he apparently forgot. According to our report the wallet was found concealed beneath the mattress of his bed, as though he feared lest anyone should read and learn what it contained. Read it, and tell me what you think."

I took the sheet of thin paper in my fingers, and, crossing the room to a brighter light, managed to decipher the writing as follows:

". . . At fourteen paces from where this wall rises from the lawn stands the ever-plashing fountain. The basin is circular, while around runs a paved path, hemmed in by smoke-blackened laurels and cut off from the public way by iron railings. The water falls with pleasant cadence into a small basin set upon a base of moss-grown rockwork. Looking south one meets a vista of green grass, of never-ceasing London traffic, and one tall distant factory chimney away in the grey haze, while around the fountain are four stunted trees. On the right stretches a strip of garden, in spring green and gay with bulbs which bloom and die unnoticed by the hundreds upon hundreds of London's workers who pass and re-pass daily in their mad, reckless hurry to earn the wherewithal to live.

"Halt upon the gravel at that spot on the twenty-third of the month punctually at noon, and she will pass wearing the yellow flower. It is the only trysting-place. She has kept it religiously for one whole year without—alas!—effecting a meeting. Go there—tell her that I still live, shake her hand in greeting and assure her that I will come there as soon as ever I am given strength so to do.

"I have been at that spot once only, yet every detail of its appearance is impressed indelibly upon my memory. Alas! that I do not know its name. Search and you will assuredly find it—and you will see her. You will speak, and give her courage."

I bit my lip.
A sudden thought illuminated my mind.
The yellow flower!
Was not the mysterious woman whom I was to meet on the night of the fourteenth also to wear a yellow flower—the mimosa!

IV

"Dear Old Dig"

I told Edwards nothing of Sir Digby's curious request, of his strange confidences, or of the mysterious letter to "E. P. K.", which now reposed in a locked drawer in my writing-table.

My friend, be he impostor or not, had always treated me strictly honourably and well. Therefore, I did not intend to betray him, although he might be a fugitive hunted by the police.

Yet was he a fugitive? Did not his words to me and his marvellous disguise prior to the tragedy imply an intention to disappear?

The enigma was indeed beyond solution.

At seven o'clock my visitor, finding necessity to revisit Harrington Gardens, I eagerly accompanied him.

There is a briskness and brightness in Piccadilly at seven o'clock on a clear, cold, winter's night unequalled in any thoroughfare in the world. On the pavements and in the motor-buses are thousands of London's workers hurrying to their homes in western suburbs, mostly the female employees of the hundreds of shops and work-rooms which supply the world's fashions—for, after all, London has now ousted Paris as the centre of the feminine mode—the shops are still gaily lit, the club windows have not yet drawn their blinds, and as motors and taxis flash past eastward, one catches glimpses of pretty women in gay evening gowns, accompanied by their male escorts on pleasure bent: the restaurant, the theatre, and the supper, until the unwelcome cry—that cry which resounds at half-past twelve from end to end of Greater London, "Time, please, ladies and gentlemen. Time!"—the pharisaical decree that further harmless merriment is forbidden. How the foreigner laughs at our childish obedience to the decree of the killjoys. And well he may, especially when we know full well that while the good people of the middle class are forced to return to the dulness of their particular suburb, the people of the class above them can sneak in by back doors of unsuspected places, and indulge in drinking, gambling, and dancing till daylight. Truly the middle-class Londoner is a meek, obedient person. One day, however, he may revolt.

Piccadilly was particularly bright and gay that night, as, passing the end of St. James's Street, we sped forward in the taxi towards Brompton Road and past the Natural History Museum to Gloucester Road.

On our arrival the door of the flat was opened by a constable without a helmet. Recognising the famous inspector, he saluted.

The body of the unknown girl had been removed to the mortuary for a post-mortem examination, but nothing else had been moved, and two officers of the C.I.D. were busy making examination for finger-prints.

I allowed them to take mine for comparison, but some they found upon the mahogany table and upon the back of a chair were undoubtedly those of the victim herself.

The small glass-topped specimen-table still lay where it had been overturned, and the fragments of the two green-glass flower-vases were strewn upon the carpet with the drooping red anemones themselves.

Regarding the overturned table the two detectives held that it had separated the assassin from his victim; that the girl had been chased around it several times before her assailant had thrown it down, suddenly sprung upon her, and delivered the fatal blow, full in her chest.

"We've thoroughly examined it for finger-prints, sir," the elder of the two officers explained to my companion. "Both on the glass top and on the mahogany edge there are a number of prints of the victim herself, as well as a number made by another hand."

"A man's?" I asked.

"No; curiously enough, it seems to be a woman's," was the reply.

"A woman's!"

I thought of that sweet perfume, and of the person who had lurked in the shadow of the stairs!

"That's interesting," remarked Edwards. "They may be those of the woman who wore green combs in her hair, or else of the porter's wife."

"The owner's man-servant is away abroad on business for his master, we've found out," answered the man addressed. "So of late the porter's wife, who lives in the basement of the next house, has been in the habit of coming in every day and tidying up the room. We took her prints this morning, and have found quite a lot about the place. No," added the man emphatically, "the finger-prints on that little table yonder are not those of the porter's wife, but of another woman who's been here recently. We only find them upon the door-handle and on the edge of the writing-table, against which the woman must have leaned. We'll have them photographed to-morrow."

The men then showed us the marks in question—distinct impressions of small finger-tips, which they had rendered vivid and undeniable by the application of a finely-powdered chalk of a pale green colour.

Apparently the two experts had devoted the whole day to the search for finger-print clues, and they had established the fact that two women had been there—the victim and another.

Who was she?

The investigation of the papers in my friend's writing-table had not yet been made. Inspector Edwards had telephoned earlier in the day, stating that he would himself go through them.

Therefore, exercising every care not to obliterate the three finger-marks upon the edge of the table, the officers proceeded to break open drawer after drawer and methodically examine the contents while I looked on.

The work was exciting. At any moment we might discover something which would throw light upon the tragedy, the grim evidence of which remained in that dark, still damp stain upon the carpet—the life-blood of the unknown victim.

Already the face of the dead girl had been photographed, and would, before morning, be circulated everywhere in an endeavour to secure identification.

I had learnt from Edwards that before noon that morning, upon the notice-board outside Bow Street Police Station, there had been posted one of those pale, buff-coloured bills headed in great, bold capitals: "Body found," in which the description had been filled in by a clerkish hand, and at the bottom a statement that the corpse was lying at the Kensington Mortuary awaiting identification.

That she was a lady seemed established by her dress, her well-kept hands, innocent of manual labour, by the costly rings and bracelet she was wearing, and the fact that, in the pocket of her coat was found her purse containing eleven pounds in gold and some silver.

Sir Digby's papers promised to be extremely interesting, as we cleared the books off a side-table and sat down to carefully investigate them.

The writing-table was a pedestal one, with a centre drawer and four drawers on either side. The first drawer burst open was the top one on the left, and from it Edwards drew two bundles of letters, each secured by faded pink tape.

These bundles he handed to me, saying—

"See what you think of these, Mr. Royle!"

One after another I opened them. They were all in the same sprawly handwriting of a woman—a woman who simply signed herself "Mittie."

They were love-letters written in the long ago, many commencing "My darling," or "Dearest," and some with "Dear old Dig."

Though it seemed mean of me to peer into the closed chapter of my friend's history, I quickly found myself absorbed in them. They were the passionate outpourings of a brave but overburdened heart. Most of them were dated from hotels in the South of England and in Ireland, and were apparently written at the end of the eighties. But as no envelopes had been preserved they gave no clue to where the addressee had been at the time.

Nearly all were on foreign notepaper, so we agreed that he must have been abroad.

As I read, it became apparent that the writer and the addressee had been deeply in love with one another, but the lady's parents had forbidden their marriage; and as, alas! in so many like cases, she had been induced to make an odious but wealthier marriage. The man's name was Francis.

"He is, alas! just the same," she wrote in one letter dated "Mount Ephraim Hotel, at Tunbridge Wells, Thursday": "We have nothing in common. He only thinks of his dividends, his stocks and shares, and his business in the City always. I am simply an ornament of his life, a woman who acts as his hostess and relieves him of much trouble in social anxieties. If father had not owed him seventeen thousand pounds he would, I feel certain, never have allowed me to marry him. But I paid my father's debt with my happiness, with my very life. And you, dear old Dig, are the only person who knows the secret of my broken heart. You will be home in London seven weeks from to-day. I will meet you at the old place at three o'clock on the first of October, for I have much—so very much—to tell you. Father knows now how I hate this dull, impossible life of mine, and how dearly I love your own kind self. I told him so to-day, and he pities me. I hope you will get this letter before you leave, but I shall watch the movements of your ship, and I shall meet you on the first of October. Till then adieu.—Ever your own Mittie."

At the old place! Where was it, I wondered? At what spot had the secret meeting been effected between the man who had returned from abroad and the woman who loved him so well, though she had been forced to become the wife of another.

That meeting had taken place more than twenty years ago. What had been its result was shown in the next letter I opened.

Written from the Queen's Hotel at Hastings on the fourth of October, the unfortunate "Mittie," who seemed to spend her life travelling on the South Coast, penned the following in a thin, uncertain hand:—

"Our meeting was a mistake, Dig, a grave mistake. We were watched by somebody in the employ of Francis. When I returned to Tunbridge Wells he taxed me with having met you, described our trysting-place—the fountain—and how we had walked and walked until, becoming too tired, we had entered that quiet little restaurant to dine. He has misjudged me horribly. The sneak who watched us must have lied to him, or he would never have spoken to me as he did—he would not have insulted me. That night I left him, and am here alone. Do not come near me, do not reply to this. It might make matters worse. Though we are parted, Dig, you know I love you and only you—*you*! Still your own MITTIE."

I sat staring at that half-faded letter, taking no heed of what Edwards was saying.

The fountain! They had met at the fountain, and had been seen!

Could that spot be the same as mentioned in the mysterious letter left behind by the fugitive Cane after the sudden death of the Englishman away in far-off Peru?

Did someone, after all the lapse of years, go there on every twenty-third of the month at noon wearing a yellow flower, to wait for a person who, alas! never came?

The thought filled me with romance, even though we were at that moment investigating a very remarkable tragedy. Yet surely in no city in this world is there so much romance, so much pathos, such whole-hearted love and affection, or such deep and deadly hatred as in our great palpitating metropolis, where secret assassinations are of daily occurrence, and where the most unpardonable sin is that of being found out.

WILLIAM LE QUEUX

"What's that you've got hold of?" Edwards asked me, as he crossed to the table and bent over me.

I started.

Then, recovering myself—for I had no desire that he should know—replied, quite coolly:

"Oh, only a few old letters—written long ago, in the eighties."

"Ah! Ancient history, eh?"

"Yes," I replied, packing them together and retying them with the soiled, pink tape. "But have you discovered anything?"

"Well," he replied with a self-conscious smile, "I've found a letter here which rather alters my theory," and I saw that he held a piece of grey notepaper in his hand. "Here is a note addressed to him as long ago as 1900 in the name of Sir Digby Kemsley! Perhaps, after all, the man who died so mysteriously in Peru was an impostor, and the owner of this place was the real Sir Digby!"

"Exactly my own theory," I declared.

"But that fountain!" he remarked. "The fountain mentioned in the letter left behind by the man Cane. We must take immediate steps to identify it, and it must be watched on the twenty-third for the coming of the woman who wears a yellow flower. When we find her, we shall be able to discover something very interesting, Mr. Royle. Don't you agree?"

V

"Time will Prove"

These are truly the fevered days of journalistic enterprise the world over.

There are no smarter journalists than those of Fleet Street, and none, not even in New York, with scent more keen for sensational news. "The day's story" is the first thought in every newspaper office, and surely no story would have been a greater "scoop" for any journal than the curious facts which I have related in the foregoing pages.

But even though the gentlemen of the Press are ubiquitous, many a curious happening, and many a remarkable coroner's inquiry, often remain unreported.

And so in this case. When, on the following morning, the coroner for the borough of Kensington held his inquiry in the little court off the High Street, no reporter was present, and only half a dozen idlers were seated in the back of the gloomy room.

When the jury had taken their seats after viewing the remains, according to custom, the police inspector reported to the coroner that the body remained unidentified, though the description had been telegraphed everywhere.

"I might add, sir," went on the inspector, "that there is strong belief that the young lady may be a foreigner. Upon the tab of her coat she was wearing was the name of a costumier: 'Sartori, Via Roma.' Only the name of the street, and not the town is given. But it must be somewhere in Italy. We are in communication with the Italian police with a view to ascertaining the name of the town, and hope thus to identify the deceased."

"Very well!" said the coroner, a shrewd, middle-aged, clean-shaven man in gold pince-nez. "Let us have the evidence," and he arranged his papers with business-like exactitude.

The procedure differed in no way from that in any other coroner's court in the kingdom, the relation of dry details by matter-of-fact persons spoken slowly in order that they might be carefully taken down.

The scene was, indeed, a gloomy one, for the morning was dark, and the place was lit by electric light. The jury—twelve honest householders of Kensington—appeared from the outset eager to get back to their daily avocations. They were unaware of the curious enigma about to be presented to them.

Not until I began to give my evidence did they appear to evince any curiosity regarding the case. But presently, when I had related my midnight interview with my friend, who was now a fugitive, the foreman put to me several questions.

"You say that after your return from your visit from this man, Sir Digby Kemsley, he rang you up on the telephone?"

"Yes."

"What did he say?" inquired the foreman, a thin, white-headed man whose social standing was no doubt slightly above that of his fellow jurymen.

"He asked me to return to him at once," was my reply.

"But this appears extraordinary—"

"We are not here to criticise the evidence, sir!" interrupted the coroner sharply. "We are only here to decide how the deceased came by her death—by accident, or by violence. Have you any doubt?"

The foreman replied in the negative, and refrained from further cross-examining me.

The coroner himself, however, put one or two pointed questions. He asked me whether I believed that it had actually been Sir Digby speaking on the second occasion, when I had been rung up, to which I replied:

"At first, the voice sounded unfamiliar."

"At first! Did you recognise it afterwards?"

I paused for a few seconds, and then was compelled to admit that I had not been entirely certain.

"Voices are, of course, often distorted by the telephone," remarked the coroner. "But in this case you may have believed the voice to have been your friend's because he spoke of things which you had been discussing in private only half-an-hour before. It may have been the voice of a stranger."

"That is my own opinion, sir," I replied.

"Ah!" he exclaimed, "and I entirely agree with you, for if your friend had contemplated the crime of murder he would scarcely have telephoned to you to come back. He would be most anxious to get the longest start he could before the raising of any hue and cry."

This remark further aroused the curiosity of the hitherto apathetic jury, who sat and listened intently to the medical evidence which followed.

The result of the doctor's examination was quickly told, and not of great interest. He had been called by the police and found the young woman dying from a deep wound under the breast, which had penetrated to the heart, the result of a savage blow with some long, thin, and very sharp instrument. The girl was not dead when he first saw her, but she expired about ten minutes afterwards.

"I should think that the weapon used was a knife with a very sharp, triangular blade judging from the wound," the spruce-looking doctor explained. "The police, however, have failed to discover it."

The words of the witness held me dumbfounded.

"Have you ever met with knives with triangular blades, doctor?" inquired the coroner.

"Oh, yes!" was the reply. "One sees them in collections of mediæval arms. In ancient days they were carried almost universally in Southern Europe—the blade about nine inches long, and sometimes perforated. Along the blade, grease impregnated with mineral poison was placed, so that, on striking, some of the grease would remain in the wound. This form of knife was most deadly, and in Italy it was known as a misericordia."

I sat there listening with open mouth. Why? Because I knew where one of those curious knives had been—one with a carved handle of cracked, yellow ivory. I had often taken it up and looked at the coat of arms carved upon the ivory—the shield with the six balls of the princely house of the Medici.

"And in your opinion, doctor, the deceased came by her death from a blow from such a weapon as you describe?" the coroner was asking.

"That is my firm opinion. The wound penetrated to the heart, and death was probably almost instantaneous."

"Would she utter a cry?"

"I think she would."

"And yet no one seems to have heard any noise!" remarked the coroner. "Is that so?" he asked, turning to the police inspector.

"We have no evidence of any cry being heard," replied the officer. "I purposely asked the other tenants of the flats above and below. But they heard no unusual sound."

One of the detective-sergeants was then called; Inspector Edwards, though present, being purposely omitted. In reply to the coroner, he described the finding of the body, its examination, and the investigation which ensued.

"I need not ask you if you have any clue to the assassin," said the coroner, when he had concluded writing down the depositions. "I presume you are actively prosecuting inquiries?"

"Yes, sir," was the brief response.

"I think, gentlemen," the coroner said, turning at last to the jury, "that we can go no further with this inquiry to-day. We must leave it for the police to investigate, and if we adjourn, let us say for a fortnight, we may then, I hope, have evidence of identification before us. The case certainly presents a number of curious features, not the least being the fact that the owner of the flat has mysteriously fled. When he is found he will, no doubt, throw some light upon the puzzling affair. I have to thank you for your attendance to-day, gentlemen," he added, addressing the dozen respectable householders, "and ask you to be present again this day fortnight—at noon."

There was evident dissatisfaction among the jury, as there is always when a coroner's inquest is ever adjourned.

It is certainly the reverse of pleasant to be compelled to keep an appointment which may mean considerable out-of-pocket expense and much personal inconvenience.

One juror, indeed, raised an objection, as he had to go to do business in Scotland. Whereupon the coroner, as he rose, expressed his regret but declared himself unable to assist him. It was, he remarked, his duty as a citizen to assist in this inquiry, and to arrive at a verdict.

After that the court rose, and every one broke up into small groups to discuss the strange affair of which the Press were at present in ignorance.

Edwards had crossed the room and was speaking to me. But I heard him not. I was thinking of that triangular-bladed weapon—the "misericordia" of the middle ages—so frequently used for stealthy knife-thrusts.

"Coming?" he asked at last. This aroused me to a sense of my surroundings, and I followed him blindly out into the afternoon shopping bustle of High Street, Kensington.

Outside the Underground Station were the flower-sellers. Some were offering that tribute which the Riviera never fails to send to us Londoners in spring—sprigs of mimosa: the yellow flower which would be worn by the mysterious "E. P. K.," the written message to whom reposed in my writing-table at home.

Personally, I am not a man of mystery, but just an ordinary London business man, differing in no way to thousands of others who are at the head of prosperous commercial concerns. London with all its garish glitter, its moods of dulness and of gaiety, its petrol-smelling streets, its farces of passing life, and its hard and bitter dramas always appealed to me. It was my home, the atmosphere in which I had been born and bred, nay, my very existence. I loved London and was ever true to the city of my birth, even though its climate might be derided, and Paris claimed as the one city in which to find the acme of comfort and enjoyment.

I had not sought mystery—far from it. It had been thrust upon me, and now, as we went along the High Street in Kensington, towards the police-station, I found myself a sudden but important factor in a stern chase—a man-hunt—such as London had seldom known, for Edwards was saying to me:

"At all hazards we must find your friend Kemsley, and you, Mr. Royle, must help us. You know him, and can identify him. There are grave suspicions against him, and these must be cleared up in view of the mysterious tragedy in Harrington Gardens."

"You surely don't expect me to denounce my friend!" I cried.

"It is not a question of denouncing him. His own actions have rendered the truth patent to every one. The girl was brutally killed, and he disappeared. Therefore he must be found," Edwards said.

"But who was it who telephoned to me, do you think?" I asked.

"Himself, perhaps. He was full of inventiveness, and he may have adopted that course hoping, when the time came, to prove an alibi. Who knows?" asked the famous inspector.

"Look here!" I said as we crossed the threshold of the police-station, "I don't believe Sir Digby was either an impostor or an assassin."

"Time will prove, Mr. Royle," he laughed with an incredulous air. "A man don't take all these precautions before disappearing unless he has a deeper motive. Your friend evidently knew of the lady's impending visit. Indeed, how could she have entered the flat had he not admitted her?"

"She might have had a key," I hazarded.

"Might—but not very likely," he said. "No, my firm conviction is that the man you know as Sir Digby Kemsley struck the fatal blow, and took the knife away with him."

I shrugged my shoulders, but did not reply.

Inside the station, we passed into the long room devoted to the officers of the Criminal Investigation Department attached to the division, and there met two sergeants who had given evidence.

I was shown the photograph of the dead unknown, calm, and even pretty, just as I had seen her lying stretched in Digby's room.

"The medical evidence was curious, Mr. Royle, wasn't it?" Edwards remarked. "That triangular knife ought not to be very difficult to trace. There surely are not many of them about."

"No," I replied faintly, for the recollection of one which I had seen only a few days prior to the tragic occurrence—the one with the arms of the Medici carved upon its hilt, arose vividly before me.

To me, alas! the awful truth was now plain.

My suspicion regarding the culprit had, by the doctor's evidence, become entirely confirmed.

I set my jaws hard in agony of mind. What was a mystery of London was to me no longer a mystery!

VI

The Piece of Conviction

The morning of the tenth of January was one of those of gloom and darkness which are, on occasions, the blots upon London's reputation.

There seemed no fog, only a heavy, threatening cloud of night fell suddenly upon the city, and at three o'clock it might have been midnight. Streets, shops, and offices were lit everywhere, and buses and taxis compelled to light up, while in the atmosphere was a sulphurous odour with a black deposit which caused the eyes to smart and the lungs to irritate.

Londoners know those periods of unpleasant darkness only too well.

I was sitting in my room in Albemarle Street, watching Haines, who was cleaning a piece of old silver I had bought at an auction on the previous day. The collecting of old silver is, I may say, my hobby, and the piece was a very fine old Italian reliquary, about ten inches in height, with the Sicilian mark of the seventeenth century.

Haines, under my tuition, had become an expert and careful cleaner of silver, and I was watching and exhorting him to exercise the greatest care, as the ornamentation was thin, and some of the scrollwork around the top extremely fragile. It had, according to the inscription at its base, contained a bone of a certain saint—a local saint of Palermo it seemed—but the relic had disappeared long ago. Yet the silver case which, for centuries, had stood upon an altar somewhere, was a really exquisite piece of the silversmith's art.

Suddenly the telephone-bell rang, and on answering it I heard Phrida's voice asking—

"I say, Teddy, is that you? Why haven't you been over since Thursday?"

I started, recollecting that I had not been to Cromwell Road since the afternoon of the inquest—three days ago.

"Dear, do forgive me," I craved. "I—I've been so horribly busy. Had to be at the works each day."

"But you might have been over in the evening," she responded in a tone of complaint. "You remember you promised to take me to the St. James's last night, and I expected you."

"Oh, dearest, I'm so sorry," I said. "But I've been awfully worried, you know. Do forgive me!"

"Yes, I know!" she answered. "Well, I'll forgive you if you'll run over now and take me to tea at the Leslies. I've ordered the car for four o'clock. Will that suit you?"

The Leslies! They were snobbish folk with whom I had but little in common. Yet what could I do but agree?

And then my well-beloved rang off.

When I got down to Cromwell Road just before four o'clock, the darkness had not lifted.

My feelings as I passed along the big, old-fashioned hall and up the thickly-carpeted stairs to the drawing-room were mixed ones of doubt, and yet of deep affection.

Ah, I loved Phrida—loved her better than my own life—and yet—?

Fresh in my memory was the doctor's evidence that the crime in Harrington Gardens had been committed with a thin, triangular knife—a knife such as that I had often seen lying upon the old-fashioned, walnut what-not in the corner of the room I was just about to enter. I had known it lying in the same place for years.

Was it still there?

Purposely, because I felt that it could no longer be there, I had refrained from calling upon my love, and now, when I paused and turned the handle of the drawing-room door, I hardly dared to cast my eyes upon that antiquated piece of furniture.

Phrida, who was sitting with her hat and coat already on, jumped up gaily to meet me.

"Oh, you really are prompt, Teddy!" she cried with a flush of pleasure.

Then, as I bent over her mother's hand, the latter said—

"You're quite a stranger, Mr. Royle. I expect you have been very upset over the curious disappearance of your friend. We've searched the papers every day, but could find nothing whatever about it."

Phrida had turned towards the fire, her pretty head bent as she buttoned her glove.

"No," I replied. "Up to the present the newspapers are in complete ignorance of the affair. But no doubt they'll learn all about it before long."

Then, crossing the room to pick up a magazine lying upon a chair, I halted against the old walnut what-not.

Yes, the mediæval poignard was still lying there, just as I had always seen it!

Had it been used, and afterwards replaced?

I scarcely dared to glance at it, lest I should betray any unusual interest. I felt that Phrida's eyes were watching me, that she suspected my knowledge.

I took up the magazine idly, glanced at it, and, replacing it, returned to her side.

"Well," she asked, "are you ready?"

And then together we descended to the car.

All the way up to Abbey Road she hardly spoke. She seemed unusually pale and haggard. I asked her what was the matter, but she only replied in a faint, unnatural voice—

"Matter? Why nothing—nothing, I assure you, Teddy!"

I did not reply. I gazed upon the pretty, pale-faced figure at my side in wonder and yet in fear. I loved her—ah! I loved her well and truly, with all my soul. Yet was it possible that by means of that knife lying there so openly in that West-End drawing-room a woman's life had been treacherously taken.

Had my friend Digby, the fugitive, actually committed the crime?

When I put the whole matter clearly and with common-sense before myself, I was bound to admit that I had a strong belief of his innocence.

What would those finger-prints reveal?

The thought held me breathless. Yes, to satisfy myself I would surreptitiously secure finger-prints of my well-beloved and then in secret compare them with those found in Sir Digby's rooms.

But how? I was reflecting as the car passed by Apsley House and into the Park on its way to St. John's Wood.

Was I acting honestly? I doubted her, I quite admit. Yet I felt that if I took some object—a glass, or something with a polished surface—that she had touched, and submitted it to examination, I would be acting as a sneak.

The idea was repugnant to me. Yet with that horrible suspicion obsessing me I felt that I must do something in order to satisfy myself.

What inane small talk I uttered in the Leslies' big, over-furnished drawing-room I know not. All I remember is that I sat with some insipid girl whose hair was flaxen and as colourless as her mind, sipping my tea while I listened to her silly chatter about a Cook's tour she had just taken through Holland and Belgium. The estimable Cook is, alas! responsible for much tea-table chatter among the fair sex.

Our hostess was an obese, flashily-dressed, dogmatic lady, the wife of the chairman of a big drapery concern who, having married her eldest daughter to a purchased knighthood, fondly believed herself to be in society—thanks to the "paid paragraphs" in the social columns of certain morning newspapers. It is really wonderful what half-guineas will do towards social advancement in these days! For a guinea one's presence can be recorded at a dinner, or an at home, or one's departure from town can be notified to the world in general in a paragraph all to one's self—a paragraph which rubs shoulders with those concerning the highest in the land. The snobbery of the "social column" would really be amusing were it not so painfully apparent. A good press-agent will, for a fee, give one as much publicity and newspaper popularity as that enjoyed by a duke, and most amazing is it that such paragraphs are swallowed with keen avidity by Suburbia.

The Leslies were an average specimen of the upper middle-class, who were struggling frantically to get into a good set. The old man was bald, pompous, and always wore gold pince-nez and a fancy waistcoat. He carried his shop manners into his drawing-room, retaining his habit of rubbing his hands in true shop-walker style when he wished to be polite to his guests.

His wife was a loud-tongued and altogether impossible person, who, it was said, had once served behind the counter in a small shop in Cardiff, but who now regarded the poor workers in her husband's huge emporium as mere money-making machines.

By dint of careful cultivation at bazaars and such-like charitable functions she had scraped acquaintance with a few women of title, to whom she referred in conversation as "dear Lady So and So, who said to me the other day," or "as my friend Lady Violet always says."

She had buttonholed me at last, though I had endeavoured to escape her, and was standing before me like a pouter-pigeon pluming herself and endeavouring to be humorous at the expense of a very modest little married woman who had been her guest that afternoon and had just left after shaking my hand.

Women of Mrs. Leslie's stamp are perhaps the most evil-tongued of all. They rise from obscurity, and finding wealth at their command, imagine that they can command obeisance and popularity. Woe betide other women who arouse their jealousy, for they will scandalise and blight the reputation of the purest of their sex in the suburban belief that the invention of scandal is the hallmark of smartness.

At last I got rid of her, thanks to the arrival of an elegant young man, the younger son of a well-known peer, to whom, of course, she was at once all smiles, and, presently, I found myself out in the hall with Phrida. I breathed more freely when at last I passed into the keen air and entered the car.

"Those people are impossible, dearest," I blurted out when the car had moved away from the door. "They are the most vulgar pair I know."

"I quite agree," replied my well-beloved, pulling the fur rug over her knees. "But they are old friends of mother's, so I'm compelled to go and see them sometimes."

"Ah!" I sighed. "I suppose the old draper will buy a knighthood at this year's sale for the King's Birthday, and then his fat wife will have a tin handle to her name."

"Really, Teddy, you're simply awful," replied my companion. "If they heard you I wonder what they would say?"

"I don't care," I replied frankly. "I only speak the truth. The Government sell their titles to anybody who cares to buy. Ah! I fear that few men who really deserve honour ever get it in these days. No man can become great unless he has the influence of money to back him. The biggest swindler who ever walked up Threadneedle Street can buy a peerage, always providing he is married and has no son. As old Leslie buys his calicoes, ribbons and women's frills, so he'll buy his title. He hasn't a son, so perhaps he'll fancy a peerage and become the Lord Bargain of Sale."

Phrida laughed heartily at my biting sarcasm.

Truth to tell, though I was uttering bitter sentiments, my thoughts were running in a very different direction. I was wondering how I could best obtain the finger-prints of the woman who held my future so irrevocably in her hands.

I had become determined to satisfy myself of my love's innocence—or—can I write the words?—of her guilt!

And as I sat there beside her, my nostrils again became filled by that sweet subtle perfume—the perfume of tragedy.

WILLIAM LE QUEUX

VII

FATAL FINGERS

Two days passed.

Those finger-prints—impressions left by a woman—upon the glass-topped specimen table in Sir Digby's room and on the door handle, were puzzling the police as they puzzled me. They had already been proved not to be those of the porter's wife, the lines being lighter and more refined.

According to Edwards, after the finger-prints had been photographed, search had been made in the archives at Scotland Yard, but no record could be found that they were those of any person previously convicted.

Were they imprints of the hand of my well-beloved?

I held my breath each time that black and terrible suspicion filled my mind. I tried to put them aside, but, like a nightmare, they would recur to me hourly until I felt impelled to endeavour to satisfy myself as to her guilt or her innocence.

I loved her. Yes, passionately and truly. Yet, somehow, I could not prevent this ever-recurring suspicion to fill my mind. There were so many small points to be elucidated—the jingle of the golden bangles, and especially the perfume, which each time I entered her presence recalled to me all the strange and unaccountable happenings of that fatal night.

Again, who was the poor, unidentified victim—the pale-faced, pretty young woman who had visited Digby clandestinely, and gone to her death?

Up to the present the police notices circulated throughout the country had failed to establish who she was. Yet, if she were a foreigner, as seemed so likely, identification might be extremely difficult; indeed, she might ever remain a mystery.

It was nearly ten o'clock at night when I called at Cromwell Road, for I had excused myself for not coming earlier, having an object in view.

I found Phrida in the library, sweet and attractive in a pale blue gown cut slightly *décolletée*. She and her mother had been out to dinner somewhere in Holland Park, and had only just returned.

Mrs. Shand drew an armchair for me to the fire, and we all three sat down to chat in the cosiness of the sombre little book-lined den. Bain, the old butler, who had known me almost since childhood, placed the tantalus, a syphon and glasses near my elbow, and at Phrida's invitation I poured myself out a drink and lit a cigarette.

"Come," I said, "you will have your usual lemonade"; and at my suggestion her mother ordered Bain to bring a syphon of that harmless beverage.

My love reached forward for one of the glasses, whereupon I took one and, with a word of apology, declared that it was not quite clean.

"Not clean!" exclaimed Mrs. Shand quickly.

"There are a few smears upon it," I said, and adding "Excuse my handkerchief. It is quite clean," I took the silk handkerchief I carried with me purposely, and polished it with the air of a professional waiter.

Both Phrida and her mother laughed.

"Really, Mr. Royle, you are full of eccentricities," declared Mrs. Shand. "You always remind me of your poor father. He was most particular."

"One cannot be too careful, or guard sufficiently against germs, you know," I said, handling the clean glass carefully and pouring out the lemonade from the syphon.

Phrida took the glass from my hand, and laughing happily across its edge, drank. Her fingers were leaving tell-tale impressions upon its surface. And yet she was unconscious of my duplicity. Ah! yes, I hated myself for my double dealing. And yet so filled was I now by dark and breathless suspicion, that I found myself quite unable to resist an opportunity of establishing proof.

I watched her as she, in all innocence, leaned back in the big saddle-bag chair holding her glass in her hand and now and then contemplating it. The impressions—impressions which could not lie—would be the means of exonerating her—or of condemning her.

Those golden bangles upon her slim white wrist and that irritating perfume held me entranced. What did she know concerning that strange tragedy in Harrington Gardens. What, indeed, was the secret?

My chief difficulty was to remain apparently indifferent. But to do so was indeed a task. I loved her, aye, with all my strength, and all my soul. Yet the black cloud which had fallen upon her was one of impenetrable mystery, and as I sat gazing upon her through the haze of my cigarette smoke, I fell to wondering, just as I had wondered during all those hours which had elapsed since I had scented that first whiff of Parfait d'Amour, with which her chiffons seemed impregnated.

At last she put down her empty glass upon the bookshelf near her. Several books had been removed, leaving a vacant space.

Mrs. Shand had already risen and bade me good-night; therefore, we were alone. So I rose from my chair and, bending over her, kissed her fondly upon the brow.

No. I would believe her innocent. That white hand—the soft little hand I held in mine could never have taken a woman's life. I refused to believe it, and yet!

Did she know more of Sir Digby Kemsley than she had admitted? Why had she gone to his flat at that hour, lurking upon the stairs until he should be alone, and, no doubt, in ignorance that I was his visitor?

As I bent over her, stroking her soft hair with my hand, I tried to conjure up the scene which had taken place in Sir Digby's room—the tragedy which had caused my friend to flee and hide himself. Surely, something of a very terrible nature must have happened, or my friend—impostor or not—would have remained, faced the music, and told the truth.

I knew Digby better than most men. The police had declared him to be an impostor; nevertheless, I still believed in him, even though he was now a fugitive. Edwards had laughed at my faith in the man who was my friend, but I felt within me a strong conviction that he was not so black as pigheaded officialdom had painted him.

The Council of Seven at Scotland Yard might be a clever combination of expert brains, but they were not infallible, as had been proved so many times in the recent annals of London crime.

Phrida had not referred to the tragedy, and I had not therefore mentioned it.

My sole object at the moment was to obtain possession of the empty glass and carry it with me from the house.

But how could I effect this without arousing her suspicion?

She had risen and stood with her back to the blazing fire, her pretty lips parted in a sweet smile. We were discussing a play at which she had been on the previous evening, a comedy that had taken the town by storm.

Her golden bangles jingled as she moved—that same light metallic sound I had heard in the darkness of the staircase at Harrington Gardens. My eager fingers itched to obtain possession of that glass which stood so tantalisingly within a couple of feet of my hand. By its means I could establish the truth.

"Well, Teddy," my beloved said at last, as she glanced at the chiming clock upon the mantelshelf. "It's past eleven, so I suppose I must go to bed. Mallock is always in a bad temper if I keep her up after eleven."

"I suppose that is only natural," I laughed. "She often waits hours and hours for you. That I know."

"Yes," she sighed. "But Mallock is really a model maid. So much better than Rayne."

Personally, I did not like the woman Mallock. She was a thin-nosed, angular person, who wore pince-nez, and was of a decidedly inquisitive disposition. But I, of course, had never shown any antagonism towards her; indeed, I considered it diplomatic to treat her with tact and consideration. She had been maid to the oldest daughter of a well-known and popular countess before entering Phrida's service, and I could well imagine that her principal topic of conversation in the servants' hall was the superiority of her late mistress, whose service she had left on her marriage to a wealthy peer.

"I'm glad she is an improvement upon Rayne," I said, for want of something else to say, and, rising, I took her little hand and pressed it to my lips in farewell.

When she had kissed me I said:

"I'll just finish my cigarette, and I can let myself out."

"Very well. But look in to-morrow, dear, won't you?" she replied, as I opened the door for her to pass. "Better still, I'll ring you up about three o'clock and see what you are doing. Oh! by the way, mother wants to remind you of your promise to dine with us on Wednesday night. I quite forgot. Of course you will—eight o'clock as usual."

"Wednesday!" I exclaimed vaguely, recollecting the acceptance of Mrs. Shand's invitation about a week previously. "What date is that?"

"Why, the fourteenth."

"The fourteenth!" I echoed.

"Yes, why? Really, you look quite scared, Freddy. What's the matter. Is anything terrible going to happen on that date?" she asked, looking at me with some concern.

"Going to happen—why?" I asked, striving to calm myself.

"Oh—well, because you look so horribly pale. When I told you the date you gave quite a jump!"

"A jump? Did I?" I asked, striving to remain calm. "I didn't know, but, really, I'm filled with great disappointment. I'm so sorry, but it will be quite impossible for me to dine with you."

"Another engagement?" she said in a rather irritated tone. "Going to some people whom you like better than us, of course. You might tell the truth, Teddy."

"The truth is that I have a prior engagement," I said. "One that I cannot break. I have to fulfill faithfully a promise I gave to a very dear friend."

"Couldn't you do it some other time?"

"No," I answered. "Only on the evening of the fourteenth."

"Then you can't come to us?" she asked with a pout.

"I'll look in after," I promised. "But to dine is entirely out of the question."

I saw that she was annoyed, but next moment her lips parted again in a pretty smile, and she said:

"Very well, then. But remember, you will not be later than ten, will you?"

"I promise not to be, dearest," I answered, and kissing her, she ascended to her room.

The fourteenth! It was on that evening I had to carry out the promise made to Digby and meet the mysterious lady at the Piccadilly Circus Tube Station—the person whose initials were "E. P. K." and who would wear in her breast a spray of mimosa.

I returned to the library, and for a second stood thinking deeply. Would I, by that romantic meeting, be placed in possession of some further fact which might throw light upon the mystery? Ah! would I, I wondered?

The empty glass caught my eye, and I was about to cross and secure it when Bain suddenly entered. Seeing me, he drew back quickly, saying: "I beg pardon, sir. I thought you had gone. Will you take anything more, sir?"

"No, not to-night, Bain," was my reply.

Whereupon the old servant glanced around for the missing glass, and I saw with heart-sinking that he placed it upon the tray to carry it back to the servants' quarters.

The link which I had been so careful in preparing was already vanishing from my gaze, when of a sudden I said:

"I'll change my mind, Bain. I wonder if you have a lemon in the house?"

"I'll go to the kitchen and see if cook has one, sir," replied the old man, who, placing down the tray, left to do my bidding.

In an instant I sprang forward and seized the empty tumbler, handling it carefully. Swiftly, I tore a piece off the evening paper, and wrapping it around the glass, placed it in the pocket of my dinner jacket.

Then, going into the hall, I put on my overcoat and hat, and awaited Bain's return.

"I shan't want that lemon!" I cried to him as he came up from the lower regions. "Good-night, Bain!" and a few moments later I was in a taxi speeding towards Albemarle Street, with the evidence I wanted safe in my keeping.

That finger-prints remained on the polished surface of the glass I knew full well—the prints of my beloved's fingers.

But would they turn out to be the same as the fingers which had rested upon the glass-topped specimen-table in Digby's room?

Opening the door with my latch-key, I dashed upstairs, eager to put my evidence to the proof by means of the finely-powdered green chalk I had already secured—the same as that used by the police.

But on the threshold of my chambers Haines met me with a message—a message which caused me to halt breathless and staggered.

VIII

Contains Further Evidence

S ir Digby Kemsley was here an hour ago, sir. He couldn't wait!" Haines exclaimed, bringing himself to attention.

"Sir Digby!" I gasped, starting. "Why, in heaven's name, didn't you ring me up at Mrs. Shand's?" I cried.

"Because he wouldn't allow me, sir. He came to see you in strictest secrecy, sir. When I opened the door I didn't know him. He's shaved off his beard and moustache, and was dressed like a clergyman."

"A clergyman!"

"Yes, sir. He looked just like a parson. I wouldn't have known him in the street."

"An excellent ruse!" I exclaimed. "Of course, Haines, you know that—well—that the police are looking for him—eh?"

"Perfectly well, but you can trust me, sir. I'll say nothing. Sir Digby's a friend of yours."

"Yes, a great friend, and I feel that he's falsely accused of that terrible affair which happened at his flat," I said. "Did he promise to call again?"

"He scribbled this note for you," Haines said, taking up a letter from my blotting-pad.

With trembling fingers I tore it open, and upon a sheet of my own notepaper read the hurriedly written words—

Sorry you were out. Wanted to see you most urgently.
Keep your promise at Piccadilly Circus, and know nothing
concerning me. My movements are most uncertain, as
something amazing has occurred which prevents me making
explanation. I will, however, send you my address in secret
as soon as I have one. I trust you, Teddy, for you are my only
friend.

Digby

I read the note several times, and gathered that he was in hourly fear of arrest. Every corner held for him a grave danger. Yet what could have occurred that was so amazing and which prevented him speaking the truth.

That I had not been in when he called was truly unfortunate. But by the fact that he was in clerical attire I surmised that he was living in obscurity—perhaps somewhere in the suburbs. London is the safest city in the world in which to hide, unless, of course, creditors or plaintiffs make it necessary to seek peace "beyond the jurisdiction of the Court."

Many a good man is driven to the latter course through no fault of his own, but by the inexorable demands of the Commissioners of Income Tax, or by undue pressure from antagonistic creditors. Every English colony on the Continent contains some who have fallen victims—good, honest Englishmen—who are dragging out the remainder of their lives in obscurity, men whose names are perhaps household words, but who conceal them beneath one assumed.

Digby would probably join the throng of the exiled. So I could do naught else than wait for his promised message, even though I was frantic in my anxiety to see and to question him regarding the reason of the presence of my well-beloved at his flat on that fatal night.

Imagine my bitter chagrin that I had not been present to receive him! It might be many months before I heard from him again, for his promise was surely very vague.

Presently I took the glass very carefully from my pocket, unwrapped it from its paper, and locked it in a little cabinet in the corner of my room, until next morning I brought it forth, and placing it upon a newspaper powdered it well with the pale green chalk which revealed at once a number of finger-marks—mine, Bain's, and Phrida's.

I am something of a photographer, as everybody is in these days of photo competitions. Therefore, I brought out my Kodak with its anastigmat lens,—a camera which I had carried for some years up and down Europe, and after considerable arrangement of the light, succeeded in taking a number of pictures. It occupied me all the morning, and even then I was not satisfied with the result. My films might, for aught I know, be hopelessly fogged.

Therefore, with infinite care, I took the glass to a professional photographer I knew in Bond Street, and he also made a number of pictures, which were duly developed and enlarged some hours later, and showed the distinctive lines and curves of each finger-print.

Not until the morning of the day following was I able to take these latter to Edwards, and then a great difficulty presented itself. How was I to explain how I had obtained the prints?

I sat for an hour smoking cigarettes furiously and thinking deeply.

At last a plan presented itself, and taking a taxi I went down to Scotland Yard, where I had no difficulty in obtaining an interview in his airy, barely-furnished business-like room.

"Hulloa, Mr. Royle!" he exclaimed cheerily as I entered. "Sit down—well, do you know anything more of that mysterious friend of yours—eh?"

I did not reply. Why should I lie? Instead, I said:

"I've been doing some amateur detective work. Have you the photographs of those finger-prints found on the specimen-table in Sir Digby's room?"

"Yes, of course," was his prompt reply, and going over to a cupboard he brought out a pile of papers concerning the case, and from it produced a number of photographic prints.

My heart stood still when I saw them. Were either of them exactly similar to any of those I carried with me? I almost feared to allow comparison to be made.

Edwards, noticing my hesitation, asked in what quarter my efforts had been directed.

"I've been getting some finger-prints, that's all," I blurted forth, and from my pocket drew the large envelope containing the prints.

The detective took them across to the window and regarded them very closely for some time, while I looked eagerly over his shoulder.

The curves and lines were extremely puzzling to me, unaccustomed as I was to them. Edwards, too, remained in silent indecision.

"We'll send them along to Inspector Tirrell in the Finger-print Department," my friend said at last. "He's an expert, and will tell at a glance if any marks are the same as ours."

Then he rang a bell, and a constable, at his instructions, carried all the prints to the department in question.

"Well, Mr. Royle," exclaimed the inspector when the door had closed; "how did you obtain those prints?"

I was ready for his question, and a lie was at once glibly upon my lips.

"Sir Digby, on the night of his disappearance, returned to me a small steel despatch box which he had borrowed some weeks before; therefore, after the affair, I examined it for finger-prints, with the result I have shown you," I said.

"Ah! but whatever prints were upon it were there before the entrance of the victim to your friend's rooms," he exclaimed. "He gave it to you when you bade him good-night, I suppose?"

"Yes."

"And you carried the box home with you?"

"Yes," I repeated; in fear nevertheless, that my lie might in some way incriminate me. Yet how could I tell him of my suspicion of Phrida. That secret was mine—and mine alone, and, if necessary, I would carry it with me to the grave.

Edwards was again silent for some minutes.

"No, Mr. Royle, I can't see that your evidence helps us in the least. If there should be the same prints on your despatch box as we found upon the specimen-table, then what do they prove?—why, nothing. If the box had been in the room at the time of the tragedy, then it might have given us an important clue, because such an object would probably be touched by any malefactor or assassin. But—"

"Ah!" I cried, interrupting. "Then you do not suspect Sir Digby, after all—eh?"

"Pardon me, Mr. Royle, but I did not say that I held no suspicion," was his quiet answer. "Yet, if you wish to know the actual truth, I, at present, am without suspicion of anyone—except of that second woman, the mysterious woman whose finger-prints we have, and who was apparently in the room at the same time as the unidentified victim."

"You suspect her, then?" I asked breathlessly.

"Not without further proof," he replied, with a calm, irritating smile. "I never suspect unless I have good grounds for doing so. At present we have three clear finger-prints of a woman whom nobody saw enter or leave, just as nobody saw the victim enter. Your friend Sir Digby seems to have held a midnight reception of persons of mysterious character, and with tragic result."

"I feel sure he is no assassin," I cried.

"It may have been a drama of jealousy—who knows?" said Edwards, standing erect near the window and gazing across at me. "Your friend, in any case, did not care to remain and explain what happened. A girl—an unknown girl—was struck down and killed."

"By whom, do you think?"

"Ah! Mr. Royle, the identity of the assassin is what we are endeavouring to discover," he replied gravely. "We must first find this man who has

WILLIAM LE QUEUX

so successfully posed as Sir Digby Kemsley. He is a clever and elusive scoundrel, without a doubt. But his portrait is already circulated both here and on the Continent. The ports are all being watched, while I have five of the best men I can get engaged on persistent inquiry. He'll try to get abroad, no doubt. No doubt, also, he has a banking account somewhere, and through that we shall eventually trace him. Every man entrusts his banker with his address. He has to, in order to obtain money."

"Unless he draws his money out in cash and then goes to a tourist agency and gets a letter of credit."

"Ah, yes, that's often done," my friend admitted. "The tourist agencies are of greatest use to thieves and forgers. They take stolen notes, change them into foreign money, and before the numbers can be circulated are off across the Channel with their booty. If we look for stolen notes we are nearly certain to find them in the hands of a tourist agency or a money-changer."

"Then you anticipate that you may find my friend Digby through his bankers?"

"Perhaps," was his vague answer. "But as he is your friend, Mr. Royle, I perhaps ought not to tell you of the channels of information we are trying," he added, with a dry laugh.

"Oh, I assure you I'm entirely ignorant of his whereabouts," I said. "If I knew, I should certainly advise him to come and see you."

"Ah! you believe in his innocence, I see?"

"I most certainly do!"

"Well,—we shall see—we shall see," he said in that pessimistic tone which he so often adopted.

"What are you doing about those letters—that letter which mentions the fountain?" I asked.

"Nothing. I've dismissed those as private correspondence regarding some love episode of the long ago," he replied. "They form no clue, and are not worth following."

At that moment the constable re-entered bearing the photographs.

"Well, what does Inspector Tirrell say?" Edwards asked quickly of the man.

"He has examined them under the glass, sir, and says that they are the same prints in both sets of photographs—the thumb and index-finger of a woman—probably a young and refined woman. He's written a memo there, sir."

Edwards took it quickly, and after glancing at it, handed it to me to read.

It was a mere scribbled line signed with the initials "W. H. T.," to the effect that the same prints appeared in both photographs, and concluded with the words "No record of this person is known in this department."

I know I stood pale and breathless at the revelation—at the incontestable proof that my well-beloved had actually been present in Digby's room after my departure on that fatal night.

Why?

By dint of a great effort I succeeded in suppressing the flood of emotions which so nearly overcame me, and listened to Edwards as he remarked:

"Well, after all, Mr. Royle, it doesn't carry us any further. Our one object is to discover the identity of the woman in question, and I think we can only do that from your absconding friend himself. If the marks are upon your despatch-box as you state, then the evidence it furnishes rather disproves the theory that the unknown woman was actually present at the time of the tragedy."

I hardly know what words I uttered.

I had successfully misled the great detective of crime, but as I rode along in the taxi back to my rooms, I was in a frenzy of despair, for I had proved beyond a shadow of doubt that Phrida was aware of what had occurred—that a black shadow of guilt lay upon her.

The woman I had loved and trusted, she who was all the world to me, had deceived me, though she smiled upon me so sweetly. She, alas! held within her breast a guilty secret.

Ah! in that hour of my bitterness and distress the sun of my life became eclipsed. Only before me was outspread a limitless grey sea of dark despair.

IX

Describes the Yellow Sign

The night of my mysterious tryst—the night of January the fourteenth—was dark, rainy, and unpleasant.

That afternoon I had taken out the sealed letter addressed to "E. P. K." and turned it over thoughtfully in my hand.

I recollected the words of the fugitive. He had said:

"On the night of the fourteenth just at eight o'clock precisely, go to the Piccadilly Tube Station and stand at the first telephone box numbered four, on the Haymarket side, when a lady in black will approach you and ask news of me. In response you will give her this note. But there is a further condition. You may be watched and recognised. Therefore, be extremely careful that you are not followed on that day, and, above all, adopt some effective disguise. Go there dressed as a working man, I would suggest."

Very strange was that request of his. It filled me with eager curiosity. What should I learn from the mysterious woman in black who was to come to me for a message from my fugitive friend.

Had he already contemplated flight when he had addressed the note to her and made the appointment, I wondered.

If so, the crime at Harrington Gardens must have been premeditated.

I recollected, too, those strange, prophetic words which my friend had afterwards uttered, namely:

"I want you to give me your promise, Royle. I ask you to make a solemn vow to me that if any suspicion arises within your mind, that you will believe nothing without absolute and decisive proof. I mean, that you will not misjudge her."

By "her" he had indicated the lady whose initials were "E. P. K."

It was certainly mysterious, and my whole mind was centred upon the affair that day.

As I stood before my glass at seven o'clock that evening, I presented a strange, uncanny figure, dressed as I was in a shabby suit which I had obtained during the day from a theatrical costumier's in Covent Garden.

Haines, to whom I had invented a story that I was about to play a practical joke, stood by much amused at my appearance.

"Well, sir," he exclaimed; "you look just like a bricklayer's labourer!"

The faded suit, frayed at the wrists and elbows, had once been grey, but it was now patched, brown, smeared with plaster, and ingrained with white dust, as was the ragged cap; while the trousers were ragged at the knees and bottoms. Around my neck was a dirty white scarf and in my hand I carried a tin tea-bottle as though I had just returned from work.

"Yes," I remarked, regarding myself critically. "Not even Miss Shand would recognise me—eh, Haines?"

"No, sir. I'm sure she wouldn't. But you'll have to dirty your face and hands a bit. Your hands will give you away if you're not careful."

"Yes. I can't wear gloves, can I?" I remarked.

Thereupon, I went to the grate and succeeded in rubbing ashes over my hands and applying some of it to my cheeks—hardly a pleasant face powder, I can assure you.

At a quarter to eight, with the precious letter in the pocket of my ragged jacket, I left Albemarle Street and sauntered along Piccadilly towards the Circus. The rain had ceased, but it was wet underfoot, and the motor buses plashed foot passengers from head to foot with liquid mud. In my walk I passed, outside the Piccadilly Hotel, two men I knew. One of them looked me straight in the face but failed to recognise me.

Piccadilly Circus, the centre of the night-life of London, is unique, with its jostling crowds on pleasure bent, its congestion of traffic, its myriad lights, its flashing, illuminated signs, and the bright façade of the Criterion on the one side and the Pavilion on the other. Surely one sees the lure of London there more than at any other spot in the whole of our great metropolis.

Passing the Criterion and turning into the Haymarket, I halted for a moment on the kerb, and for the first time in my life, perhaps, gazed philosophically upon the frantic, hurrying panorama of human life passing before my eyes.

From where I stood I could see into the well-lit station entrance with the row to the telephone boxes, at the end of which sat the smart young operator, who was getting numbers and collecting fees. All the boxes were engaged, and several persons were waiting, but in vain my eyes searched for a lady in black wearing mimosa.

The winter wind was bitterly cold, and as I was without an overcoat it cut through my thin, shabby clothes, causing me to shiver. Nevertheless, I kept my watchful vigil. By a neighbouring clock I could see that it was already five minutes past the hour of the appointment. Still, I waited in eager expectation of her coming.

The only other person who seemed to loiter there was a thin, shivering Oriental, who bore some rugs upon his shoulder—a hawker of shawls.

Past me there went men and women of every grade and every station. Boys were crying "Extrur spe-shull," and evil-looking loafers, those foreign scoundrels who infest the West End, lurked about, sometimes casting a suspicious glance at me, with the thought, perhaps, that I might be a detective.

Ah! the phantasmagora of life outside the Piccadilly Tube at eight o'clock in the evening is indeed a strangely complex one. The world of London has then ceased to work and has given itself over to pleasure, and, alas! in so many cases, to evil.

In patience I waited. The moments seemed hours, for in my suspense I was dubious whether, after all, she would appear. Perhaps she already knew, by some secret means, of Sir Digby's flight, and if so, she would not keep the appointment.

I strolled up and down the pavement, for a policeman, noticing me hanging about, had gruffly ordered me to "Move on!" He, perhaps, suspected me of "loitering for the purpose of committing a felony."

Everywhere my eager eyes searched to catch sight of some person in black wearing a spray of yellow blossom, but among that hurrying crowd there was not one woman, young or old, wearing that flower so reminiscent of the Riviera.

I entered the station, and for some moments stood outside the telephone box numbered 4. Then, with failing heart, I turned and went along to the spacious booking-hall, where the lifts were ever descending with their crowds of passengers.

Would she ever come? Or, was my carefully planned errand entirely in vain?

I could not have mistaken the date, for I had made a note of it in my diary directly on my return from Harrington Gardens, and before I had learned of the tragedy. No. It now wanted a quarter to nine and she had not appeared. At nine I would relinquish my vigil, and assume my normal identity. I was sick to death of lounging there in the cutting east wind with the smoke-blackened tin bottle in my hand.

I had been idly reading an advertisement on the wall, and turned, when my quick eyes suddenly caught sight of a tall, well-dressed woman of middle age, who, standing with her back to me, was speaking to the telephone-operator.

I hurried eagerly past her, when my heart gave a great bound. In the corsage of her fur-trimmed coat she wore the sign for which I had been searching for an hour—a sprig of mimosa!

With my heart beating quickly in wild excitement, I drew back to watch her movements.

She had asked the operator for a number, paid him, and was told that she was "on" at box No. 4.

I saw her enter, and watched her through the glass door speaking vehemently with some gesticulation. The answer she received over the wire seemed to cause her the greatest surprise, for I saw how her dark, handsome face fell when she heard the response.

In a second her manner changed. From a bold, commanding attitude she at once became apprehensive and appealing. Though I could not hear the words amid all that hubbub and noise, I knew that she was begging the person at the other end to tell her something, but was being met with a flat refusal.

I saw how the black-gloved hand, resting upon the little ledge, clenched itself tightly as she listened. I fancied that tears had come into her big, dark eyes, but perhaps it was only my imagination.

At last she put down the receiver and emerged from the box, with a strange look of despair upon her handsome countenance.

What, I wondered, had happened?

She halted outside the box for a moment, gazing about her as though in expectation of meeting someone. She saw me, but seeing only a labourer, took no heed of my presence. Then she glanced at the tiny gold watch in her bracelet, and noting that it was just upon nine, drew a long breath—a sigh as though of despair.

I waited until she slowly walked out towards the street, and following, came up beside her and said in a low voice:

"I wonder, madame, if you are looking for me?"

She glanced at me quickly, with distinct suspicion, and noting my dress, regarded me with some disdain.

Her dark brows were knit for a second in distinct displeasure, even of apprehension, and then in an instant I recollected my friend's injunction that I might be watched and followed. In giving her the message the greatest secrecy was to be observed.

She halted, as though in hesitation, took from her bag a tiny lace handkerchief and dabbed her face, then beneath her breath, and without glancing further at me, said:

"Follow me, and I will speak to you presently—when there is no danger."

Upon that I moved away and leisurely lit my pipe, as though entirely unconcerned, while she still stood in the doorway leading to the Haymarket, looking up and down as though awaiting somebody.

Yes, she was a distinctly handsome woman; tall, erect, and well preserved. Her gown fitted her perfectly, and her black jacket, trimmed with some rich dark fur, was a garment which gave her the stamp of a woman of wealth and refinement. She wore a neat felt hat also trimmed with fur, white gloves, and smart shoes, extremely small, even girlish, for a woman so well developed.

Presently she sauntered forth down the Haymarket, and a few moments afterwards, still smoking and carrying my bottle, I lounged lazily after her.

At the corner, by the Carlton, she turned into Pall Mall, continuing along that thoroughfare without once looking back. Opposite the United Service Club she crossed the road, and passing across the square in front of the Athenæum, descended the long flight of steps which led into the Mall.

There in the darkness, beneath the trees, where there were no onlookers—for at that hour the Mall is practically deserted, save for a few loving couples and a stray taxi or two—she suddenly paused, and I quickly approached and raised my cap politely.

"Well?" she asked sharply, almost in a tone of annoyance. "What is it? What do you want with me, my man?"

X

Cherchez La Femme

I confess that her attitude took me aback.

I was certainly unprepared for such a reception.

"I believed, madame, that you were in search of me?" I said, with polite apology.

"I certainly was not. I don't know you in the least," was her reply. "I went to the Tube to meet a friend who did not keep his appointment. Is it possible that you have been sent by him? In any case, it was very injudicious for you to approach me in that crowd. One never knows who might have been watching."

"I come as messenger from my friend, Sir Digby Kemsley," I said in a low voice.

"From him?" she gasped eagerly. "I—ah! I expected him. Is he prevented from coming? It was so very important, so highly essential, that we should meet," she added in frantic anxiety as we stood there in the darkness beneath the bare trees, through the branches of which the wind whistled weirdly.

"I have this letter," I said, drawing it from my pocket. "It is addressed 'For E. P. K.'"

"For me?" she cried with eagerness, as she took it in her gloved hand, and then leaving my side she hurried to a street lamp, where she tore it open and read the contents.

From where I stood I heard her utter an ejaculation of sudden terror. I saw how she crushed the paper in one hand while with the other she pressed her brow. Whatever the letter contained it was news which caused her the greatest apprehension and fear, for dashing back to me she asked:

"When did he give you this? How long ago?"

"On the night of January the sixth," was my reply. "The night when he left Harrington Gardens in mysterious circumstances."

"Mysterious circumstances!" she echoed. "What do you mean? Is he no longer there?"

"No, madame. He has left, and though I am, perhaps, his most intimate friend, I am unaware of his whereabouts. There were," I added, "reasons, I fear, for his disappearance."

"Who are you? Tell me, first."

"My name is Edward Royle," was my brief response.

"Ah! Mr. Royle," the woman cried, "he has spoken of you many times. You were his best friend, he said. I am glad, indeed, to meet you, but—but tell me why he has disappeared—what has occurred?"

"I thought you would probably know that my friend is wanted by the police," I replied gravely. "His description has been circulated everywhere."

"But why?" she gasped, staring at me. "Why are the police in search of him?"

For a few seconds I hesitated, disinclined to repeat the grave charge against him.

"Well," I said at last in a low, earnest voice, "the fact is the police have discovered that Sir Digby Kemsley died in South America some months ago."

"I don't follow you," she said.

"Then I will be more plain. The police, having had a report of the death of Sir Digby, believe our mutual friend to be an impostor!"

"An impostor! How utterly ridiculous. Why, I myself can prove his identity. The dead man must have been some adventurer who used his name."

"That is a point which I hope with your assistance to prove," I said. "The police at present regard our friend with distinct suspicion."

"And I suppose his worst enemy has made some serious allegation against him—that woman who hates him so. Ah! I see it all now. I see why he has written this to me—this confession which astounds me. Ah! Mr. Royle," she added, her gloved hands tightly clenched in her despair. "You do not know in what deadly peril Sir Digby now is. Yes, I see it plainly. There is a charge against him—a grave and terrible charge—which he is unable to refute, and yet he is perfectly innocent. Oh, what can I do? How can I act to save him?" and her voice became broken by emotion.

"First tell me the name of this woman who was such a deadly enemy of his. If you reveal this to me, I may be able to throw some light upon circumstances which are at the present moment a complete mystery."

"No, that is his secret," was her low, calm reply. "He made me swear never to reveal the woman's name."

"But his honour—nay, his liberty—is now at stake," I urged.

"That does not exonerate me from breaking my word of honour, Mr. Royle."

"Then he probably entertains affection for the woman, and is hence loth to do anything which might cause her pain. Strangely enough, men often love women whom they know are their bitterest enemies."

"Quite so. But the present case is full of strange and romantic facts—facts, which if written down, would never be believed. I know many of them myself, and can vouch for them."

"Well, is this unnamed woman a very vengeful person?" I asked, remembering the victim who had been found dead at Harrington Gardens.

"Probably so. All women, when they hate a man, are vengeful."

"Why did she hate him so?"

"Because she believed a story told of him—an entirely false story—of how he had treated the man she loved. I taxed him with it, and he denied it, and brought me conclusive proof that the allegation was a pure invention."

"Is she young or middle-aged?"

"Young, and distinctly pretty," was her reply.

Was it possible that this woman was speaking of that girl whom I had seen lying dead in my friend's flat? Had he killed her because he feared what she might reveal? How dearly I wished that I had with me at that moment a copy of the police photographs of the unidentified body.

But even then she would probably declare it not to be the same person, so deeply had Sir Digby impressed upon her the necessity of regarding the affair as strictly secret.

Indeed, as I walked slowly at her side, I saw that, whatever the note contained, it certainly had the effect upon her of preserving her silence.

In that case, could the crime have been premeditated by my friend? Had he written her that secret message well knowing that he intended to kill the mysterious woman who was his deadliest enemy.

That theory flashed across my brain as I walked with her, and I believed it to be the correct one. I accepted it the more readily because it removed from my mind those dark suspicions concerning Phrida, and, also, in face of facts which this unknown lady had dropped, it seemed to be entirely feasible.

Either the unsuspecting woman fell by the hand of Digby Kemsley or—how can I pen the words—by the hand of Phrida, the woman I loved. There was the evidence that a knife with a triangular blade had been used, and such a knife had been, and was still, in the possession of my well-beloved; but from what I had learned that night it seemed that, little as I had dreamed the truth, my friend Digby had been held in bondage by a woman, whose tongue he feared.

Ah! How very many men in London are the slaves of women whom they fear. All of us are human, and the woman with evil heart is, alas! only too ready to seize the opportunity of the frailty of the opposite sex, and whatever may be the secret she learns, of business or of private life, she will most certainly turn it to her advantage.

It was similar circumstances I feared in the case of dear old Digby.

I was wondering, as I walked, whether I should reveal to my companion—whose name she had told me was Mrs. Petre—the whole of the tragic circumstances.

"Is it long ago since you last saw Digby?" I asked her presently, as we strolled slowly together, and after I had given her my address, and we had laughed together over my effective disguise.

"Nearly two months," she replied. "I've been in Egypt since the beginning of November—at Assuan."

"I was there two seasons ago," I said. "How delightful it is in Upper Egypt—and what a climate in winter! Why, it is said that it has never rained there for thirty years!"

"I had a most awfully jolly time at the Cataract. It was full of smart people, for only the suburbs, the demi-monde, and Germans go to the Riviera nowadays. It's so terribly played out, and the Carnival gaiety is so childish and artificial."

"It amuses the Cookites," I laughed; "and it puts money in the pockets of the hotel-keepers of Nice and the neighbourhood."

"Monte is no longer *chic*," she declared. "German women in blouses predominate; and the really smart world has forsaken the Rooms for Cairo, Heliopolis, and Assuan. They are too far off and too expensive for the bearer of Cook's coupons."

I laughed. She spoke with the nonchalant air of the smart woman of the world, evidently much travelled and cosmopolitan.

But I again turned the conversation to our mutual friend, and strove with all the diplomatic powers I possessed to induce her to reveal the name or give me a description of the woman whom she had alleged to be his enemy—the woman who was under a delusion that he had wronged her lover. To all my questions, however, she remained dumb. That letter which I had placed in her hand had, no doubt, put a seal of silence upon her lips.

At one moment she assumed a haughtiness of demeanour which suited her manner and bearing, at the next she became sympathetic and eager. She was, I gauged, a woman of strangely complex character. Yet whom could she be? I knew most, perhaps even all, of Digby's friends, I believed. He often used to give cosy little tea parties, to which women—many of them well known in society—came. Towards them he always assumed quite a paternal attitude, for he was nothing if not a ladies' man.

She seemed very anxious to know in what circumstances he had handed me the note, and what instructions he had given me. To her questions I replied quite frankly. Indeed, I repeated his words.

"Ah! yes," she cried. "He urged you not to misjudge me. Then you will not, Mr. Royle—will you?" she asked me with sudden earnestness.

"I have no reason to misjudge you, Mrs. Petre," I said, quietly. "Why should I?"

"Ah! but you may. Indeed, you most certainly will."

"When?" I asked, in some surprise.

"When—when you know the bitter truth."

"The truth of what?" I gasped, my thoughts reverting to the tragedy in Harrington Gardens. Though I had not referred to it I felt that she must be aware of what had occurred, and of the real reason of Digby's flight.

"The truth which you must know ere long," she answered hoarsely as we halted again beneath the leafless trees. "And when you learn it you will most certainly condemn me. But believe me, Mr. Royle, I am like your friend, Sir Digby, more sinned against than sinning."

"You speak in enigmas," I said.

"Because I cannot—I dare not tell you what I know. I dare not reveal the terrible and astounding secret entrusted to me. You will know it all soon enough. But—there," she added in a voice broken in despair, "what can matter now that Digby has shown the white feather—and fled."

"He was not a coward, Mrs. Petre," I remarked very calmly.

"No. He was a brave and honest man until—" and she paused, her low voice fading to a whisper that I did not catch.

"Until what?" I asked. "Did something happen?"

"Yes, it did," she replied in a hard, dry tone. "Something happened which changed his life."

"Then he is not the impostor the police believe?" I demanded.

"Certainly not," was her prompt reply. "Why he has thought fit to disappear fills me with anger. And yet—yet from this letter he has sent to me I can now see the reason. He was, no doubt, compelled to fly, poor fellow. His enemy forced him to do so."

"The woman—eh?"

"Yes, the woman," she admitted, bitter hatred in her voice.

Then, after a pause, I said: "If I can be of any service to you, Mrs. Petre, for we are both friends of Digby's, I trust you will not fail to command me."

And I handed her a card from my case, which I had carried expressly.

"You are very kind, Mr. Royle," she replied. "Perhaps I may be very glad of your services one day. Who knows? I live at Park Mansions."

"And may I call?"

"For the present, no. I let my flat while I went abroad, and it is still occupied for several weeks. I shall not be there before the first week in March."

"But I want to find Digby—I want to see him most urgently," I said.

"And so do I!"

"How can we trace him?" I asked.

"Ah! I am afraid he is far too elusive. If he wishes to hide himself we need not hope to find him until he allows us to," she replied. "No, all we can do is to remain patient and hopeful."

Again a silence fell between us. I felt instinctively that she wished to confide in me, but dare not do so.

Therefore I exclaimed suddenly:

"Will you not tell me, Mrs. Petre, the identity of this great enemy of our friend—this woman? Upon information which you yourself may give, Digby's future entirely depends," I added earnestly.

"His future!" she echoed. "What do you mean?"

"I mean only that I am trying to clear his good name of the stigma now resting upon it."

The handsome woman bit her lip.

"No," she replied with a great effort. "I'm sorry—deeply sorry—but I am now in a most embarrassing position. I have made a vow to him, and that vow I cannot break without first obtaining his permission. I am upon my honour."

I was silent. What could I say?

This woman certainly knew something—something which, if revealed, would place me in possession of the truth of what had actually occurred at Harrington Gardens on that fatal night. If she spoke she might clear Phrida of all suspicion.

Suddenly, after a pause, I made up my mind to try and clear up one point—that serious, crucial point which had for days so obsessed me.

"Mrs. Petre," I said, "I wonder if you will answer me a single question, one which does not really affect the situation much. Indeed, as we are, I hope, friends, I ask it more out of curiosity than anything else."

"Well, what is it?" she asked, regarding me strangely.

"I want to know whether, being a friend of Digby's, you have ever met or ever heard of a certain young lady living in Kensington named Phrida Shand."

The effect of my words was almost electrical. She sprung towards me, with fire in her big, dark eyes.

"Phrida Shand!" she cried wildly, her white-gloved hands again clenched. "Phrida Shand! You know that woman, eh? You know her, Mr. Royle. Is she a friend of yours?—or—or is she your enemy? Your friend, perhaps, because she is pretty. Oh, yes!" she laughed, hysterically. "Oh, yes! Of course, she is your friend. If she is—then curse her, Mr. Royle—invoke all the curses of hell upon her, as she so richly deserves!"

And from her lips came a peal of laughter that was little short of demoniacal, while I stood glaring at her in blank dismay.

What did she mean? Aye, what, indeed?

XI

In Which an Allegation is Made

I stood aghast at her words.

I strove to induce her to speak more openly, and to tell me why I should not regard Phrida as my friend.

But she only laughed mysteriously, saying:

"Wait, and you will see."

"You make a distinct charge against her, therefore I think you ought to substantiate it," I said in a tone of distinct annoyance.

"Ah! Mr. Royle. Heed my words, I beg of you."

"But, tell me, is Miss Shand the same person as you have denounced as Digby's enemy?" I asked in breathless apprehension. "Surely you will tell me, Mrs. Petre, now that we are friends."

"Ah! but are we friends?" she asked, looking at me strangely beneath the light of the street-lamp in that deserted thoroughfare, where all was silence save the distant hum of the traffic. The dark trees above stood out distinct against the dull red night-glare of London, as the mysterious woman stood before me uttering that query.

"Because we are mutual friends of Sir Digby's. I hope I may call you a friend," I replied, as calmly as I was able.

She paused for a moment in indecision. Then she said:

"You admit that you are friendly with the girl Shand—eh?"

"Certainly."

"More than friendly, I wonder?" she asked in a sharp tone.

"Well—I'll be perfectly frank," was my answer. "I am engaged to be married to her."

"Married," she gasped, "to her! Are you mad, Mr. Royle?"

"I think not," I answered, greatly surprised at her sudden attitude. "Why?"

"Because—because," she replied in a low, earnest voice, scarce above a whisper, "because, before you take such a step make further inquiry."

"Inquiry about what?" I demanded.

"About—well, about what has occurred at Harrington Gardens."

"Then you know!" I cried. "You know the truth, Mrs. Petre?"

"No," she replied quite calmly. "I know from this letter what must have occurred there. But who killed the girl I cannot say."

"Who was the girl they found dead?" I asked breathlessly.

"Ah! How can I tell? I did not see her."

In a few quick words I described the deceased, but either she did not recognise her from the description, or she refused to tell me. In any case, she declared herself in ignorance.

The situation was galling and tantalising. I was so near discovering the truth, and yet my inquiries had only plunged me more deeply into a quagmire of suspicion and horror. The more I tried to extricate myself the deeper I sank.

"But whoever the poor girl may have been, you still maintain that Phrida Shand was Digby's most deadly enemy?" I asked quickly, setting a trap for her.

I took her unawares, and she fell into it.

"Yes," was her prompt response. An instant later, however, realising how she had been led to make an allegation which she had not intended, she hastened to correct herself, saying: "Ah, no! Of course, I do not allege that. I—I only know that Digby was acquainted with her, and that—"

"Well?" I asked slowly, when she paused.

"That—that he regretted the acquaintanceship."

"Regretted? Why?"

The woman shrugged her shoulders. All along she had been cognisant of the tragedy, yet with her innate cleverness she had not admitted her knowledge.

"A man often regrets his friendship with a woman," she said, with a mysterious air.

"What!" I cried fiercely. "Do you make an insinuation that—"

"My dear Mr. Royle," she laughed, "I make no insinuation. It was you who have endeavoured to compel me to condemn her as Digby's enemy. You yourself suggested it!"

"But you have told me that his fiercest and most bitter enemy was a woman!"

"Certainly. But I have not told you that woman's name, nor do I intend to break my vow of secrecy to Digby—fugitive that he may be at this moment. Yet, depend upon it, he will return and crush his enemies in the dust."

"I hope he will," was my fervent reply. "Yet I love Phrida Shand, and upon her there rests a terrible cloud of suspicion."

She was silent for a moment, still standing beneath the lamp, gazing at me with those big, dark eyes.

At last she said:

"The way out is quite easy."

"How?"

"If you have any regard for your future put your love aside," was her hard response.

"You hate her!" I said, knitting my brows, yet recollecting the proof I had secured of her presence in Digby's flat.

"Yes," was her prompt response. "I hate her—I have cause to hate her!"

"What cause?"

"That is my own affair, Mr. Royle—my own secret. Find Digby, and he will, no doubt, tell you the truth."

"The truth concerning Phrida?"

"Yes."

"But he knew I was engaged to her! Why did he not speak?"

"And expose her secret?" she asked. "Would he have acted as a gentleman had he done so? Does a man so lightly betray a woman's honour?"

"A woman's honour!" I gasped, staring at her, staggered as though she had struck me a blow. "What do you mean?"

"I mean nothing," was her cold reply. "Take it as you may, Mr. Royle, only be warned."

"But if Digby knew that she was worthless, he would surely have made some remark to arouse my suspicion?" I exclaimed.

"Why should he?" she queried. "A true gentleman does not usually expose a woman's secret."

I saw her point, and my heart sank within me. Were these scandalous allegations of hers based upon truth, or was she actuated by ill-feeling, perhaps, indeed, of jealousy?

We walked on again slowly until we reached St. James's Palace, and passed out into the end of Pall Mall, where it joined St. James's Street. Yet her attitude was one of complete mystery. I was uncertain whether the admission she had so unconsciously made regarding Phrida—that she was Digby's worst enemy—was the actual truth or not.

One thing was plain. This Mrs. Petre was a clever, far-seeing woman of the world, who had with great ingenuity held from me her knowledge of the crime.

A problem was, therefore, presented to me. By what means could she be aware of it? First, she had expected to meet Digby that evening; secondly, the letter I had brought was written before the assassination of the unknown girl.

How could she have obtained knowledge of the affair if it were not premeditated and hinted at in the letter I had so faithfully delivered?

Half way up St. James's Street my companion suddenly exclaimed:

"I must be going! Would you please hail me a taxi, Mr. Royle?"

"I will—when you have answered my question," I said, with great politeness.

"I have already replied to it," was her response. "You love Phrida Shand, but if you have any self-respect, any regard for your future, break off Whatever infatuation she has exercised over you. If you are Digby's friend, you will be a man, and act as such!"

"I really don't follow you," I said, bewildered.

"Perhaps not. But surely my words are plain enough!"

"Is she the enemy of Digby, of whom you have spoken?"

"That question I am not permitted to answer."

I was silent a few seconds. Then I asked earnestly:

"Tell me openly and frankly, Mrs. Petre. Is she the person you suspect of having committed the crime?"

She gave vent to a short dry laugh.

"Really, Mr. Royle," she exclaimed, "you put to me the most difficult riddles. How can I possibly suspect anyone of a crime of which I know nothing, and of which even the papers appear to be in ignorance?"

"But you are not in ignorance," I said. "How, pray, did you learn that a tragedy had occurred?"

"Ah!" she laughed. "That is my secret. You were very careful not to tell me the true cause of poor Digby's flight. Yes, Mr. Royle, I congratulate you upon your ingenuity in protecting the honour of your friend. Rest assured he will not forget the great services you have already rendered him."

"I look for no reward. He was my friend," was my reply.

"Then, if he was your friend and you are still his, heed my warning concerning Phrida Shand."

"But tell me what you know?" I cried, clutching her arm as we walked together. "You don't understand that you are making allegations—terrible allegations—against the woman I love dearest in all the world.

WILLIAM LE QUEUX

You have made an assertion, and I demand that you shall substantiate it," I added in frantic anxiety.

She shook off my hand angrily, declaring that nothing more need be said, and adding that if I refused to heed her, then the peril would be mine.

"But you shall not leave me until you have furnished me with proof of these perfidious actions of my love!" I declared vehemently.

"Mr. Royle, we really cannot use high words in the public street," she replied in a low tone of reproof. "I am sorry that I am not permitted to say more."

"But you shall!" I persisted. "Tell me—what do you know? Is Digby the real Sir Digby?"

"Of course he is!"

"And what are his exact relations with Phrida?"

"Ah!" she laughed. "You had better ask her yourself, Mr. Royle. She will, no doubt, tell you. Of course, she will—well, if you are to marry her. But there, I see that you are not quite responsible for your words this evening. It is, perhaps, natural in the circumstances; therefore I will forgive you."

"Natural!" I echoed. "I should think it is natural that I should resent such dastardly allegations when made against the woman I love."

"All I repeat is—go and ask her for yourself," was the woman's quiet response as she drew herself up, and pulled her fur more closely about her throat. "I really can't be seen here talking with you in that garb," she added.

"But you must tell me," I persisted.

"I can tell you no more than I have done. The girl you love will tell you everything, or—at least, if you have a grain of ingenuity, as you no doubt have—you will find out everything for yourself."

"Ah! but—"

"No, not another word, please, Mr. Royle—not to-night. If after making inquiry into the matter you care to come and see me when I am back in Park Mansions, I shall be very happy to receive you. By that time, however, I hope we shall have had news of poor Digby's whereabouts."

"If I hear from him—as I expect to—how can I communicate with you?" I asked.

For a few seconds she stood wondering.

"Write to me to Park Mansions," she replied. "My letters are always forwarded."

And raising her umbrella she herself hailed a passing taxi.

"Remember my warning," were her final words as she gave the man an address in Regent's Park, and entered the conveyance. "Go and see Phrida Shand at once and tell her what I have said."

"May I mention your name?" I asked hoarsely.

"Yes," she replied. "Good-night."

And a moment later I was gazing at the red back-lamp of the taxi, while soon afterwards I again caught a glimpse of the same lonely seller of shawls whom I had seen at the Tube station, trudging wearily homeward, there being no business doing at that hour of the evening.

XII

PHRIDA MAKES CONFESSION

I sat in my rooms in Albemarle Street utterly bewildered.

My meeting with the mysterious woman who wore the spray of mimosa had, instead of assisting to clear up the mystery, increased it a hundredfold.

The grave suspicions I had entertained of Phrida had been corroborated by her strangely direct insinuations and her suggestion that I should go to her and tell her plainly what had been alleged.

Therefore, after a sleepless night, I went to Cromwell Road next morning, determined to know the truth. You can well imagine my state of mind when I entered Mrs. Shand's pretty morning-room, where great bowls of daffodils lent colour to the otherwise rather dull apartment.

Phrida entered, gay, fresh, and charming, in a dark skirt and white blouse, having just risen from breakfast.

"Really, Teddy," she laughed, "you ought to be awarded a prize for early rising. I fear I'm horribly late. It's ten o'clock. But mother and I went last night to the Aldwych, and afterwards with the Baileys to supper at the Savoy. So I may be forgiven, may I not—eh?"

"Certainly, dear," I replied, placing my hand upon her shoulder. "What are you doing to-day?"

"Oh! I'm quite full up with engagements," she replied, crossing to the writing-table and consulting a porcelain writing tablet.

"I'm due at my dressmaker's at half-past eleven, then I've to call in Mount Street at half-past twelve, lunch at the Berkeley, where mother has two women to lunch with her, and a concert at Queen's Hall at three—quite a day, isn't it?" she laughed.

"Yes," I said. "You are very busy—too busy even to talk seriously with me—eh?"

"Talk seriously!" she echoed, looking me straight in the face. "What do you mean, Teddy? Why, what's the matter?"

"Oh! nothing very much, dearest," was my reply, for I was striving to remain calm, notwithstanding my great anxiety and tortured mind.

"But there is," she persisted, clutching at my hand and looking eagerly into my face. "What is amiss? Tell me," she added, in low earnestness.

I was silent for a moment, and leaving her I crossed to the window and gazed out into the broad, grey thoroughfare, grim and dispiriting on that chilly January morning.

For a moment I held my breath, then, with sudden determination, I walked back to where she was standing, and placing both hands upon her shoulders, kissed her passionately upon the lips.

"You are upset to-day, Teddy," she said, with deep concern. "What has happened? Tell me, dear."

"I—I hardly know what's happened," I replied in a low voice. "But, Phrida," I said, looking straight into her great eyes, "I want to—to ask you a question."

"A question—what?" she demanded, her cheeks paling slightly.

"Yes. I want you to tell me what you know of a Mrs. Petre, a—"

"Mrs. Petre!" she gasped, stepping back from me, her face pale as death in an instant. "That woman!"

"Yes, that woman, Phrida. Who is she—what is she?"

"Please don't ask me, Teddy," my love cried in distress, covering her pretty face with her hands and bursting suddenly into tears.

"But I must, Phrida—I must, for my own peace of mind," I said.

"Why? Do you know the woman?"

"I met her last night," I explained. "I delivered to her a note which my friend Digby had entrusted to me."

"I thought your friend had disappeared?" she said quickly.

"It was given to me before his flight," was my response. "I fulfilled a confidential mission with which he entrusted me. And—and I met her. She knows you—isn't that so?"

I stood with my eyes full upon the white face of the woman I loved, surveying her coldly and critically, so full of black suspicion. Was my heart at that moment wholly hers? In imagination, place yourself, my reader, in a similar position. Put before yourself the problem with which, at that second, I found myself face to face.

I loved Phrida, and yet had I not obtained proof positive of her clandestine visit to my friend on that fateful night? Were her finger-prints not upon the little glass-topped specimen-table in his room?

And yet so clever, so ingenious had she been, so subtle was her woman's wit, that she had never admitted to me any knowledge of him further than a formal introduction I had once made long ago.

I had trusted her—aye, trusted her with all the open sincerity of an honourable man—for I loved her better than anything else on earth. And with what result?

With my own senses of smell and of hearing I had detected her presence on the stairs—waiting, it seemed, to visit my friend in secret after I had left.

No doubt she had been unaware of my identity as his visitor, or she would never dared to have lurked there.

As I stood with my hand tenderly upon her arm, the gaze of my well-beloved was directed to the ground. Guilt seemed written upon her white brow, for she dared not raise her eyes to mine.

"Phrida, you know that woman—you can't deny knowledge of her—can you?"

She stood like a statue, with her hands clenched, her mouth half open, her jaws fixed.

"I—I—I don't know what you mean," she faltered at last, in a hard voice quite unusual to her.

"I mean that I have a suspicion, Phrida—a horrible suspicion—that you have deceived me," I said.

"How?" she asked, with her harsh, forced laugh.

I paused. How should I tell her? How should I begin?

"You have suppressed from me certain knowledge of which you know I ought to have been in possession for my friend Digby's sake, and—"

"Ah! Digby Kemsley again!" she cried impatiently. "You've not been the same to me since that man disappeared."

"Because you know more concerning him than you have ever admitted to me, Phrida," I said in a firm, earnest voice, grasping her by the arm and whispering into her ear. "Now, be open and frank with me—tell me the truth."

"Of what?" she faltered, raising her eyes to mine with a frightened look.

"Of what Mrs. Petre has told me."

"That woman! What has she said against me?" my love demanded with quick resentment.

"She is not your friend, in any case," I said slowly.

"My friend!" she echoed. "I should think not. She—"

And my love's little hands clenched themselves and she burst again into tears without concluding her sentence.

"I know, dearest," I said, striving to calm her, and stroking her hair from her white brow. "I tell you at once that I do not give credence to any of her foul allegations, only—well, in order to satisfy myself, I have come direct to you to hear your explanation."

"My—my explanation!" she gasped, placing her hand to her brow and bowing her head. "Ah! what explanation can I make of allegations I have never heard?" she demanded. "Surely, Teddy, you are asking too much."

I grasped her hand, and holding it in mine gazed again upon her. We were standing together near the centre of the room where the glowing fire shed a genial warmth and lit up the otherwise gloomy and solemn apartment.

Ah! how sweet she seemed to me, how dainty, how charming, how very pure. And yet? Ah! the recollection of that woman's insinuations on the previous night ate like a canker-worm into my heart. And yet how I loved the pale, agitated girl before me! Was she not all the world to me?

A long and painful silence had fallen between us, a silence only broken by the whirl of a taxi passing outside and the chiming of the long, old-fashioned clock on the stairs.

At last I summoned courage to say in a calm, low voice;

"I am not asking too much, Phrida. I am only pressing you to act with your usual honesty, and tell me the truth. Surely you can have nothing to conceal?"

"How absurd you are, Teddy!" she said in her usual voice. "What can I possibly have to conceal from you?"

"Pardon me," I said; "but you have already concealed from me certain very important facts concerning my friend Digby."

"Who has told you that? The woman Petre, I suppose," she cried in anger. "Very well, believe her, if you wish."

"But I don't believe her," I protested.

"Then why ask me for an explanation?"

"Because one is, I consider, due from you in the circumstances."

"Then you have set yourself up to be my judge, have you?" she asked, drawing herself up proudly, all traces of her tears having vanished. I saw that the attitude she had now assumed was one of defiance; therefore I knew that if I were to obtain the information I desired I must act with greatest discretion.

"No, Phrida," I answered. "I do not mistrust or misjudge you. All I ask of you is the truth. What do you know of my friend Digby Kemsley?"

WILLIAM LE QUEUX

"Know of him—why, nothing—except that you introduced us."

For a second I remained silent. Then with severity I remarked:

"Pardon me, but I think you rather misunderstood my question. I meant to ask whether you have ever been to his flat in Harrington Gardens?"

"Ah! I see," she cried instantly. "That woman Petre has endeavoured to set you against me, Teddy, because I love you. She has invented some cruel lie or other, just as she did in another case within my knowledge. Come," she added, "tell me out plainly what she has alleged against me?"

She was very firm and resolute now, and I saw in her face a hard, defiant expression—an expression of bitter hatred against the woman who had betrayed her.

"Well," I said; "loving you as intensely as I do, I can hardly bring myself to repeat her insinuations."

"But I demand to know them," she protested, standing erect and facing me. "I am attacked; therefore, I am within my right to know what charges the woman has brought against me."

"She has brought no direct charges," was my slow reply. "But she has suggested certain things—certain scandalous things."

"What are they?" she gasped, suddenly pale as death.

"First tell me the truth, Phrida," I cried, holding her in my arms and looking straight into those splendid eyes I admired so much. "Admit it—you knew Digby. He—he was a friend of yours?"

"A—a friend—" she gasped, half choking with emotion. "A—friend—yes."

"You knew him intimately. You visited him at his rooms unknown to me!" I went on fiercely.

"Ah!" she shrieked. "Don't torture me like this, Teddy, when I love you so deeply. You don't know—you can never know all I have suffered—and now this woman has sought to ruin and crush me!"

"Has she spoken the truth when she says that you visited Digby—at night—in secret!" I demanded, bitterly, between my teeth, still holding her, her white, hard-set face but a few inches from my own.

She drew a long, deep breath, and in her eyes was a strange half-fascinated look—a look that I had never seen in them before.

"Ah! Teddy," she gasped. "This—this is the death of all our love. I foresee only darkness and ruin before me. But I will not lie to you. No! I—I—"

Then she paused, and a shudder ran through her slim frame which I held within my grasp. "I'll tell you the truth. Yes. I—I—went to see your friend unknown to you."

"You did!" I cried hoarsely, with fierce anger possessing my soul.

"Yes, dear," she faltered in a voice so low that I could scarce catch her reply. "Yes—I—I went there," she faltered, "because—because he—he compelled me."

"Compelled you!" I echoed in blank dismay.

But at that instant I saw that the blackness of unconsciousness had fallen upon my love even as I held her in my embrace.

And for me, too, alas! the sun of life had ceased to shine, and the world was dead.

XIII

THE FUGITIVE'S SECRET

Tenderly I placed my love upon the couch, and then rang the bell.

In answer to my summons the young Italian man-servant appeared.

"Send Mallock here quickly," I said. "Miss Shand is not well. But say nothing of this to your mistress, or to the other servants. You understand, Egisto?"

"Cer-tainly, sare," replied the smart young Tuscan, and a few moments later the door re-opened to admit the thin-faced maid in black, wearing her muslin apron and gold-rimmed glasses.

She dashed across to the couch in an instant, and bent, looking into the white, immobile face of my well-beloved.

"I fear your mistress has fainted, Mallock, so I thought it best to call you. I have, unfortunately, imparted to her some news which has upset her. Will you please see after her?"

"Of course, sir. I'll go and get some smelling salts and some water."

And quickly the girl disappeared. Then, when she had gone, I stood before the inanimate form of the woman I loved so well, and wondered what could be the real, actual truth.

Her admission had taken me aback. She had confessed to visiting my friend, but had alleged that he had compelled her. Was she actually beneath some mysterious thraldom—was she held in some secret bondage by the man I had trusted and who was my best friend?

The very suspicion of it filled me with a fierce irresponsible anger, and I clenched my fists.

Ah! I would find him and face him. I would clutch his throat and force the truth from his lips.

And if he had betrayed me—if he had exercised any evil influence over Phrida—then, by heaven! I would take his life!

Mallock bustled in the next moment, and sinking upon her knees began to apply restoratives.

"Tell your mistress that I will return after luncheon, if she will see me," I said.

"Yes, sir."

"And—and tell her, Mallock, to remain calm until I see her. Will you?"

"Yes, sir," answered the maid, and then I went out into the hall, struggled into my overcoat, and left the house.

Out in Cromwell Road the scene, grey, dull and dismal, was, alas! in accord with my own feelings.

The blow I had feared had fallen. The terrible suspicion I had held from that moment when, upon the stairs at Harrington Gardens, I had smelt that sweet, unusual perfume and heard the jingle of golden bangles, had been proved.

She had actually admitted her presence there—with the man I had believed to be my friend, the man, whom, up to the present, I had sought to shield and protect!

I hailed a taxi, and not knowing what I did, drove to the Reform. As I passed up the steps from Pall Mall the porter handed me my letters, and then, heedless of where my footsteps carried me, I entered the big, square hall and turned into the writing-room on the left—a room historic in the annals of British politics, for many a State secret had been discussed there by Ministers of the Crown, many a point of the Cabinet's policy had been decided, and also the fate of many a bill.

The long, sombre room with the writing tables covered with blue cloth, was empty, as it usually is, and I flung myself down to scribble a note—an apology for not keeping an appointment that afternoon.

My overburdened heart was full of chagrin and grief, for my idol had been shattered by a single blow, and only the wreck of all my hopes and aspirations now remained.

In a week's time the coroner would hold his adjourned inquiry into the tragedy at Harrington Gardens, and then what startling revelations might be made! By that time it was probable that the police would be able to establish the identity of the accused, and, moreover, with Mrs. Petre vengeful and incensed against Phrida, might she not make a statement to the authorities?

If so, what then?

I sat with my elbows upon the table staring out into Pall Mall, which wore such a cold and cheerless aspect that morning.

What could I do? How should I act? Ah! yes, at that moment I sat utterly bewildered, and trying in vain to discern some way out of that maze of mystery.

I had not looked at the unopened letters beneath my hand, but suddenly chancing to glance at them, I noticed one in an unfamiliar feminine handwriting.

I tore it open carelessly, expecting to find some invitation or other, when, within, I found three hastily scrawled lines written on the notepaper of the Great Eastern Hotel at Liverpool Street. It read:

"Since I saw you something has happened. Can you meet me again as soon as possible? Please wire me, Mrs. Petre, Melbourne House, Colchester."

I gazed at the note in extreme satisfaction. At least, I had the woman's address. Yes, after I had again seen Phrida I would see her and force from her lips the truth.

I rose quickly, placed the other letters in my pocket without opening them, and drove down to the City, where I was compelled to keep a business appointment.

At half-past three Egisto admitted me to Mrs. Shand's, and in reply to my question, told me that the "Signorina," as he always called Phrida, was in the morning-room.

Dressed in a pale grey gown, relieved with lace at the collar and wrists, she rose slowly from a big armchair as I entered, and came across to me, her face pale, drawn, and anxious.

"Ah! dearest," I cried. "I'm glad to see you better. Are you quite yourself again now?"

"Quite, thanks," was her low, rather weak reply. "I—I felt very unwell this morning. I—I don't know what was the matter." Then clinging to me suddenly, she added, "Ah! forgive me, Teddy, won't you?"

"There is nothing to forgive, dear," was my reply, as, placing my arm tenderly about her slim waist, I looked into the depths of those wonderful dark eyes of hers, trying to fathom what secret lay hidden there.

"Ah!" she exclaimed. "I know, dear, that though you affect to have forgiven me—that you have not. How could you possibly forgive?"

"I am not angry with you in the least, Phrida!" I assured her quite calmly. "Because you have not yet told me the truth. I am here to learn it."

"Yes," she gasped, sinking into a chair and staring straight into the fire. The short winter's day was dying, and already the light had nearly faded. But the fire threw a mellow glow upon her pale, hard-set features, and she presented a strangely dramatic picture as she sat there with head bent in shame. "Ah! yes. You are here again to torture me, I suppose," she sighed bitterly.

"I have no desire in the least to torture you," I said, standing erect before her. "But I certainly think that some explanation of your conduct is due to me—the man whom you are to marry."

"Marry!" she echoed in a blank voice, with a shrug of her shoulders, her eyes still fixed upon the fire.

"Yes, marry," I repeated. "You made an admission to me this morning—one of which any man would in such circumstances demand explanation. You said that my friend had forced you to go to Harrington Gardens. Tell me why? What power does that man hold over you?"

"Ah, no! Teddy!" she cried, starting wildly to her feet. "No, no!" she protested, grasping my hands frantically. "Don't ask that question. Spare me that! Spare me that, for the sake of the love you once bore for me."

"No. I repeat my question," I said slowly, but very determinedly.

"Ah! no. I—I can't answer it. I—"

For a few moments a silence fell between us.

Then I said in a low, meaning tone:

"You can't answer it, Phrida, because you are ashamed, eh?"

She sprang upon me in an instant, her face full of resentful fire.

"No!" she declared vehemently. "I am not ashamed—only I—I cannot tell you the reason I went to Harrington Gardens. That's all."

"Yours is, to say the least, a rather thin excuse, is it not?" I asked.

"What else can I say? Simply I can tell you nothing."

"But you admit that you went to Harrington Gardens. Did you go more than once?" I asked very quietly.

She nodded in the affirmative.

"And the last occasion was on the night when my friend was forced to fly, eh?" I suggested.

I saw that she was about to elude answering my question. Therefore, I added:

"I already know you were there. I have established your presence beyond the shadow of doubt. So you may just as well admit it."

"I—I do," she faltered, sinking again into her chair and resting her elbows upon her knees.

"You were there—you were present when the crime was committed," I said, looking straight at her as I stood before her with folded arms.

"Whoever has said that tells wicked lies," was her quick response.

"You were in Digby's room that night—after I left," I declared.

"How do you know."

"Because the police have photographs of your finger-prints," was my quiet reply.

The effect of my words upon her was electrical.

"The police!" she gasped, her face instantly pale as death. "Do they know?"

"Inspector Edwards is in possession of your finger-prints," I replied briefly.

"Then—then they will suspect me!" she shrieked in despair. "Ah! Teddy! If you love me, save me!"

And she flung herself wildly at my feet, clutching my hands and raising her face to mine in frantic appeal.

"For that very reason I have returned here to you to-day, Phrida," I replied in a low tone of sympathy. "If I can save you from being implicated in this terrible affair, I will. But you must tell me the whole truth from the start. Then I may be able to devise a plan to ensure your security."

And I slowly assisted her to her feet and led her back to her chair.

She sat without moving or speaking for some moments, gravely thinking. Then of a sudden, she said in a hard, hoarse voice:

"Ah! you don't know, Teddy, what I have suffered—how I have been the innocent victim of a foul and dastardly plot. I—I was entrapped—I—"

"Entrapped!" I echoed. "By whom? Not by Digby Kemsley? He was not the sort of man."

"He is your friend, I know. But if you knew the truth you would hate him—hate him, with as deep and fierce a hatred as I do now," she declared, with a strange look in her great eyes.

"You told me he had forced you to go to his flat."

"He did."

"Why?"

"Because he wanted to tell me something—to—"

"To tell you what?"

"I refuse to explain—I can't tell you, Teddy."

"Because it would be betraying his secret—eh?" I remarked with bitterness. "And, yet, in the same breath you have told me you hate him. Surely, this attitude of yours is an unusual one—is it not? You cannot hate him and strive to shield him at the same moment!"

She paused for a second before replying. Then she said:

"I admit that my attitude towards your friend is a somewhat strange one, but there are reasons—strong, personal reasons of my own—which prevent me revealing to you the whole of what is a strange and ghastly story. Surely it will suffice you to know that I did not conceal all knowledge of your friend and call upon him in secret all of my own free will. No, Teddy, I loved you—and I still love you, dear—far too well for that."

"I trusted you, Phrida, but you deceived me," I replied, with a poignant bitterness in my heart.

"Under compulsion. Because—" and she paused with a look of terror in her eyes.

"Because what?" I asked slowly, placing my hand tenderly upon her shoulder.

She shrank from contact with me.

"No. I—I can't tell you. It—it's all too terrible, too horrible!" she whispered hoarsely, covering her white face with her hands. "I loved you, but, alas! all my happiness, all the joy of which I have so long dreamed, has slipped away from me because of the one false step—my one foolish action—of which I have so long repented."

"Tell me, Phrida," I urged, in deep earnestness, bending down to her. "Confide in me."

"No," she replied, with an air of determination. "It is my own affair. I have acted foolishly and must bear the consequences."

"But surely you will not sacrifice our love rather than tell me the truth!" I cried.

Hot tears welled in her eyes, and I felt her frail form tremble beneath my touch.

"Alas! I am compelled," she faltered.

"Then you refuse to tell me—you refuse to explain why this man whom I believed to be my friend, and to whom I have rendered many services, has held you in his thraldom?" I exclaimed bitterly.

XIV

Reveals a Further Deception

My love paused. She remained silent for a long time. Then, with her head bowed, she faltered:

"Yes. I—I am compelled to refuse."

"Why compelled?" I demanded.

"I—I cannot tell you," she whispered hoarsely. "I dare not."

"Dare not? Is your secret so terrible, then?"

"Yes. It is all a mystery. I do not know the truth myself," she replied. "I only know that I—that I love you, and that now, because that woman has spoken, I have lost you and am left to face the world—the police—alone!"

"Have I not told you, dearest, that I will do my best to protect and defend you if you will only reveal the truth to me," I said.

"But I can't."

"You still wish to shield this blackguard who has held you in secret in his hands?" I cried in anger.

"No, I don't," she cried in despair. "I tell you, Teddy, now—even if this is the last time we ever meet—that I love you and you alone. I have fallen the victim of a clever and dastardly plot, believe me, or believe me not. What I tell you is the truth."

"I do believe you," I replied fervently. "But if you love me, Phrida, as you declare, you will surely reveal to me the perfidy of this man I have trusted!"

"I—I can't now," she said in a voice of excuse. "It is impossible. But you may know some day."

"You knew that I visited him on that fatal night. Answer me?"

She hesitated. Then presently, in a low tone, replied—

"Yes, Teddy, I knew. Ah!" she went on, her face white and haggard. "You cannot know the torture I have undergone—fearing that you might be aware of my presence there. Each time I met you I feared to look you in the face."

"Because your secret is a guilty one—eh?"

"I fell into a trap, and I cannot extricate myself," she declared hoarsely. "Now that the police know, there is only one way out for me," she added, in a tone of blank despair. "I cannot face it—no—I—now that I have lost your love, dear. I care for naught more. My enemies will hound me to my death!"

And she burst into a torrent of bitter tears.

"No, no," I answered her, placing my hand tenderly upon her shoulder. "Reveal the truth to me, and I will protect you and shield you from them. At present, though the police are in possession of your finger-prints, as being those of a person who had entered the flat on that night, they have no knowledge of your identity, therefore, dear, have no fear."

"Ah! but I am in peril!" she cried, and I felt her shudder beneath my touch. "That woman—ah!—she may tell the police!"

"What woman?"

"Mrs. Petre, the woman who has already betrayed me to you."

"Then she knows—she knows your secret?" I gasped.

She bent her head slowly in the affirmative.

I saw in her eyes a look of terror and despair, such as I had never before seen in the eyes of any person before—a haunted, agonised expression that caused my heart to go out in sympathy for her—for even though she might be guilty—guilty of that crime of vengeance, yet, after all, she was mine and she possessed my heart.

"Is there no way of closing that woman's lips?" I asked very slowly.

She was silent, for, apparently, the suggestion had not before occurred to her. Of a sudden, she looked up into my face earnestly, and asked:

"Tell me, Teddy. Will you promise me—promise not to prejudge me?"

"I do not prejudge you at all, dearest," I declared with a smile. "My annoyance is due to your refusal to reveal to me anything concerning the man who has falsely posed as my friend."

"I would tell you all, dearest," she assured me, "but it is impossible. If I spoke I should only further arouse your suspicions, for you would never believe that I spoke the truth."

"Then you prefer that I should remain in ignorance, and by doing so your own peril becomes increased!" I remarked, rather harshly.

"Alas! my silence is imperative," was all she would reply.

Again and again I pressed her to tell me the reason of the evil influence held over her by the man who was now a fugitive, but with the greatest ingenuity she evaded my questions, afterwards declaring that all my inquiries were futile. The secret was hers.

"And so you intend to shield this man, Phrida," I remarked at last, in bitter reproach.

WILLIAM LE QUEUX

"I am not silent for his sake!" my love cried, starting up in quick resentment. "I hate him too much. No, I refuse to reveal the truth because I am compelled."

"But supposing you were compelled to clear yourself in a criminal court," I said. "Supposing that this woman went to the police! What then? You would be compelled to speak the truth."

"No. I—I'd rather kill myself!" she declared, in frantic despair. "Indeed, that is what I intend to do—now that I know I have lost you!"

"No, no," I cried. "You have not lost me, Phrida. I still believe in your purity and honesty," I went on, clasping her passionately to my heart, she sobbing bitterly the while. "I love you and I still believe in you," I whispered into her ear.

She heaved a great sigh.

"Ah! I wonder if you really speak the truth?" she murmured. "If I thought you still believed in me, how happy I should be. I would face my enemies, and defy them."

"I repeat, Phrida, that notwithstanding this suspicion upon you, I love you," I said very earnestly.

"Then you will not prejudge me!" she asked, raising her tear-stained eyes to mine. "You will not believe evil of me until—until I can prove to you the contrary. You will not believe what Mrs. Petre has told you?" she implored.

"I promise, dearest, that I will believe nothing against you," I said fervently, kissing her cold, hard lips. "But cannot you, in return, assist me in solving the mystery of Harrington Gardens. Who was the girl found there? Surely you know?"

"No, I don't. I swear I don't," was her quick reply, though her face was blanched to the lips.

"But Mrs. Petre gave me to understand that you knew her," I said.

"Yes—that woman!" she cried in anger. "She has lied to you, as to the others. Have I not told you that she is my most deadly enemy?"

"Then she may go to the police—who knows! How can we close her mouth?"

My love drew a long breath and shook her head. The light had faded, and only the fitful flames of the fire illuminated the sombre room. In the dark shadows she presented a pale, pathetic little figure, her face white as death, her thin, delicate hands clasped before her in dismay and despair.

"Have you any idea where Digby is at this moment?" I asked her slowly, wondering whether if he were an intimate friend he had let her know his hiding-place.

"No. I have not the slightest idea," was her faint reply.

"Ah! If only I could discover him I would wring the truth from him," I exclaimed between my teeth.

"And if you did so, I myself would be imperilled," she remarked. "No, Teddy, you must not do that if—if you love me and would protect me."

"Why?"

"If you went to him he would know that I had spoken, and then he would fulfil the threats he has so often made. No, you must not utter a single word. You must, for my sake, still remain his friend. Will you, dear?"

"After what you have told me!" I cried. "Never!"

"But you must," she implored, grasping both my hands in hers. "If he had the slightest suspicion that I had admitted my friendship with him, he would act as he has always declared he would."

"How would he act?"

"He would reveal something—he would bring proofs that even you would consider irrefutable," she answered in a low, hard whisper. "No, dear," and her grip upon my hands tightened. "In any case there only remains to me one course—to end it all, for in any case, I must lose you. Your confidence and love can never be restored."

"You must not speak like that," I said very gravely. "I have not yet lost confidence in you, Phrida. I—"

"Ah! I know how generous you are, dear," she interrupted, "but how can I conceal from myself the true position? You have discovered that I visited that man's flat clandestinely, that—that we were friends—and that—"

She paused, not concluding her sentence, and bursting again into tears, rushed from the room before I could grasp and detain her.

I stood silent, utterly dumbfounded.

Were those words an admission of her guilt?

Was it by her hand, as that woman had insinuated, the unknown girl's life had been taken?

I recollected the nature of the wound, as revealed by the medical evidence, and I recalled that knife which was lying upon the table in the drawing-room above.

Why did Phrida so carefully conceal from me the exact truth

concerning her friendship with the man I had trusted? What secret power did he exercise over her? And why did she fear to reveal anything to me—even though I had assured her that my confidence in her remained unshaken.

Was not guilt written upon that hard, white face?

I stood staring out of the window in blank indecision. What I had all along half feared had been proved. Between my love and the man of whom I had never had the slightest suspicion, some secret—some guilty secret—existed.

And even now, even at risk of losing my affection, she was seeking to shield him!

My blood boiled within me, and I clenched my fists as I strode angrily up and down that dark room.

All her admissions came back to me—her frantic appeal to me not to prejudge her, and her final and out-spoken decision to take her own life rather than reveal the truth.

What could it mean? What was the real solution of that strange problem of crime in which, quite unwittingly, I had become so deeply implicated?

I was passing the grate in pacing the room, as I had already done several times, when my eyes fell upon a piece of paper which had been screwed up and flung there. Curiosity prompted me to pick it out of the cinders, for it struck me that it must have been thrown there by Phrida before I had entered the room.

To my surprise I saw the moment I held it in my hand that it was a telegram. Opening it carefully I found that it was addressed to her, therefore she had no doubt cast it upon the fire when I had so suddenly entered.

I read it, and stood open-mouthed and amazed.

By it the perfidy of the woman I loved, alas! became revealed.

She had deceived me!

XV

An Effaced Identity

The telegram was signed with the initial "D."—Digby!
The words I read were—"Have discovered T suspects.
Exercise greatest care, and remember your promise. We shall meet
again soon."

The message showed that it had been handed in at Brussels at one
o'clock that afternoon.

Brussels! So he was hiding there. Yes, I would lose no time in
crossing to the gay little Belgian capital and search him out.

Before giving him up to the police I would meet him face to face and
demand the truth. I would compel him to speak.

Should I retain possession of the message? I reflected. But, on
consideration, I saw that when I had left, Phrida might return to recover
it. If I replaced it where I had found it she would remain in ignorance of
the knowledge I had gained.

So I screwed it up again and put it back among the cinders in the
grate, afterwards leaving the house.

Next morning I stepped out upon the platform of the great Gare
du Nord in Brussels—a city I knew well, as I had often been there
on business—and drove in a taxi along the busy, bustling Boulevard
Auspach to the Grand Hotel.

In the courtyard, as I got out, the frock-coated and urbane manager
welcomed me warmly, for I had frequently been his guest, and I was
shown to a large room overlooking the Boulevard where I had a wash
and changed.

Then descending, I called a taxi and immediately began a tour of
the various hotels where I thought it most likely that the man I sought
might be.

The morning was crisp and cold, with a perfect sky and brilliant
sunshine, bright and cheerful indeed after the mist and gloom of January
in London.

Somehow the aspect, even in winter, is always brighter across the
channel than in our much maligned little island. They know not the
"pea-souper" on the other side of the Straits of Dover, and the light,

invigorating atmosphere is markedly apparent directly one enters France or Belgium.

The business boulevards, the Boulevarde Auspach, and the Boulevard du Nord, with their smart shops, their big cafés, and their hustling crowds, were bright and gay as my taxi sped on, first to the Métropole, in the Place de Brouckere.

The name of Kemsley was unknown there. The old concierge glanced at his book, shook his head, and elevating his shoulders, replied:

"Non, m'sieur."

Thence I went to the Palace, in front of the station, the great new hotel and one of the finest in Europe, a huge, garish place of gilt and luxury. But there I met with equal success.

Then I made the tour of the tree-lined outer boulevards, up past the Botanical Gardens and along the Rue Royale, first to the Hotel de France, then to the Europe, the Belle Vue, the Carlton in the Avenue Louise, the new Wiltscher's a few doors away, and a very noted English house from the Boulevard Waterloo, as well as a dozen other houses in various parts of the town—the Cecil in the Boulevard du Nord, the Astoria in the Rue Royale, and even one or two of the cheaper pensions—the Dufour, De Boek's, and Nettell's, but all to no purpose.

Though I spent the whole of that day making investigations I met with no success.

Though I administered judicious tips to concierge after concierge, I could not stir the memory of a single one that within the past ten days any English gentleman answering the description I gave had stayed at their establishment.

Until the day faded, and the street lamps were lit, I continued my search, my taxi-driver having entered into the spirit of my quest, and from time to time suggesting other and more obscure hotels of which I had never heard.

But the reply was the same—a regretful "Non, m'sieur."

It had, of course, occurred to me that if the fugitive was hiding from the Belgian police, who no doubt had received his description from Scotland Yard, he would most certainly assume a false name.

But I hoped by my minute description to be able to stir the memory of one or other of the dozens of uniformed hall-porters whom I interviewed. The majority of such men have a remarkably retentive memory for a face, due to long cultivation, just as that possessed by one's club hall-porter, who can at once address any of the thousand or so members by name.

I confess, however, when at five o'clock, I sat in the huge, noisy Café Métropole over a glass of coffee and a liqueur of cognac, I began to realise the utter hopelessness of my search.

Digby Kemsley was ever an evasive person—a past master in avoiding observation, as I well knew. It had always been a hobby of his, he had told me, of watching persons without himself being seen.

Once he had remarked to me while we had been smoking together in that well-remembered room wherein the tragedy had taken place:

"I should make a really successful detective, Royle. I've had at certain periods of my life to efface myself and watch unseen. Now I've brought it to a fine art. If ever circumstances make it imperative for me to disappear—which I hope not," he laughed, "well—nobody will ever find me, I'm positive."

These words of his now came back to me as I sat there pensively smoking, and wondering if, after all, I had better not return again to London and remain patient for the additional police evidence which would no doubt be forthcoming at the adjourned inquest in a week's time.

I thought of the clever cunning exercised by the girl whom I so dearly loved and in whose innocence I had so confidently believed, of her blank refusal to satisfy me, and alas! of her avowed determination to shield the scoundrel who had posed as my friend, and whom the police had declared to be only a vulgar impostor.

My bitter reflection maddened me.

The jingle and chatter of that noisy café, full to overflowing at that hour, for rain had commenced to fall outside in the boulevard, irritated me. From where I sat in the window I could see the crowds of business people, hurrying through the rain to their trams and trains—the neat-waisted little modistes, the felt-hatted young clerks, the obese and over-dressed and whiskered men from their offices on the Bourse, the hawkers crying the "Soir," and the "Dernière Heure," with strident voices, the poor girls with rusty shawls and pinched faces, selling flowers, and the gaping, idling Cookites who seem to eternally pass and re-pass the Métropole at all hours of the day and the night.

Before my eyes was there presented the whole phantasmagoria of the life of the thrifty, hard-working Bruxellois, that active, energetic race which the French have so sarcastically designated "the brave Belgians."

After a lonely dinner in the big, glaring salle-à-manger, at the Grand, I went forth again upon my quest. That the fugitive had been in Brussels on the previous day was proved by his telegram, yet evasive as he was, he might have already left. Yet I hoped he still remained in the capital, and if so he would, I anticipated, probably go to one of the music-halls or variety theatres. Therefore I set out upon another round.

I strolled eagerly through the crowded promenade of the chief music-hall of Brussels—the Pole Nord, the lounge wherein men and women were promenading, laughing, and drinking, but I saw nothing of the man of whom I was in search.

I knew that he had shaved off his beard and otherwise altered his appearance. Therefore my attention upon those about me was compelled to be most acute.

I surveyed both stalls and boxes, but amid that gay, well-dressed crowd I could discover nobody the least resembling him.

From the Pole Nord I went to the Scala, where I watched part of an amusing revue; but my search there was likewise in vain, as it was also at Olympia, the Capucines, and the Folies Bergères, which I visited in turn. Then, at midnight, I turned my attention to the big cafés, wandering from the Bourse along the Boulevard Auspach, entering each café and glancing around, until at two o'clock in the morning I returned to the Grand, utterly fagged out by my long vigil of over fifteen hours.

In my room I threw off my overcoat and flung myself upon the bed in utter despair.

Until I met that man face to face I could not, I saw, learn the truth concerning my love's friendship with him.

Mrs. Petre had made foul insinuations, and now that my suspicions had been aroused that Phrida might actually be guilty of that terrible crime at Harrington Gardens, the whole attitude of my well-beloved seemed to prove that my suspicions were well grounded.

Indeed, her last unfinished sentence as she had rushed from the room seemed conclusive proof of the guilty secret by which her mind was now overburdened.

She had never dreamed that I held the slightest suspicion. It was only when she knew that the woman Petre had met me and had talked with me that she saw herself betrayed. Then, when I had spoken frankly, and told her what the woman had said, she saw that to further conceal her friendship with Digby was impossible.

Every word she had spoken, every evasive sentence, every protest that she was compelled to remain silent, recurred to me as I lay there staring blankly at the painted ceiling.

She had told me that she was unaware of the fugitive's whereabouts, and yet not half an hour before she had received a telegram from him.

Yes, Phrida—the woman I trusted and loved with such a fierce, passionate affection, had lied to me deliberately and barefacedly.

But I was on the fellow's track, and cost what it might in time, or in money, I did not intend to relinquish my search until I came face to face with him.

That night, as I tossed restlessly in bed, it occurred to me that even though he might be in Brussels, it was most probable in the circumstances that he would exercise every precaution in his movements, and knowing that the police were in search of him, would perhaps not go forth in the daytime.

Many are the Englishmen living "under a cloud" in Brussels, as well as in Paris, and there is not a Continental city of note which does not contain one or more of those who have "gone under" at home.

Seedy and down-at-heel, they lounge about the cafés and hotels frequented by English travellers. Sometimes they sit apart, pretend to sip their cup of coffee and read a newspaper, but in reality they are listening with avidity to their own language being spoken by their own people—poor, lonely, solitary exiles.

Every man who knows the by-ways of the Continent has met them often in far-off, obscure towns, where they bury themselves in the lonely wilderness of a drab back street and live high-up for the sake of fresh air and that single streak of sunshine which is the sole pleasure of their broken, blighted lives.

Yes, the more I reflected, the more apparent did it become that if the man whom Inspector Edwards had declared to be a gross impostor was still in the Belgian capital, he would most probably be in safe concealment in one or other of the cheaper suburbs.

But how could I trace him?

To go to the bureau of police and make a statement would only defeat my own ends.

No; if I intended to learn the truth I must act upon my own initiative. Official interference would only thwart my own endeavours.

I knew Digby Kemsley. He was as shrewd and cunning as any of the famous detectives, whether in real life or in fiction. Therefore, to be a match for him, I would, I already realised, be compelled to fight him with his own weapons.

I did not intend that he should escape me before he told me, with his own lips, the secret of my well-beloved.

XVI

Reveals another Enigma

The identity of the victim has not yet been established, sir."

These words were spoken to the coroner by Inspector Edwards at the adjourned inquest held on January the twenty-second.

Few people were in court, for, until the present, the public had had no inkling as to what had occurred on that fatal night in Harrington Gardens. The first inquest had not been "covered" by any reporter, as the police had exercised considerable ingenuity in keeping the affair a secret.

But now, at the adjourned inquiry, secrecy was no longer possible, and the three reporters present were full of inquisitiveness regarding the evidence given on the previous occasion, and listened with attention while it was being read over.

Inspector Edwards, however, had dealt with them in his usually genial manner, and by the exercise of considerable diplomacy had succeeded in allaying their suspicions that there was any really good newspaper "story" in connection with it.

The medical witnesses were recalled, but neither had anything to add to the depositions they had already made. The deceased had been fatally stabbed by a very keen knife with a blade of peculiar shape. That was all.

The unknown had been buried, and all that remained in evidence was a bundle of blood-stained clothing, some articles of jewellery, a pair of boots, hat, coat, gloves, and a green leather vanity-bag.

"Endeavours had been made, sir, to trace some of the articles worn by the deceased, and also to establish the laundry marks on the underclothing," the inspector went on, "but, unfortunately, the marks have been pronounced by experts to be foreign ones, and the whole of the young lady's clothes appear to have been made abroad—in France or Belgium, it is thought."

"The laundry marks are foreign, eh?" remarked the coroner, peering at the witness through his pince-nez, and poising his pen in his hand. "Are you endeavouring to make inquiry abroad concerning them?"

"Every inquiry is being made, sir, in a dozen cities on the continent. In fact, in all the capitals."

WILLIAM LE QUEUX

"And the description of the deceased has been circulated?"

"Yes, sir. Photographs have been sent through all the channels in Europe. But up to the present we have met with no success," Edwards replied. "There is a suspicion because of a name upon a tab in the young girl's coat that she may be Italian. Hence the most ardent search is being made by the Italian authorities into the manner and descriptions of females lately reported as missing."

"The affair seems remarkably curious," said the coroner. "It would certainly appear that the lady who lost her life was a stranger to London."

"That is what we believe, sir," Edwards replied. Seated near him, I saw how keen and shrewd was the expression upon his face. "We have evidence that certain persons visited the flat on the night in question, but these have not yet been identified. The owner of the flat has not yet been found, he having absconded."

"Gone abroad, I suppose?"

"It would appear so, sir."

"And his description has been circulated also?" asked the coroner.

"Yes, a detailed description, together with a recent photograph," was Edwards' reply. Then he added: "We have received this at Scotland Yard, sir—an anonymous communication which may or may not throw considerable light on to the affair," and he handed a letter on blue paper to the coroner, which the latter perused curiously, afterwards passing it over to the foreman of the jury.

"Rather remarkable!" he exclaimed.

Then, when the jury had completed reading the anonymous letter, addressing them, he said:

"It is not for you, gentlemen, to regard that letter in the light of evidence, but, nevertheless, it raises a very curious and mysterious point. The writer, as you will note, is prepared to reveal the truth of the whole affair in return for a monetary reward. It is, of course, a matter to be left entirely at the discretion of the police."

I started at this statement, and gazed across the court—dull and cheerless on that cold winter's afternoon.

Who had written that anonymous letter? Who could it be who was ready to reveal the truth if paid for doing so?

Was Phrida's terrible secret known?

I held my breath, and listened to the slow, hard words of the coroner, as he again addressed some questions to the great detective.

"Yes, sir," Edwards was saying. "There is distinct evidence of the presence at the flat on the night in question of some person—a woman whose identity we have not yet been successful in establishing. We, however, have formed a theory which certainly appears to be borne out by the writer of the letter I have just handed you."

"That the unknown was struck down by the hand of a woman—eh?" asked the Coroner, looking sharply across at the Inspector, who briefly replied in the affirmative, while I sat staring straight before me, like a man in a dream.

I heard the Coroner addressing the jury in hard, business-like tones, but I know not what he said. My heart was too full to think of anything else besides the peril of the one whom I loved.

I know that the verdict returned by the jury was one of "Wilful murder." Then I went out into the fading light of that brief London day, and, seeking Edwards, walked at his side towards the busy Kensington High Street.

We had not met for several days, and he, of course, had no knowledge of my visit to Brussels. Our greeting was a cordial one, whereupon I asked him what was contained in the anonymous letter addressed to "The Yard"?

"Ah! Mr. Royle. It's very curious," he said. "The Coroner has it at this moment, or I'd show it to you. The handwriting is a woman's, and it has been posted at Colchester."

"At Colchester!" I echoed in dismay.

"Yes, why?" he asked, looking at me in surprise.

"Oh, nothing. Only—well, Colchester is a curious place for anyone to live who knows the truth about an affair in Kensington," was my reply, for fortunately I quickly recovered myself.

"Why not Colchester as well as Clapham—eh?"

"Yes, of course," I laughed. "But, tell me, what does the woman say?"

"She simply declares that she can elucidate the mystery and give us the correct clue—even bring evidence if required—as to the actual person who committed the crime, if we, on our part, will pay for the information."

"And what shall you do?" I asked eagerly.

"I don't exactly know. The letter only arrived this morning. To-morrow the Council of Seven will decide what action we take."

"Does the woman give her name?" I asked with affected carelessness.

"No. She only gives the name of 'G. Payne,' and the address as 'The G.P.O., London.' She's evidently a rather cute person."

"G. Payne"—the woman Petre without a doubt.

I recollected her telegram asking me to meet her. She had said that something had "happened," and she had urged me to see her as soon as possible. Was it because I had not replied that she had penned that anonymous letter to the police?

The letter bore the Colchester post-mark, and she, I knew, lived at Melbourne House in that town.

"I suppose you will get into communication with her," I exclaimed presently.

"Of course. Any line of action in the elucidation of the mystery is worth trying. But what I cannot quite understand is, why she requires blood-money," remarked the detective as we strolled together in the arcaded entrance to the Underground Station at High Street, Kensington. "I always look askance at such letters. We receive many of them at the Yard. Not a single murder mystery comes before us, but we receive letters from cranks and others offering to point out the guilty person."

"But may not the writers of such letters be endeavouring to fasten guilt upon perfectly innocent persons against whom they have spite?" I suggested.

"Ah! That's just it, Mr. Royle," exclaimed my companion gravely. "Yet it is so terribly difficult to discriminate, and I fear we often, in our hesitation, place aside letters, the writers of which could really give valuable information."

"But in this case, what are your natural inclinations?" I asked. "I know that you possess a curious, almost unique, intuition as to what is fact and what is fiction. What is, may I term it, your private opinion?"

He halted against the long shop-windows of Derry & Toms, and paused for several minutes.

"Well," he said at last in a deeply earnest tone, "I tell you frankly, Mr. Royle, what I believe. First, I don't think that the man Kemsley, although an impostor, was the actual assassin."

"Why?" I gasped.

"Well—I've very carefully studied the whole problem. I've looked at it from every point of view," he said. "I confess the one fact puzzles me, that this man Kemsley could live so long in London and pose as the dead Sir Digby if he were not the actual man himself, has amazed me! In his position as Sir Digby, the great engineer, he must have met in society many persons who knew him. We have evidence that he constantly moved in the best circles in Mayfair, and apparently without the slightest compunction. Yet, in contradiction, we have the remarkable fact that the real Sir Digby died in South America in very mysterious and tragic circumstances."

I saw that a problem was presented to Inspector Edwards which sorely puzzled him, as it certainly did myself.

"Well," I asked after a pause, and then with some trepidation put the question, "what do you intend doing?"

"Doing!" he echoed. "There is but one course to pursue. We must get in touch with this woman who says she knows the truth, and obtain what information we can from her. Perhaps she can reveal the identity of the woman whose fingers touched that glass-topped table in the room where the crime was committed. If so, that will tell us a great deal, Mr. Royle." Then, taking a cigarette from his pocket and tapping it, he added, "Do you know, I've been wondering of late how it is that you got those finger-prints which so exactly corresponded with the ones which we secured in the flat. How did you obtain them?"

His question non-plussed me.

"I had a suspicion," I replied in a faltering voice, "and I tried to corroborate it."

"But you have corroborated it," he declared. "Why, Mr. Royle, those prints you brought to the Yard are a most important clue. Where did you get them?"

I was silent for a moment, jostled by the crowd of passers-by.

"Well," I said with a faint smile, realising what a grave mistake I had made in inculpating my well-beloved, "I simply made some experiments as an amateur in solving the mystery."

"Yes, but those prints were the same as those we got from the flat. Whence did they come?"

"I obtained them upon my own initiative," I replied, with a forced laugh.

"But you must surely tell me, Mr. Royle," he urged quickly. "It's a most important point."

"No," I replied. "I'm not a detective, remember. I simply put to the test a suspicion I have entertained."

"Suspicion of what?"

"Whether my theory was correct or not."

"Whatever theory you hold, Mr. Royle, the truth remains the same. I truly believe," he said, looking hard at me, "namely that the unknown victim was struck down by the hand which imprinted the marks you brought to me—a woman's hand. And if I am not mistaken, sir—you know the identity of the guilty woman!"

XVII

Concerns Mrs. Petre

Days, weeks, passed, but I could obtain no further clue. The month of March lengthened into April, but we were as far as ever from a solution of the mystery.

Since my return from Brussels I had, of course seen Phrida, many, many times, and though I had never reverted again to the painful subject, yet her manner and bearing showed only too plainly that she existed in constant dread!

Her face had become thin and haggard, with dark rings around her eyes and upon it was a wild, hunted expression, which she strove to disguise, but in vain.

She now treated me with a strange, cold indifference, so unlike her real self, while her attitude was one of constant attention and strained alertness.

The woman Petre had apparently not been approached by Scotland Yard, therefore as the days went by I became more and more anxious to see her, to speak with her—and, if necessary, to come to terms with her.

Therefore, without a word to anyone, I one evening caught the six o'clock train from Liverpool Street, and before eight was eating my dinner in the big upstairs room of The Cups Hotel, while the hall-porter was endeavouring to discover for me the whereabouts of Melbourne House.

I had nearly finished my meal when the uniformed servant entered, cap in hand, saying:

"I've found, sir, that the house you've been inquiring for is out on the road to Marks Tey, about a mile. An old lady named Miss Morgan lived there for many years, but she died last autumn, and the place has, they say, been let furnished to a lady—a Mrs. Petre. Is that the lady you are trying to find?"

"It certainly is," I replied, much gratified at the man's success. Then, placing a tip in his palm, I drank off my coffee, put on my overcoat, and descended to the taxi which he had summoned for me.

He gave directions to the driver, and soon we were whirling along the broad streets of Colchester, and out of the town on the dark, open road which led towards London. Presently we pulled up, and getting out, I found myself before a long, low, ivy-covered house standing back behind a high hedge of clipped box, which divided the small, bare front garden from the road. Lonely and completely isolated, it stood on the top of a hill with high, leafless trees behind, and on the left a thick copse. In front were wide, bare, open fields.

Opening the iron gate I walked up the gravelled path to the door and rang. In a window on the right a light showed, and as I listened I heard the tramp of a man's foot upon the oilcloth of the hall, and next moment the door was unlocked and opened.

A tall, thin-faced young man of somewhat sallow complexion confronted me. He had keen, deep-set eyes, broad forehead, and pointed chin.

"Is Mrs. Petre at home?" I inquired briefly.

In a second he looked at me as though with distrust, then apparently seeing the taxi waiting, and satisfying himself that I was a person of respectability, he replied in a refined voice:

"I really don't know, but I'll see, if you will step in?" and he ushered me into a small room at the rear of the house, a cosy but plainly-furnished little sitting-room, wherein a wood fire burned with pleasant glow.

I handed him my card and sat down to wait, in the meanwhile inspecting my surroundings with some curiosity.

Now, even as I recall that night, I cannot tell why I should have experienced such a sense of grave insecurity as I did when I sat there awaiting the woman's coming. I suppose we all of us possess in some degree that strange intuition of impending danger. It was so with me that night—just as I have on other occasions been obsessed by that curious, indescribable feeling that "something is about to happen."

There was about that house an air of mystery which caused me to hesitate in suspicion. Whether it was owing to its lonely position, to the heavy mantle of ivy which hid its walls, to the rather weird and unusual appearance of the young man who had admitted me, or to the mere fact that I was there to meet the woman who undoubtedly knew the truth concerning the tragic affair, I know not. But I recollect a distinct feeling of personal insecurity.

I knew the woman I was about to meet to be a cold, hard, unscrupulous person, who, no doubt, held my love's liberty—perhaps her life—in the hollow of her hand.

That horrifying thought had just crossed my mind when my reflections were interrupted by the door opening suddenly and there swept into the room the lady upon whom I had called.

"Ah! Mr. Royle!" she cried in warm welcome, extending her rather large hand as she stood before me, dressed quietly in black, relieved by a scarlet, artificial rose in her waistband. "So you've come at last. Ah! do you know I've wanted to meet you for days. I expected you would come to me the moment you returned from Brussels."

I started, and stood staring at her without replying. She knew I had been to Belgium. Yet, as far as I was aware, nobody knew of my visit—not even Haines.

"You certainly seem very well acquainted with my movements, Mrs. Petre," I laughed.

But she only shrugged her shoulders. Then she said:

"I suppose there was no secrecy regarding your journey, was there?"

"Not in the least," I replied. "I had business over there, as I very often have. My firm do a big business in Belgium and Holland."

She smiled incredulously.

"Did your business necessitate your visiting all the hotels and music-halls?"

"How did you know that?" I asked in quick surprise.

But she only pursed her lips, refusing to give me satisfaction. I saw that I must have been watched—perhaps by Digby himself. The only explanation I could think of was that he, with his clever cunning, had watched me, and had written to this woman, his accomplice, telling her of my search.

"Oh! don't betray the source of your information if you consider it so indiscreet," I said with sarcasm a few moments later. "I came here, Mrs. Petre, in response to your invitation. You wished to see me?"

"I did. But I fear it is now too late to avert what I had intended," was her quiet response. The door was closed, the room was silent, and we were alone.

Seated in an armchair the woman leaned back and gazed at me strangely from beneath her long, half-closed lashes, as though undecided what she should say. I instantly detected her hesitation, and said:

"You told me in your message that something unexpected had occurred. What is it? Does it concern our mutual friend, Digby?"

"Friend!" she echoed. "You call him your friend, and yet at the same time you have been in search of him, intending to betray him to the police!"

"Such was certainly not my intention," I declared firmly. "I admit that I have endeavoured to find him, but it was because I wished to speak with him."

"Ah! of course," she sneered. "That girl Shand has, perhaps, made a statement to you, and now you want to be inquisitive, eh? She's been trying to clear herself by telling you some fairy-tale or another, I suppose?"

"I repeat, Mrs. Petre," I said with anger, "I have no desire nor intention to act towards Digby in any way other than with friendliness."

"Ah! You expect me to believe that, my dear sir," she laughed, snapping her fingers airily. "No, that girl is his enemy, and I am hers."

"And that is the reason why you have sent the anonymous letter to the police!" I said in a low, hard voice, my eyes full upon her.

She started at my words.

"What letter?" she asked, in pretence of ignorance.

"The one mentioned at the adjourned inquest at Kensington," I replied. "The one in which you offer to sell the life of the woman I love!"

"So you know she is guilty—eh?" the woman asked. "She has confessed it to you—has she not?"

"No. She is innocent," I cried. "I will never believe in her guilt until it is proved."

"Then it will not be long, Mr. Royle, before you will have quite sufficient proof," she replied with a triumphant smile upon her lips.

"You are prepared to sell those proofs, I understand," I said, suddenly assuming an air of extreme gravity. "Now, I'm a business man. If you wish to dispose of this information, why not sell it to me?"

She laughed in my face.

"No, not to you, my dear sir. My business is with the police, not with the girl's lover," was her quick response.

"But the price," I said. "I will outbid the police if necessary."

"No doubt you would be only too glad of the chance of saving the girl who has so cleverly deceived you. But, without offence, Mr. Royle, I certainly think you are a fool to act as you are now acting," she added. "A foul crime of jealousy has been committed, and the assassin must pay the penalty of her crime."

"And you allege jealousy as the motive?" I gasped.

"Most certainly," she answered. Then, after a pause of a few seconds, she added—"The girl you have so foolishly trusted and in whom you still believe so implicitly, left her home in Cromwell Road in the night, as she had often done before, and walked round to Harrington Gardens in order to see Digby. There, in his rooms, she met her rival—she had suspicions and went there on purpose armed with a knife. And with it she struck the girl down, and killed her."

"It's a lie!" I cried, starting to my feet. "A foul, wicked lie!"

"But what I say can be proved."

"At a price," I said bitterly.

"As you are a business man, so I am a business woman, Mr. Royle," she replied quite calmly. "When I see an opportunity of making money, I do not hesitate to seize it."

"But if you know the truth—if this is the actual truth which at present I will not believe—then it is your duty, nay, you are bound by law to go to the police and tell them what you know."

"I shall do that, never fear," she laughed. "But first I shall try and get something for my trouble."

"And whom do you intend to bring up as witness against Miss Shand?" I asked.

"Wait and see. There will be a witness—an eye-witness, who was present, and whose evidence will be corroborated," she declared in due course with a self-satisfied air. "I have not resolved to reveal the truth without fully reviewing the situation. When the police know—as they certainly will—you will then find that I have not lied, and perhaps you will alter your opinion of the girl you now hold in such high esteem."

XVIII

Discloses the Trap

The woman's words held me speechless.

She seemed so cold, so determined, so certain of her facts that I felt, when I came to consider what I already had proved, that she was actually telling me the ghastly truth.

And yet I loved Phrida. No. I refused to allow my suspicions to be increased by this woman who had approached the police openly and asked for payment for her information.

She was Phrida's enemy. Therefore it was my duty to treat her as such, and in a moment I had decided upon my course of action.

"So I am to take it that both Digby and yourself are antagonistic towards Phrida Shand?" I exclaimed, leaning against the round mahogany table and facing her.

She did not speak for a few seconds, then, springing to her feet, exclaimed:

"Would you excuse me for a few seconds? I forgot to give an order to my servant who is just going out."

And she bustled from the room, leaving me alone with my own confused thoughts.

Ah! The puzzling problem was maddening me. In my investigations I now found myself in a cul-de-sac from which there seemed no escape. The net, cleverly woven without a doubt, was slowly closing about my poor darling, now so pale, and anxious, and trembling.

Had she not already threatened to take her own life at first sign of suspicion being cast upon her by the police!

Was that not in itself, alas! a sign that her secret was a guilty one?

I knew not what to do, or how to act.

I suppose my hostess had been absent for about five minutes when the door suddenly re-opened, and she entered.

"When we were interrupted, Mrs. Petre," I said, as she advanced towards me, "I was asking you a plain question. Please give me a plain reply. You and Phrida Shand are enemies, are you not?"

"Well, we are not exactly friends," she laughed, "after all that has occurred. I think I told you that in London."

"I remember all that you told me," I replied. "But I want to know the true position, if—whether we are friends, or enemies? For myself, it matters not. I will be your friend with just as great a satisfaction as I will be your enemy. Now, let us understand each other. I have told you, I'm a man of business."

The woman, clever and resourceful, smiled sweetly, and in a calm voice replied:

"Really, Mr. Royle, I don't see why, after all, we should be enemies, that is, if what you tell me is the positive truth, that you owe my friend Digby no ill-will."

"I owe no man ill-will until his perfidy is proved," was my reply. "I merely went to Brussels to try and find him and request an explanation. He charged me with a mission which I discharged with the best of my ability, but which, it seems, has only brought upon me a grave calamity—the loss of the one I love. Hence I am entitled to some explanation from his own lips!"

"Which I promise you that you shall have in due course. So rest assured upon that point," she urged. "But that is in the future. We are, however, discussing the present. By the way—you'll take something to drink, won't you?"

"No, thank you," I protested.

"But you must have something. I'm sorry I have no whisky to offer you, but I have some rather decent port," and disregarding my repeated protests, she rang the bell, whereupon the young man who had admitted me—whom I now found to my surprise to be a servant—entered and bowed.

"Bring some port," his mistress ordered, and a few moments later he reappeared with a decanter and glasses upon a silver tray.

She poured me out a glass, but refused to have any herself.

"No, no," she laughed, "at my time of life port wine would only make me fat—and Heaven knows I'm growing horribly stout now. You don't know, Mr. Royle, what horror we women have of stoutness. In men it is a sign of ease and prosperity, in women it is suggestive of alcoholism and puts ten years on their ages."

Out of politeness, I raised my glass to her and drank. Her demeanour had altered, and we were now becoming friends, a fact which delighted me, for I saw I might, by the exercise of a little judicious diplomacy, act so as to secure protection for Phrida.

While we were chatting, I suddenly heard the engine of my taxi started, and the clutch put in with a jerk.

"Why!" I exclaimed, surprised. "I believe that's my taxi going away. I hope the man isn't tired of waiting!"

"No. I think it is my servant. I 'phoned for a cab for her, as I want her to take a message into Colchester," Mrs. Petre replied. Then, settling herself in the big chair, she asked:

"Now, why can't we be friends, Mr. Royle?"

"That I am only too anxious to be," I declared.

"It is only your absurd infatuation for Phrida Shand that prevents you," she said. "Ah!" she sighed. "How grossly that girl has deceived you!"

I bit my lip. My suspicions were surely bitter enough without the sore being re-opened by this woman.

Had not Phrida's admissions been a self-condemnation to which, even though loving her as fervently as I did, I could not altogether blind myself.

I did not speak. My heart was too full, and strangely enough my head seemed swimming, but certainly not on account of the wine I had drunk, for I had not swallowed more than half the glass contained.

The little room seemed to suddenly become stifling. Yet that woman with the dark eyes seemed to watch me intently as I sat there, watch me with a strange, deep, evil glance—an expression of fierce animosity which even at that moment she could not conceal.

She had openly avowed that the hand of my well-beloved had killed the unknown victim because of jealousy. Well, when I considered all the facts calmly and deliberately, her words certainly seemed to bear the impress of truth.

Phrida had confessed to me that, rather than face inquiry and condemnation she would take her own life. Was not that in itself sufficient evidence of guilt?

But no! I strove to put such thoughts behind me. My brain was awhirl, nay, even aflame, for gradually there crept over me a strange, uncanny feeling of giddiness such as I had never before experienced, a faint, sinking feeling, as though the chair was giving way beneath me.

"I don't know why, but I'm feeling rather unwell," I remarked to my hostess. Surely it could not be due to my overwrought senses and my strained anxiety for Phrida's safety.

"Oh! Perhaps it's the heat of the room," the woman replied. "This place gets unpleasantly warm at night. You'll be better in a minute or two, no doubt. I'll run and get some smelling salts. It is really terribly close in here," and, rising quickly, she left me alone.

I remember that instantly she had disappeared a red mist gathered before my eyes, and with a fearful feeling of asphyxiation I struggled violently, and fell back exhausted into my chair, while my limbs grew suddenly icy cold, though my brow was burning.

To what could it be due?

I recollect striving to think, to recall facts, to reason within myself, but in vain. My thoughts were so confused that grim, weird shadows and grotesque forms arose within my imagination. Scenes, ludicrous and tragic, wildly fantastic and yet horrible, were conjured up in my disordered brain, and with them all, pains—excruciating pains, which shot through from the sockets of my eyes to the back of my skull, inflicting upon me tortures indescribable.

I set my teeth in determination not to lose consciousness beneath the strain, and my eyes were fixed upon the wall opposite. I remember now the exact pattern of the wallpaper, a design of pale blue trellis-work with crimson rambler roses.

I suppose I must have remained in that position, sunk into a heap in the chair, for fully five minutes, though to me it seemed hours when I suddenly became conscious of the presence of persons behind me.

I tried to move—to turn and look—but found that every muscle in my body had become paralysed. I could not lift a finger, neither would my lips articulate any sound other than a gurgle when I tried to cry out. And yet I remained in a state of consciousness, half blotted out by those weird, fantastic and dreamy shapes, due apparently to the effect of that wine upon my brain.

Had I been deliberately poisoned? The startling truth flashed across my mind just as I heard a low stealthy movement behind me.

Yes. I was helpless there, in the hands of my enemies. I, wary as I believed myself to be, had fallen into a trap cunningly prepared by that clever woman who was Digby's accomplice.

I now believed all that Edwards had told me of the man's cunning and his imposture. How that he had assumed the identity of a clever and renowned man who had died so mysteriously in South America. Perhaps he had killed him—who could tell?

As these bitter thoughts regarding the man whom I had looked upon as a friend flitted through my brain, I saw to my amazement, standing boldly before me, the woman Petre with two men, one a dark-bearded, beetle-browed, middle-aged man of Hindu type—a half-caste probably—while the other was the young man who had admitted me.

The Hindu bent until his scraggy whiskers almost touched my cheek, looking straight into my eyes with keen, intent gaze, but without speaking.

I saw that the young man had carried a small deal box about eighteen inches square, which he had placed upon the round mahogany table in the centre of the room.

This table the woman pushed towards my chair until I was seated before it. But she hardly gave me a glance.

I tried to speak, to inquire the reason of such strange proceedings, but it seemed that the drug which had been given me in that wine had produced entire muscular paralysis. I could not move, neither could I speak. My brain was on fire and swimming, yet I remained perfectly conscious, horrified to find myself so utterly and entirely helpless.

The sallow-faced man, in whose black eyes was an evil, murderous look, and upon whose thin lips there played a slight, but triumphant smile, took both my arms and laid them straight upon the table.

I tried with all my power to move them, but to no purpose. As he placed them, so they remained.

Then, for the first time, the woman spoke, and addressing me, said in a hard, harsh tone:

"You are Digby's enemy, and mine, Mr. Royle. Therefore you will now see the manner in which we treat those who endeavour to thwart our ends. You have been brave, but your valour has not availed you much. The secret of Digby Kemsley is still a secret—and will ever be a secret," she added in a slow, meaning voice.

And as she uttered those words the half-bred Indian took my head in his hands and forced my body forward until my head rested upon the table between my outstretched arms.

Again I tried to raise myself, and to utter protest, but only a low gurgling escaped my parched lips. My jaws were set and I could not move them.

Ah! the situation was the strangest in which I have ever found myself in all my life.

Suddenly, while my head lay upon the polished table I saw the Hindu put a short double-reed pipe to his mouth, and next instant the room was filled with weird, shrill music, while at the same moment he unfastened the side of the little box and let down the hinged flap.

Again the native music sounded more shrill than before, while the woman and the young man-servant had retreated backward towards the door, their eyes fixed upon the mysterious box upon the table.

I, too, had my eyes upon the box.

Suddenly I caught sight of something within, and next second held my breath, realising the horrible torture that was intended.

I lay there helpless, powerless to draw back and save myself.

Again the sounds of the pipe rose and then died away slowly in a long drawn-out wail.

My eyes were fixed upon that innocent-looking little box in horror and fascination.

Ah! Something moved again within.

I saw it—saw it quite plainly.

I tried to cry out—to protest, to shout for help. But in vain.

Surely this woman's vengeance was indeed a fiendish and relentless one.

My face was not more than a foot away from the mysterious box, and when I fully realised, in my terror, what was intended, I think my brain must have given way.

I became insane!

XIX

The Seal of Silence

Yes, there was no doubt about it. Terror and horror had driven me mad.

And surely the deadly peril in which I found myself was in itself sufficient to cause the cheek of the bravest man to pale, for from that box there slowly issued forth a large, hideous cobra, which, coiling with sinuous slowness in front of my face held its hooded head erect, ready to strike.

While the Hindu played that weird music on the pipes its head with the two beady eyes and flickering tongue, moved slowly to and fro. It was watching me and ready to deal its fatal blow.

The woman saw the perspiration standing upon my white brow, and burst out laughing, still standing at a safe distance near the door.

"Ah! Mr. Royle, you won't have much further opportunity of investigation," she exclaimed. "You have become far too inquisitive, and you constitute a danger—hence this action. I'm very sorry, but it must be so," declared the brutal, inhuman woman.

She was watching, gloating over her triumph; waiting, indeed, for my death.

Surely I was not their first victim! All had been carried out in a method which showed that the paralysing drug and the deadly reptile had been used before by this strange trio.

The music, now being played incessantly, apparently prevented the snake from darting at me, as it was, no doubt, under the hypnotic influence of its master. But I knew that the moment the music ceased it would be my last.

With frantic efforts I struggled to withdraw my head and hands from the reptile's reach, but every muscle seemed powerless. I could not budge an inch.

Again I tried to speak, to shout for help, but no word could I articulate. I was dead in all save consciousness.

"Oh, yes," laughed Mrs. Petre hoarsely; "we're just playing you a little music—to send you to sleep—to put the seal of silence upon you, Mr. Royle. And I hope you'll sleep very well to-night—very well—as no doubt you will!" and she gave vent to a loud peal of harsh laughter.

Then, for a moment she hesitated, until suddenly she cried to the Hindu:

"Enough!"

The music ceased instantly, and the snake, whose hooded head had been swaying to and fro slowly, suddenly shot up erect.

The spell of the music was broken, and I knew my doom was sealed.

Those small, brilliant eyes were fastened upon mine, staring straight at me, the head moving very slowly, while those three brutes actually watched my agony of terror, and exchanged smiles as they waited for the reptile to strike its fatal blow.

In an instant its fangs would, I knew, be in my face, and into my blood would be injected that deadly venom which must inevitably prove fatal.

Yes, I had been entrapped, and they held the honours in the game. After my death Phrida would be denounced, accused, and convicted as an assassin. Because, perhaps, I might be a witness in her favour, or even assist her to escape arrest, this woman had taken the drastic step of closing my lips for ever.

But was it with Digby's knowledge? Had he ever been her accomplice in similar deeds to this?

Suddenly I recollected with a start what Edwards had told me—that the real Sir Digby Kemsley, an invalid, had died of snake-bite in mysterious circumstances, in Peru; and that his friend, a somewhat shady Englishman named Cane, had been suspected of placing the reptile near him, owing to the shouts of terror of the doomed man being overheard by a Peruvian man-servant.

Was it possible that the man whom I had known as Digby was actually Cane?

The method of the snake was the same as that practised at Huacho!

These, and other thoughts, flashed across my brain in an instant, for I knew that the agony of a fearful death would be quickly upon me.

I tried to utter a curse upon those three brutes who stood looking on without raising a hand to save me, but still I could not speak.

Suddenly, something black shot across my startled eyes. The reptile had darted.

The horror of that moment held me transfixed.

WILLIAM LE QUEUX

I felt a sharp sting upon my left cheek, and next instant, petrified by a terror indescribable, I lost consciousness.

What happened afterwards I have no idea. I can only surmise.

How long I remained senseless I cannot tell. All I am aware of is that when I returned to a knowledge of things about me I had a feeling that my limbs were benumbed and cramped. Against my head was a cold, slimy wall, and my body was lying in water.

For a time, dazed as I was, I could not distinguish my position. My thoughts were all confused; all seemed pitch darkness, and the silence was complete save for the slow trickling of water somewhere near my head.

I must have lain there a full hour, slowly gathering my senses. The back of my head was very sore, for it seemed as though I had received a heavy blow, while my elbows and knees seemed cut and bruised.

In the close darkness I tried to discover where I was, but my brain was swimming with an excruciating pain in the top of my skull.

Slowly, very slowly, recollections of the past came back to me— remembrance of that terrible, final half-hour.

Yes, Joy! I was still alive; the loathsome reptile's fang had not produced death. It may have bitten some object and evacuated its venom just prior to biting me. That was the theory which occurred to me, and I believe it to be the correct one.

I could raise my hand, too. I was no longer paralysed. I could speak. I shouted, but my voice seemed deadened and stifled.

On feeling my head I found that I had a long scalp-wound, upon which the blood was congealed. My clothes were rent, and as I groped about I quickly found that my prison was a circular wall of stone, wet and slimy, about four feet across, and that I was half reclining in water with soft, yielding mud beneath me, while the air seemed close and foul.

The roof above me seemed high, for my voice appeared to ascend very far. I looked above me and high up, so high that I could only just distinguish it was a tiny ray of light—the light of day.

With frantic fingers I felt those circular walls, thick with the encrustations and slime of ages. Then all of a sudden the truth flashed upon me. My enemies, believing me dead, had thrown me down a well!

I shouted and shouted, yelled again and again. But my voice only echoed high up, and no one came to my assistance.

My legs, immersed as they were in icy-cold water, were cramped and benumbed, so that I had no feeling in them, while my hands were wet and cold, and my head hot as fire.

As far as I could judge in the darkness, the well must have been fully eighty feet or so deep, and after I had been flung headlong down it the wooden trap-door had been re-closed. It was through the chink between the two flaps that I could see the blessed light of day.

I shouted again, yelling with all my might: "Help! Help!" in the hope that somebody in the vicinity might hear me and investigate.

I was struggling in order to shift into a more comfortable position, and in doing so my feet sank deeper into the mud at the bottom of the well—the accumulation of many years, no doubt.

Two perils faced me—starvation, or the rising of the water: for if it should rain above, the water percolating through the earth would cause it to rise in the well and overwhelm me. By the dampness of the wall I could feel that it was not long since the water was much higher than my head, as I now stood upright.

Would assistance come?

My heart sank within me when I thought of the possibility that I had been precipitated into the well in the garden of Melbourne House, in which case I could certainly not hope for succour.

Again I put out my hands, frantically groping about me, when something I touched in the darkness caused me to withdraw my hand with a start.

Cautiously I felt again. My eager fingers touched it, for it seemed to be floating on the surface of the water. It was cold, round, and long—the body of a snake!

I drew my hand away. Its contact thrilled me.

The cobra had been killed and flung in after me! In that case the precious trio had, without a doubt, fled.

Realisation of the utter hopelessness of the situation sent a cold shudder through me. I had miraculously escaped death by the snake's fangs, and was I now to die of starvation deep in that narrow well?

Again and again I shouted with all my might, straining my eyes to that narrow chink which showed so far above. Would assistance never come? I felt faint and hungry, while my wounds gave me considerable pain, and my head throbbed so that I felt it would burst at any moment.

I found a large stone in the mud, and with it struck hard against the wall. But the sound was not such as might attract the attention of anybody who happened to be near the vicinity of the well. Therefore I shouted and shouted again until my voice grew hoarse, and I was compelled to desist on account of my exhaustion.

WILLIAM LE QUEUX

For fully another half-hour I was compelled to remain in impatience and anxiety in order to recover my voice and strength for, weak as I was, the exertion had almost proved too much for me. So I stood there with my back to the slimy wall, water reaching beyond my knees, waiting and hoping against hope.

At last I shouted again, as loudly as before, but, alas! only the weird echo came back to me in the silence of that deeply-sunk shaft. I felt stifled, but, fortunately for me, the air was not foul.

Yes, my assassins had hidden me, together with the repulsive instrument of their crime, in that disused well, confident that no one would descend to investigate and discover my remains. How many persons, I wonder, are yearly thrown down wells where the water is known to be impure, or where the existence of the well itself is a secret to all but the assassin?

I saw it all now. My taxi-man must have been paid and dismissed by that thin-faced young man, yet how cleverly the woman had evaded my question, and how glib her explanation of her servant going into the town in a taxi.

When she had risen from her chair and left me, it was, no doubt, to swiftly arrange how my death should be encompassed.

Surely that isolated, ivy-covered house was a house of grim shadows—nay, a house of death—for I certainly was not the first person who had been foully done to death within its walls.

As I waited, trying to possess myself with patience, and hoping against hope that I might still be rescued from my living tomb, the little streak of light grew brighter high above, as though the wintry sun was shining.

I strained my ears to catch any sound beyond the slow trickling of the water from the spring, but, alas! could distinguish nothing.

Suddenly, however, I heard a dull report above, followed quickly by a second, and then another in the distance, and another. At first I listened much puzzled; but next moment I realised the truth.

There was a shooting-party in the vicinity!

XX

From the Tomb

Again I shouted—yelled aloud with all my might. I placed my hands to my mouth, making a trumpet of them, and shouted upwards:

"Help! For God's sake! Help! I'm down here—dying! Help!—*Help!*"

A dozen times I yelled my appeal, but with the same negative result. Whoever had fired in the vicinity was either too far away, or too occupied with his sport to hear me.

I heard another shot fired—more distant than the rest. Then my heart sank within me—the party were receding.

I don't know how long I waited—perhaps another hour—when I thought I would try again. Therefore I recommenced my shouts for assistance, yelling frantically towards the high-up opening.

Suddenly the streak of light became obscured, and dust and gravel fell upon me, the latter striking my head with great force from such a height.

I heard a noise above—a footstep upon the wooden flap of the well. My heart gave a bound.

"Help!" I yelled. "Open the well! I'm down here—dying. Save me! Fetch assistance!"

The feet above moved, and a moment later I saw above me a round disc of daylight and a head—a girl's head—silhouetted within it.

"Who's there?" she asked in a timid, half-frightened voice.

"It's me!" I cried. "Get me out of this! I'm dying. Get me a rope or something, quickly!"

"Who are you?" asked the girl, still frightened at her discovery.

"I'm a man who's been thrown down here, and I can't get out. Get somebody to help me, I beg of you!"

"All right!" she replied. "There's some men, shooting here. I'll run and tell them."

And her face disappeared from the disc of daylight.

At last! Help was forthcoming, and I breathed more freely.

I suppose about five minutes must have elapsed before I saw above me the heads of two men in golf-caps, peering over the edge of the well.

"Hulloa!" cried one in a refined voice, "what are you doing down there?"

"Doing!" I echoed, "you should come down and see!" I said with some sarcasm. "But, I say! Send me down a rope, will you? I'm a prisoner here."

"Have you been thrown in there?" asked the voice. "This lady says you have."

"Yes, I have. I'll tell you a strange story when you get me out."

"All right!" exclaimed the other. "Hold on! We'll go over to the farm and get a rope. Why, I was here half-an-hour ago, and never dreamt you were down there. Hold on!"

And the two faces disappeared, their places being taken by the silhouette of the girl.

"I say!" I cried. "Where am I? What do they call this place?"

"Well, this is one of the fields of Coppin's Farm, just outside Lexden Park."

"Do you know Melbourne House?" I asked.

"Oh, yes. Miss Morgan's. She's dead," replied the girl's voice from above. "It's out on the high road—close by."

"Is this well in the middle of a field, then?" I asked.

"In the corner. Some old, half-ruined cottages stood here till a couple of years ago, when they were pulled down."

"And this was the well belonging to them?"

"I suppose so," she replied, and a few minutes later I heard voices and saw several heads peering down at me, while now and then gravel fell upon my unprotected head, causing me to put my hands up to protect it.

"I say!" cried the man's voice who had first addressed me, "We're sending down a rope. Can you fasten it round you, and then we'll haul you up? I expect you're in a pretty state, aren't you?"

"Yes; I'm not very presentable, I fear," I laughed.

Then down came a stout farmer's rope, several lengths of which were knotted together after some delay, until its end dangled before me.

"I hope you've joined it all right," I cried. "I don't want to drop down!"

"No, it's all right!" one of the men—evidently a labourer—declared. "You needn't fear, mister."

I made a knot in the end, then, placing it around both my thighs, made a slip knot and clung to the rope above. This took me some minutes. Then, when all was ready, I gave the signal to haul.

"Slowly!" I shouted, for I was swinging from side to side of the well, bruising my elbows and knees. "Haul slower! I'm getting smashed to pieces!"

They heeded me, and with care I was gradually drawn up to the blessed light of day—a light which, for a few minutes, nearly blinded me, so exhausted and dazed was I.

Naturally I was beset by a hundred queries as to how I came to be imprisoned in such a place.

But I sat down upon the ground, a strange, begrimed and muddy figure, no doubt, gazing about me for a few moments unable to speak.

I was in the corner of a bare, brown field, with a high hedgerow close by. Around were the foundations of demolished cottages, and I was seated upon a heap of brick-rubbish and plaster.

The two who were dressed in rough, shooting kit I took to be military men, while three others were farm-hands, and the girl—a tall, rather good-looking open-air girl, was dressed in a short, tweed skirt, well-cut, a thick jacket, a soft felt hat, and heavy, serviceable boots. No second glance was needed to show that, although so roughly dressed, she was undoubtedly a lady.

One of the men called her Maisie, and later I knew that her name was Maisie Morrice, that she was his sister, who had been walking with the "guns."

My presence down the well certainly needed explanation, and as they had rescued me, it was necessary to satisfy their natural curiosity.

"I had a curious adventure here last night," I told them, after pausing to take breath. "I came from London to see a lady living at Melbourne House. A lady named Petre—but I was given some drugged wine, and—well, when I came to I found myself down there. That's all."

"A very unpleasant experience, I should say," remarked the elder of the two sportsmen, a tall, grey-moustached man, as he surveyed me. "I suppose you'll go back to Melbourne House and get even with the lady? I would!"

"Melbourne House!" echoed the other man. "Why, Maisie, that's where old Miss Morgan lived, and it's been taken by some woman with an Indian servant, hasn't it?"

"Yes," replied the girl. "She's been there a month or two, but quite a mystery. Nobody has called on her. Mother wouldn't let me."

"Apparently she's not a very desirable acquaintance," remarked her brother grimly.

"I want to go there," I said feebly, trying to rise.

"You seem to have hurt your head pretty badly," remarked the elder

WILLIAM LE QUEUX

sportsman. "I suppose you'd better go into Colchester and see the police—eh?"

"I'll drive him in, sir," volunteered one of the men, whom I took to be the farmer.

"Yes, Mr. Cuppin," exclaimed the girl. "Get your trap and drive this gentleman to the doctor and the police."

"Thank you," I replied. "But I don't want the people at Melbourne House to know that I'm alive. They believe me dead, and it will be a pretty surprise for them when I return, after seeing the doctor. So I ask you all to remain silent about this affair—at least for an hour or so. Will you?"

They all agreed to do so, and, being supported by two of the men, I made my way across the field to the farm; and ten minutes later was driving into Colchester in the farmer's dog-cart.

At the "Cups" my appearance caused some sensation, but, ascending to my room, I quickly washed, changed my ruined suit, and made myself presentable, and then went to see an elderly and rather fussy doctor, who put on his most serious professional air, and who was probably the most renowned medical man in the town. The provincial medico, when he becomes a consultant, nearly always becomes pompous and egotistical, and in his own estimation is the only reliable man out of Harley Street.

The man I visited was one of the usual type, a man of civic honours, with the aspirations of a mayoralty, I surmised. I think he believed that I had injured my head while in a state of intoxication, so I did not undeceive him, and allowed his assistant to bathe and bandage my wound and also the bite upon my cheek, while the farmer waited outside for me.

When at last I emerged, I hesitated.

Should I go to the police and tell them what had occurred? Or should I return alone to Melbourne House, and by my presence thwart whatever sinister plans might be in progress.

If I went to the police I would be forced to explain much that I desired, at least for the present, to keep secret. And, after all, the local police could not render me much assistance. I might give the woman and her accomplices in charge for attempted murder, but would such course help in the solution of the Harrington Gardens affair?

After a few moments' reflection I decided to drive straight to the house of shadows and demand an explanation of the dastardly attempt upon me.

A quarter of an hour later Mr. Cuppin pulled up near the long, ivy-covered house, and, alighting, I made my way within the iron gate and up the gravelled path to the front door, where I rang.

I listened attentively, and heard someone moving.

Yes, the house was not empty, as I had half feared.

A moment later a neat maid-servant opened the door, and regarded me with some surprise.

"Is Mrs. Petre at home?" I inquired.

"No, sir, she isn't," replied the girl with a strong East Anglian accent.

"When will she be in?" I asked.

"I really don't know, sir," she said. "She hasn't left word where she's gone."

"Is anyone else at home?"

"No, sir."

"How long have you been with Mrs. Petre?" I asked, adding, in an apologetic tone, "I hope I'm not too inquisitive?"

"I've been here about two months—ever since she took the house."

"Don't you think your mistress a rather curious person?" I asked, slipping half-a-sovereign into her hand. She regarded the coin, and then looked at me with a smile of surprise and satisfaction.

"I—I hardly know what you mean, sir," she faltered.

"Well, I'll be quite frank with you," I said. "I'm anxious to know something about what company she keeps here. Last night, for instance, a gentleman called in a taxi. Did you see him?"

"No, sir," she answered. "Mistress sent me out on an errand to the other side of the town, and when I came back just before half-past eleven I found the front door ajar, and everybody gone. And nobody's been back here since."

After disposing of my body, then, the precious trio had fled.

I knew that Phrida must now be in hourly peril of arrest—for that woman would, now that she believed me dead, lose not an instant in making a damning statement to the police regarding what had occurred on that night in Harrington Gardens.

XXI

Records a Strange Statement

W ill you permit me to come inside a moment?" I asked the girl. "I want you to tell me one or two things, if you will."

At first she hesitated, but having surveyed me critically and finding, I suppose, that I was not a tramp she opened the door wider and admitted me to the room wherein her mistress had entertained me on the previous night.

I glanced quickly around. Yes, nothing had been altered. There was the chair in which I had sat, and the round, mahogany table upon which my head had laid so helplessly while the reptile, charmed by the Hindu's music, had sat erect with swaying head.

Ah! as that terrible scene again arose before my eyes I stood horrified. The girl noticed my demeanour, and looked askance at me.

"Does your mistress have many visitors?" I asked her. "To tell you the truth, I'm making these confidential inquiries on behalf of an insurance company in London. So you can be perfectly open with me. Mrs. Petre will never know that you have spoken."

"Well, sir," replied the dark-eyed maid, after a pause, during which time she twisted her dainty little apron in her hand, "I suppose I really ought not to say anything, but the fact is mistress acts very curiously sometimes. Besides, I don't like Ali."

"You mean the Indian?"

"Yes. He's too crafty and cunning," she replied. "Sometimes in the middle of the night I wake up and hear Ali, shut up in his room, playing on his flute—such horrible music. And on such occasions the mistress and Horton, the man, are usually with him—listening to his concert, I suppose."

"On those occasions, have there been guests in the house?" I asked quickly.

"Once, I think about a fortnight ago, a gentleman had called earlier in the evening. But I did not see him."

"Did you see him next morning?"

"Oh, no; he did not stay the night."

"But on this particular occasion, how did you know that Mrs. Petre and Horton were in the room with him?"

"Because I listened from the top of the stairs, and could hear voices. The gentleman was in there too, I believe, listening to the noise of Ali's pipes."

Had the stranger fallen a victim to the serpent, I wondered?

Who could he have been, and what was his fate?

"Has your mistress and her two servants left you suddenly like this before?" I inquired.

"Never, sir. I can't make it out. They seem to have gone out with the gentleman who called—and evidently they left all of a hurry."

"Why?"

"Because when I got back I found that my mistress had pulled out the first coat and hat she could find, and had not taken even a handbag. Besides, if she knew she was to be absent she would have left me a note." And she added in a tone of resentment: "It isn't fair to leave me by myself in a lonely house like this!"

"No, it isn't," I agreed. "But, tell me, does your mistress have many callers?"

"Very few. She has had a visitor lately—a gentleman. He stayed a few days, and then left suddenly."

"Young or old?"

"Elderly, clean-shaven, and grey hair. She used to call him Digby."

"Digby!" I echoed. "When was he here? Tell me quickly!"

"Oh, about four days ago, I think. Yes—he went away last Sunday night."

"Tell me all about him," I urged her. "He's a friend of mine."

"Oh, then perhaps I ought not to say anything," said the girl a little confused.

"On the contrary, you will be doing me the very greatest service if you tell me all that you know concerning him," I declared. "Don't think that anything you say will annoy me, for it won't. He was my friend, but he served me a very evil trick."

"Well, sir," she replied, "he arrived here very late one night, and my mistress sat with him in the drawing-room nearly all night talking to him. I crept down to try and hear what was going on, but they were speaking so low, almost whispering, so that I could catch only a few words."

"What did you hear?" I inquired breathlessly.

"Well, from what I could gather the gentleman was in some grave danger—something to do with a girl. Mistress seemed very excited

WILLIAM LE QUEUX

and talked about another girl, which she called Freda, or something like that, and then the gentleman mentioned somebody named Royle, whereon mistress seemed to fly into a passion. I heard her say distinctly, 'You are a fool, Digby! If you're not very careful you'll give the game away.' Then he said, 'If the truth comes out, she will suffer, not me.'"

"Whom did you infer he meant by she?" I asked.

"Ah, sir, that's impossible to say," was her response. "Well, they were alone there for hours. He seemed to be begging her to tell him something, but she steadily refused. And every time he mentioned the name of Royle she became angry and excited. Once I heard her say, 'As long as you keep carefully out of the way, you need not fear anything. Nobody—not even the girl—suspects the truth. So I don't see that you need have the slightest apprehension. But mind, you're going to play the straight game with me, Digby, or, by heaven! it will be the worse for you!'"

"Then she threatened him?" I remarked.

"Yes. She seemed very determined and spoke in a low, hard voice. Of course, I could only catch a few disjointed words, and out of them I tried to make sense. But I overheard sufficient to know that the visitor was in a state of great agitation and fear."

"Did he go out much?"

"All the time he was here I never knew him to go further than the garden," said the maid, who seemed to be unusually intelligent.

"What about Ali?"

"Ali was his constant companion. When they were together they spoke in some foreign language."

A sudden thought flashed across my mind.

Could Ali be a Peruvian Indian and not a Hindu? Was he the accomplice of the mysterious Englishman named Cane—the man suspected of causing the death of Sir Digby Kemsley?

What this girl was revealing was certainly amazing.

"You are quite sure that this man she called Digby left the neighbourhood last Sunday?" I asked her.

"Quite. I overheard him speaking with the mistress late on Saturday night. He said, 'By this time to-morrow I shall be back in Brussels.' And I know he went there, for next day I posted a letter to Brussels."

"To him?" I cried. "What was the address?"

"The name was Bryant, and it was addressed Poste Restante, Brussels. I remember it, because I carefully made a note of it, as the whole affair seemed so extraordinary."

"But this man she called Digby. Was he well-dressed?" I inquired.

"Oh, no—not at all. He seemed poor and shabby. He only had with him a little handbag, but I believe he came from a considerable distance, probably from abroad, expressly to see her."

"Then you think he is in Brussels now?"

"Well, I posted the letter on Monday night. To-day is Wednesday," she said.

I reflected. My first impulse was to go straight to Brussels and send a message to Mr. Bryant at the Poste Restante—a message that would trap him into an appointment with me.

But in face of Phrida's present peril could I possibly leave London?

I was at the parting of the ways. To hesitate might be to lose trace of the man who had proved such a false friend, while, by crossing to Brussels again, I would be leaving Phrida to her fate.

"You heard no other mention of the person named Royle?" I asked her after a brief pause, during which I placed a second half-sovereign in her hand.

She reflected for a moment, her eyes cast down upon the carpet, as we stood together in that sombre little room of horrors.

"Well, yes," she replied thoughtfully. "One afternoon when I was taking tea into the drawing-room where they were sitting together I heard mistress say, 'I don't like that man Royle at all. He means mischief—more especially as he loves the girl.' The gentleman only laughed and said, 'Have no fear on that score. He knows nothing, and is not likely to know, unless you tell him.' Then mistress said, 'I've been a fool, perhaps, but when we met I told him one or two things—sufficient to cause him to think.' Then the gentleman stood up angrily and cried out in quite a loud voice: 'What! you fool! You've actually told him—you've allowed your infernal tongue to wag and let out the truth!' But she said that she had not told all the truth, and started abusing him—so much so that he left the room and went out into the garden, where, a few minutes later, I saw him talking excitedly to Ali. But when the two men talked I could, of course, understand nothing," added the girl.

"Then your mistress declared that she didn't like the man Royle, eh?"

"Yes; she seemed to fear him—fear that he knew too much about some business or other," replied the maid. "And to tell you quite frankly, sir, after watching the mistress and her visitor very narrowly for a couple of days I came to the conclusion that the gentleman was hiding—that perhaps the police were after him."

"Why?" I inquired in a casual tone. "What made you think that?"

"I hardly know. Perhaps from the scraps of conversation I overheard, perhaps from his cunning, secret manner—not but what he was always nice to me, and gave me something when he left."

"You didn't hear any other names of persons mentioned?" I asked. "Try and think, as all that you tell me is of the greatest importance to me."

The girl stood silent, while I paced up and down that room in which, not many hours before, I had endured that awful mental torture. She drew her hand across her brow, trying to recall.

"Yes, there was another name," she admitted at last, "but I can't at the moment recall it."

"Ah, do!" I implored her. "Try and recall it. I am in no hurry to leave."

Again the dark-eyed maid in the dainty apron was silent—both hands upon her brow, as she had turned from me and was striving to remember.

"It was some foreign name—a woman's name," she said.

I recollected the dead girl was believed to have been a foreigner!

Suddenly she cried—

"Ah, I remember! The name was Mary Brack."

"Mary Brack!" I repeated.

"Yes. Of course I don't know how it's spelt."

"Well, if it were a foreign name it would probably be Marie B-r-a-c-q—if you are sure you've pronounced it right."

"Oh, yes. I'm quite sure. Mistress called her 'poor girl!' so I can only suppose that something must have happened to her."

I held my breath at her words.

Yes, without a doubt I had secured a clue to the identity of the girl who lost her life at Harrington Gardens.

Her name, in all probability, was Marie Bracq!

XXII

"MARIE BRACQ!"

Marie Bracq! The name rang in my ears in the express all the way from Colchester to Liverpool Street.

Just before six o'clock I alighted from a taxi in Scotland Yard, and, ascending in the lift, soon found myself sitting with Inspector Edwards.

At that moment I deemed it judicious to tell him nothing regarding my night adventure in the country, except to say:

"Well, I've had a strange experience—the strangest any man could have, because I have dared to investigate on my own account the mystery of Harrington Gardens."

"Oh! tell me about it, Mr. Royle," he urged, leaning back in his chair before the littered writing-table.

"There's nothing much to tell," was my reply. "I'll describe it all some day. At present there's no time to waste. I believe I am correct in saying that the name of the murdered girl is Marie Bracq."

Edwards looked me straight in the face. "That's not an English name, is it?" he said.

"No, Belgian, I should say."

"Belgian? Yes, most probably," he said. "A rather uncommon name, and one which ought not to be difficult to trace. How did you find this out?"

"Oh, it's a long story, Mr. Edwards," I said. "But I honestly believe that at last we are on the scent. Cannot you discover whether any girl of that name is missing?"

"Of course. I'll wire to the Brussels police at once. Perhaps it will be well to ask the Préfect of Police in Paris if they have any person of that name reported missing," he said, and, ringing a bell, a clerk appeared almost instantly with a writing-pad and pencil.

"Wire to Brussels and Paris and ask if they have any person named Marie Bracq—be careful of the spelling—missing. If so, we will send them over a photo."

"Yes, sir," the man replied, and disappeared.

"Well," I asked casually, when we were alone, "have you traced the tailor who made the dead girl's costume?"

"Not yet. The Italian police are making every inquiry."

"And what have you decided regarding that letter offering to give information?"

"Nothing," was his prompt reply. "And if this information you have obtained as to the identity of the deceased proves correct, we shall do nothing. It will be far more satisfactory to work out the problem for ourselves, rather than risk being misled by somebody who has an axe to grind."

"Ah! I'm pleased that you view the matter in that light," I said, much relieved. "I feel confident that I have gained the true name of the victim."

"But how did you manage it, Mr. Royle?" he asked, much interested.

I, however, refused to satisfy his curiosity.

"You certainly seem to know more about the affair than we do," he remarked with a smile.

"Well, was I not a friend of the man who is now a fugitive?" I remarked.

"Ah, of course! And depend upon it, Mr. Royle, when this affair is cleared up, we shall find that your friend was a man of very curious character," he said, pursing his lips. "Inquiries have shown that many mysteries concerning him remain to be explained."

For a moment I did not speak. Then I asked:

"Is anything known concerning a woman friend of his named Petre?"

"Petre?" he echoed. "No, not that I'm aware of. But it seemed that he was essentially what might be called a ladies' man."

"I know that. He used to delight in entertaining his lady friends."

"But who is this woman Petre whom you've mentioned?" he inquired with some curiosity.

"The woman who is ready to give you information for a consideration," I replied.

"How do you know that?"

"Well, I am acquainted with her. I was with her last night," was my quick response. "Her intention is to condemn a perfectly innocent woman."

"Whom?" he asked sharply. "The woman who lost that green horn comb at the flat?"

I held my breath.

"No, Edwards," I answered, "that question is unfair. As a gentleman, I cannot mention a lady's name. If she chooses to do so that's another matter. But if she does—as from motives of jealousy she easily may do—please do not take any action without first consulting me. Ere long I shall have a strange, almost incredible, story to put before you."

"Why not now?" he asked, instantly interested.

"Because I have not yet substantiated all my facts," was my reply.

"Cannot I assist you? Why keep me in the dark?" he protested.

"I'm afraid you can render me no other assistance except to hesitate to accept the allegations of that woman Petre," I replied.

"Well, we shall wait until she approaches us again," he said.

"This I feel certain she will do," I exclaimed. "But if you see her, make no mention whatever of me—you understand? She believes me to be dead, and therefore not likely to disprove her allegations."

"Dead!" he echoed. "Really, Mr. Royle, all this sounds most interesting."

"It is," I declared. "I believe I am now upon the verge of a very remarkable discovery—that ere long we shall know the details of that crime in South Kensington."

"Well, if you do succeed in elucidating the mystery you will accomplish a marvellous feat," said the great detective, placing his hands together and looking at me across his table. "I confess that I'm completely baffled. That friend of yours who called himself Kemsley has disappeared as completely as though the ground had opened and swallowed him."

"Ah, Edwards, London's a big place," I laughed, "and your men are really not very astute."

"Why not?"

"Because the man you want called at my rooms in Albemarle Street only a few days ago."

"What?" he cried, staring at me surprised.

"Yes, I was unfortunately out, but he left a message with my man that he would let me know his address later."

"Amazing impudence!" cried my friend. "He called in order to show his utter defiance of the police, I should think."

"No. My belief is that he wished to tell me something," I said. "Anyhow, he will either return or send his address."

"I very much doubt it. He's a clever rogue, but, like all men of his elusiveness and cunning, he never takes undue chances. No, Mr. Royle, depend upon it, he'll never visit you again."

"But I may be able to find him. Who knows?"

The detective moved his papers aside, and with a sigh admitted:

"Yes, you may have luck, to be sure."

Then, after some further conversation, he looked at the piece of sticking plaster on my head and remarked:

"I see you've had a knock. How did you manage it?"

I made an excuse that in bending before my own fireplace I had struck it on the corner of the mantelshelf. Afterwards I suddenly said:

"You recollect those facts you told me regarding the alleged death of the real Kemsley in Peru, don't you?"

"Of course."

"Well, they've interested me deeply. I'd so much like to know any further details."

Edwards reflected a moment, recalling the report.

"Well," he said, taking from one of the drawers in his table a voluminous official file of papers. "There really isn't very much more than what you already know. The Consul's report is a very full one, and contains a quantity of depositions taken on the spot—mostly evidence of Peruvians, in which little credence can, perhaps, be placed. Of course," he added, "the suspected man Cane seems to have been a very bad lot. He was at one time manager of a rubber plantation belonging to a Portuguese company, and some very queer stories were current regarding him."

"What kind of stories?" I asked.

"Oh, his outrageous cruelty to the natives when they did not collect sufficient rubber. He used, they said, to burn the native villages and massacre the inhabitants without the slightest compunction. He was known by the natives as 'The Red Englishman.' They were terrified by him. His name, it seems, was Herbert Cane, and so bad became his reputation that he was dismissed by the company after an inquiry by a commission sent from Lisbon, and drifted into Argentina, sinking lower and lower in the social scale."

Then, after referring to several closely-written pages of foolscap, each one bearing the blue embossed stamp of the British Consulate in Lima, he went on:

"Inquiries showed that for a few months the man Cane was in Monte Video, endeavouring to obtain a railway concession for a German group of financiers, but his reputation became noised abroad and he found it better to leave that city. Afterwards he seems to have met Sir Digby and to have become his bosom friend."

"And what were the exact circumstances of Sir Digby's death?" I asked anxiously.

"Ah! they are veiled in mystery," was the detective's response, turning again to the official report and depositions of witnesses. "As I think I told you, Sir Digby had met with an accident and injured his spine. Cane, whose acquaintance he made, brought him down to Lima, and a couple of months later, under the doctor's advice, removed him to a bungalow at Huacho. Here they lived with a couple of Peruvian men-servants, named Senos and Luis. Cane seemed devoted to his friend, leading the life of a quiet, studious, refined man—very different to his wild life on the rubber plantation. One morning, however, on a servant entering Sir Digby's room, he found him dead, and an examination showed that he had been bitten in the arm by a poisonous snake. There were signs of a struggle, showing the poor fellow's agony before he died. Cane, entering shortly afterwards, was distracted with grief, and telegraphed himself to the British Consul at Lima. And, according to custom in that country, that same evening the unfortunate man was buried."

"Without any inquiry?" I asked.

"Yes. At the time, remember, there was no suspicion. A good many people die annually in Peru of snake-bite," Edwards replied, again referring to the file of papers before him. "It seems, however, that three days later, the second Peruvian servant—a man known as Senos—declared that during the night of the tragic affair he had heard his master suddenly yell with terror and cry out 'You blackguard, Cane, you hell-fiend; take the thing away. Ah! God! You—why, you've killed me!'"

"Yes," I said. "But was this told to Cane?"

"Cane saw the man and strenuously denied his allegation. He, indeed, went to the local Commissary of Police and lodged a complaint against the man Senos for falsely accusing him, saying that he had done so out of spite, because a few days before he had had occasion to reprimand him for inattention to his duties. Further, Cane brought up a man living five miles from Huacho who swore that the accused man was at his bungalow on that night, arriving at nine o'clock. He drank so heavily that he could not get home, so he remained there the night, returning at eight o'clock next morning."

"And the police officials believed him—eh?" I asked.

"Yes. But next day he left Huacho, expressing a determination to go to Lima and make a statement to the Consul there. But he never arrived at the capital, and he has never been seen since."

"Then a grave suspicion rests upon him?" I remarked, reflecting upon my startling adventure of the previous night.

"Certainly. But the curious thing is that no attempt seems to have been made by the police authorities in Lima to trace the man. They allowed him to disappear, and took no notice of the affair, even when the British Consul reported it. I fancy police methods must be very lax ones there," he added.

"But what could have been the method of the assassin?" I asked.

"Why, simply to allow the snake to strike at the sleeping man, I presume," said the detective. "Yet, one would have thought that after the snake had bitten him he would have cried out for help. But he did not."

Had the victim, I wondered, swallowed that same tasteless drug that I had swallowed, and been paralysed, as I had been?

"And the motive of the crime?" I asked.

Edwards shrugged his shoulders, and raised his brows.

"Robbery, I should say," was his reply. "But, strangely enough, there is no suggestion of theft in this report; neither does there seem to be any woman in the case."

"You, of course, suspect that my friend Digby and the man Cane, are one and the same person!" I said. "But is it feasible that if Cane were really responsible for the death of the real Sir Digby, would he have the bold audacity to return to London and actually pose as his victim?"

"Yes, Mr. Royle," replied the detective, "I think it most feasible. Great criminals have the most remarkable audacity. Some really astounding cases of most impudent impersonation have come under my own observation during my career in this office."

"Then you adhere to the theory which you formed at first?"

"Most decidedly," he replied; "and while it seems that you have a surprise to spring upon me very shortly, so have I one to spring upon you—one which I fear, Mr. Royle," he added very slowly, looking me gravely in the face—"I fear may come as a great shock to you."

I sat staring at him, unable to utter a syllable.

He was alluding to Phrida, and to the damning evidence against her. What could he know? Ah! who had betrayed my love?

XXIII

LOVE'S CONFESSION

I dined alone at the Club, and afterwards sat over my coffee in one of the smaller white-panelled rooms, gazing up at the Adams ceiling, and my mind full of the gravest thoughts.

What had Edwards meant when he promised me an unpleasant surprise? Had the woman Petre already made a statement incriminating my well-beloved?

If so, I would at once demand the arrest of her and her accomplices for attempted murder. It had suggested itself to me to make a complete revelation to Edwards of the whole of my exciting adventure at Colchester, but on mature consideration I saw that such a course might thwart my endeavours to come face to face with Digby.

Therefore I had held my tongue.

But were Edwards' suspicions that the assassin Cane and the man I knew as Sir Digby Kemsley were one and the same, correct, or were they not?

The method by which the unfortunate Englishman in Peru had been foully done to death was similar to the means employed against myself at Colchester on the previous night. Again, the fact that the victim did not shout and call for aid was, no doubt, due to the administration of that drug which produced complete paralysis of the muscles, and yet left the senses perfectly normal.

Was that Indian whom they called Ali really a Peruvian native—the accomplice of Cane? I now felt confident that this was so.

But in what manner could the impostor have obtained power over Phrida? Why did she not take courage and reveal to me the truth?

Presently, I took a taxi down to Cromwell Road and found my well-beloved, with thin, pale, drawn face, endeavouring to do some fancy needlework by the drawing-room fire. Her mother had retired with a bad headache, she said, and she was alone.

"I expected you yesterday, Teddy," she said, taking my hand. "I waited all day, but you never came."

"I had to go into the country," I replied somewhat lamely.

Then after a brief conversation upon trivialities, during which time

I sat regarding her closely, and noting how nervous and agitated she seemed, she suddenly asked:

"Well! Have you heard anything more of that woman, Mrs. Petre?"

"I believe she's gone abroad," I replied, with evasion.

Phrida's lips twitched convulsively, and she gave vent to a slight sigh, of relief, perhaps.

"Tell me, dearest," I said, bending and stroking her soft hair from her white brow. "Are you still so full of anxiety? Do you still fear the exposure of the truth?"

She did not reply, but of a sudden buried her face upon my shoulder and burst into tears.

"Ah!" I sighed, still stroking her hair sympathetically, "I know what you must suffer, darling—of the terrible mental strain upon you. I believe in your innocence—I still believe in it, and if you will bear a stout heart and trust me, I believe I shall succeed in worsting your enemies."

In a moment her tear-stained face was raised to mine.

"Do you really believe that you can, dear?" she asked anxiously. "Do you actually anticipate extricating me from this terrible position of doubt, uncertainty, and guilt?"

"I do—if you will only trust me, and keep a brave heart, darling," I said. "Already I have made several discoveries—startling ones."

"About Mrs. Petre, perhaps?"

"About her and about others."

"What about her?"

"I have found out where she is living—down at Colchester."

"What?" she gasped, starting. "You've been down there?"

"Yes, I was there yesterday, and I saw Ali and the two servants."

"You saw them—and spoke to them?" she cried incredibly.

"Yes."

"But, Teddy—ah! You don't know how injudicious it was for you to visit them. Why, you might have—"

"Might have what?" I asked, endeavouring to betray no surprise at her words.

"Well, I mean you should not have ventured into the enemy's camp like that. It was dangerous," she declared.

"Why?"

"They are quite unscrupulous," she replied briefly.

"They are your enemies, I know. But I cannot see why they should be mine," I remarked.

"My enemies—yes!" my love cried bitterly. "It will not be long before that woman makes a charge against me, Teddy—one which I shall not be able to refute."

"But I will assist you against them. I love you, Phrida, and it is my duty to defend you," I declared.

"Ah! You were always so good and generous," she remarked wistfully. "But in this case I cannot, alas, see how you can render me any aid! The police will make inquiries, and—and then the end," she added in a voice scarce above a whisper.

"No, no!" I urged. "Don't speak in that hopeless strain, darling. I know your position is a terrible one. We need not refer to details; as they are painful to both of us. But I am straining every nerve—working night and day to clear up the mystery and lift from you this cloud of suspicion. I have already commenced by learning one or two facts— facts of which the police remain in ignorance. Although you refused to tell me—why, I cannot discern—the name of the unfortunate girl who lost her life, I have succeeded in gaining knowledge of it. Was not the girl named Marie Bracq?"

She started again at hearing the name.

"Yes," she replied at once. "Who told you?"

"I discovered it for myself," I replied. "Who was the girl—tell me?"

"A friend of Digby Kemsley's."

"A foreigner, of course?"

"Yes, Belgian, I believe."

"From Brussels, eh?"

"Perhaps. I don't know for certain."

"And she learned some great secret of Digby's, which was the motive of the crime," I suggested.

But my love only shook her pretty head blankly, saying—"I don't know. Perhaps she knew something to his detriment."

"And in order to silence her, she was killed," I suggested.

"Perhaps."

She made no protest of her own innocence, I noticed. She seemed to place herself unreservedly in my hands to judge her as I thought fit.

Yet had not her own admissions been extremely strange ones. Had she not practically avowed her guilt?

"Can you tell me nothing concerning this Belgian girl?" I asked her a few moments later.

"I only knew her but very slightly."

"Pardon me putting to you such a pointed question, Phrida. But were you jealous of her?"

"Jealous!" she exclaimed. "Why, dear me, no. Why should I be jealous? Who suggested that?"

"Mrs. Petre. She declares that your jealousy was the motive of the crime, and that Digby himself can bear witness to it."

"She said that?" cried my love, her eyes flashing in fierce anger. "She's a wicked liar."

"I know she is, and I intend to prove her so," I replied with confidence. "When she and I meet again we have an account to settle. You will see."

"Ah! Teddy, beware of her! She's a dangerous woman—highly dangerous," declared my love apprehensively. "You don't know her as I do—you do not know the grave evil and utter ruin she has brought upon others. So I beg of you to be careful not to be entrapped."

"Have others been entrapped, then?" I asked with great curiosity.

"I don't know. No. Please don't ask me," she protested. "I don't know."

Her response was unreal. My well-beloved was I knew in possession of some terrible secret which she dared not betray. Yet why were her lips sealed? What did she fear?

"I intend to find Digby, and demand the truth from him," I said after we had been silent for a long time. "I will never rest until I stand before him face to face."

"Ah! no dear!" she cried in quick alarm, starting up and flinging both her arms about my neck. "No, don't do that?" she implored.

"Why not?"

"Because he will condemn me—he will think you have learned something from me," she declared in deep distress.

"But I shall reveal to him my sources of information," I said. "Since that fatal night I have learned that the man whom I believed was my firm friend has betrayed me. An explanation is due to me, and I intend to have one."

"At my expense—eh?" she asked in bitter reproach.

"No, dearest. The result shall not fall upon you," I said. "I will see to that. A foul and dastardly crime has been committed, and the assassin shall be brought to punishment."

My well-beloved shuddered in my arms as she heard my words—as though the guilt were upon her.

I detected it, and became more than ever puzzled. Why did she seek to secure this man's freedom?

I asked her that question point-blank, whereupon in a hard, faltering voice, she replied:

"Because, dear, while he is still a fugitive from justice I feel myself safe. The hour he is arrested is the hour of my doom."

"Why speak so despondently?" I asked. "Have I not promised to protect you from those people?"

"How can you if they make allegations against me and bring up witnesses who will commit perjury—who will swear anything in order that the guilt shall be placed upon my head," she asked in despair.

"Though the justice often dispensed by country magistrates is a disgraceful travesty of right and wrong, yet we still have in England justice in the criminal courts," I said. "Rest assured that no jury will convict an innocent woman of the crime of murder."

She stood slightly away from me, staring blankly straight before her. Then suddenly she pressed both hands upon her brow and cried in a low, intense voice:

"May God have pity on me!"

"Yes," I said very earnestly. "Trust in Him, dearest, and He will help you."

"Ah!" she cried. "You don't know how I suffer—of all the terror—all the dread that haunts me night and day. Each ring at the door I fear may be the police—every man who passes the house I fear may be a detective watching. This torture is too awful. I feel I shall go mad—*mad*!"

And she paced the room in her despair, while I stood watching her, unable to still the wild, frantic terror that had gripped her young heart.

What could I do? What could I think?

"This cannot go on, Phrida!" I cried at last in desperation. "I will search out this man. I'll grip him by the throat and force the truth from him," I declared, setting my teeth hard. "I love you, and I will not stand by and see you suffer like this!"

"Ah, no!" she implored, suddenly approaching me, flinging herself upon her knees and gripping my hands. "No, I beg of you not to do that!" she cried hoarsely.

"But why?" I demanded. "Surely you can tell me the reason of your fear!" I went on—"the man is a rank impostor. That has been proved already by the police."

"Do you know that?" she asked, in an instant grave. "Are you quite certain of that? Remember, you have all along believed him to be the real Sir Digby."

WILLIAM LE QUEUX

"What is your belief, Phrida?" I asked her very earnestly.

She drew a long breath and hesitated.

"Truth to tell, dear, I don't know what to think. Sometimes I believe he must be the real person—and at other times I am filled with doubt."

"But now tell me," I urged, assisting her to rise to her feet and then placing my arm about her neck, so that her pretty head fell upon my shoulder. "Answer me truthfully this one question, for all depends upon it. How is it that this man has secured such a hold upon you—how is it that with you his word is law—that though he is a fugitive from justice you refuse to say a single word against him or to give me one clue to the solution of this mystery?"

Her face was blanched to the lips, she trembled in my embrace, drawing a long breath.

"I—I'm sorry, dear—but I—I can't tell you. I—I dare not. Can't you understand?" she asked with despair in her great, wide-open eyes. "*I dare not!*"

XXIV

Official Secrecy

The following evening was damp, grey, and dull, as I stood shivering at the corner of the narrow Rue de l'Eveque and the broad Place de la Monnie in Brussels. The lamps were lit, and around me everywhere was the bustle of business.

I had crossed by the morning service by way of Ostend, and had arrived again at the Grand only half an hour before.

The woman Petre had sent a letter to Digby Kemsley to the Poste Restante in Brussels under the name of Bryant. If this were so, the fugitive must be in the habit of calling for his letters, and it was the great black façade of the chief post-office in Brussels that I was watching.

The business-day was just drawing to a close, the streets were thronged, the traffic rattled noisily over the uneven granite paving of the big square. Opposite the Post Office the arc lamps were shedding a bright light outside the theatre, while all the shops around were a blaze of light, while on every side the streets were agog with life.

Up and down the broad flight of steps which led to the entrance of the Post Office hundreds of people ascended and descended, passing and re-passing the four swing-doors which gave entrance to the huge hall with its dozens of departments ranged around and its partitioned desks for writing.

The mails from France and England were just in, and dozens of men came with their keys to obtain their correspondence from the range of private boxes, and as I watched, the whole bustle of business life passed before me.

I was keeping a sharp eye upon all who passed up and down that long flight of granite steps, but at that hour of the evening, and in that crowd, it was no easy matter.

Would I be successful? That was the one thought which filled my mind.

As I stood there, my eager gaze upon that endless stream of people, I felt wearied and fagged. The Channel crossing had been a bad one, as it so often is in January, and I had not yet recovered from my weird experience at Colchester. The heavy overcoat I wore was, I found, not proof against the cutting east wind which swept around the corner from the Boulevard Auspach, hence I was compelled to change my position and seek shelter in a doorway opposite the point where I expected the man I sought would enter.

I had already surveyed the interior and presented the card of a friend to an official at the Poste Restante, though I knew there was no letter for him. I uttered some words of politeness to the man in order to make his acquaintance, as he might, perhaps, be of use to me ere my quest was at an end.

At the Poste Restante were two windows, one distributing correspondence for people whose surname began with the letters A to L, and the other from M to Z.

It was at the first window I inquired, the clerk there being a pleasant, fair-haired, middle-aged man in a holland coat as worn by postal employees. I longed to ask him if he had any letters for the name of Bryant, or if any Englishman of that name had called, but I dared not do so. He would, no doubt, snub me and tell me to mind my own business.

So instead, I was extremely polite, regretted to have troubled him, and, raising my hat, withdrew.

I saw that to remain within the big office for hours was impossible. The uniformed doorkeeper who sat upon a high desk overlooking everything, would quickly demand my business, and expel me.

No, my only place was out in the open street. Not a pleasant prospect in winter, and for how many days I could not tell.

For aught I knew, the fugitive had called for the woman's letter and left the capital. But he, being aware that the police were in search of him, would, I thought, if he called at the post office at all for letters, come there after dark. Hence, I had lost no time in mounting guard.

My thoughts, as I stood there, were, indeed, bitter and confused.

The woman Petre had not, as far as I could make out, made any incriminating statement to the police. Yet she undoubtedly believed me to be dead, and I reflected in triumph upon the unpleasant surprise in store for her when we met—as meet we undoubtedly would.

The amazing problem, viewed briefly, stood thus: The girl, Marie Bracq, had been killed by a knife with a three-cornered blade, such knife having been and being still in the possession of Phrida, my well-beloved, whose finger-prints were found in the room near the body of the poor girl. The grave and terrible suspicion resting upon Phrida was increased and even corroborated by her firm resolve to preserve secrecy, her admissions, and her avowed determination to take her own life rather than face accusation.

On the other hand, there was the mystery of the identity of Marie Bracq, the mystery of the identity of the man who had passed as Sir Digby Kemsley, the reason of his flight, if Phrida were guilty, and the mystery of the woman Petre, and her accomplices.

Yes. The whole affair was one great and complete problem, the extent of which even Edwards, expert as he was, had, as yet, failed to discover. The more I tried to solve it the more hopelessly complicated did it become.

I could see no light through the veil of mystery and suspicion in which my well-beloved had become enveloped.

Why had that man—the man I now hated with so fierce an hatred—held her in the hollow of his unscrupulous hands? She had admitted that, whenever he ordered her to do any action, she was bound to obey.

Yes. My love was that man's slave! I ground my teeth when the bitter thought flashed across my perturbed mind.

Ah! what a poor, ignorant fool I had been! And how that scoundrel must have laughed at me!

I was anxious to meet him face to face—to force from his lips the truth, to compel him to answer to me.

And with that object I waited—waited in the cold and rain for three long hours, until at last the great doors were closed and locked for the night, and people ascended those steps no longer.

Then I turned away faint and disheartened, chilled to the bone, and wearied out. A few steps along the Boulevard brought me to the hotel, where I ate some dinner, and retired to my room to fling myself upon the couch and think.

Why was Phrida in such fear lest I should meet the man who held her so mysteriously and completely in his power? What could she fear from our meeting if she were, as I still tried to believe, innocent?

Again, was it possible that after their dastardly attempt upon my life, Mrs. Petre and her accomplices had fled to join the fugitive? Were they with him? Perhaps so! Perhaps they were there in Brussels!

The unfortunate victim, Marie Bracq, had probably been a Belgian. Bracq was certainly a Belgian name.

The idea crossed my mind to go on the following day to the central Police Bureau I had noticed in the Rue de la Regence, and make inquiry whether they knew of any person of that name to be missing. It was not a bad suggestion, I reflected, and I felt greatly inclined to carry it out.

Next day, I was up early, but recognised the futility of watching at the Poste Restante until the daylight faded. On the other hand, if Mrs. Petre was actually in that city, she would have no fear to go about openly. Yet, after due consideration, I decided not to go to the post office till twilight set in.

The morning I spent idling on the Boulevards and in the cafés, but I became sick of such inactivity, for I was frantically eager and anxious to learn the truth.

At noon I made up my mind, and taking a taxi, alighted at the Préfecture of Police, where, after some time, I was seen by the *Chef du Sureté*, a grey-haired, dry-as-dust looking official—a narrow-eyed little man, in black, whose name was Monsieur Van Huffel, and who sat at a writing-table in a rather bare room, the walls of which were painted dark green. He eyed me with some curiosity as I entered and bowed.

"Be seated, I pray, m'sieur," he said in French, indicating a chair on the opposite side of the table, and leaning back, placed his fingers together in a judicial attitude.

The police functionary on the continent is possessed of an ultra-grave demeanour, and is always of a funereal type.

"M'sieur wishes to make an inquiry, I hear?" he began.

"Yes," I said. "I am very anxious to know whether you have any report of a young person named Marie Bracq being missing."

"Marie Bracq!" he echoed in surprise, leaning forward towards me. "And what do you know, m'sieur, regarding Marie Bracq?"

"I merely called to ascertain if any person of that name, is reported to you as missing," I said, much surprised at the effect which mention of the victim had produced upon him.

"You are English, of course?" he asked.

"Yes, m'sieur."

"Well, curiously enough, only this morning I have had a similar inquiry from your Scotland Yard. They are asking if we are acquainted with any person named Marie Bracq. And we are, m'sieur," said Monsieur Van Huffel. "But first please explain what you know of her."

"I have no personal acquaintance with her," was my reply. "I know of her—that is all. But it may not be the same person."

He opened a drawer, turned over a quantity of papers, and a few seconds later produced a photograph which he passed across to me.

It was a half-length cabinet portrait of a girl in a fur coat and hat. But no second glance was needed to tell me that it was actually the picture of the girl found murdered in London.

"I see you recognise her, m'sieur," remarked the police official in a cold, matter-of-fact tone. "Please tell me all you know."

I paused for a few seconds with the portrait in my hand. My object was to get all the facts I could from the functionary before me, and give him the least information possible.

"Unfortunately, I know but very little," was my rather lame reply. "This lady was a friend of a lady friend of mine."

"An English lady was your friend—eh?"

"Yes."

"In London?"

I nodded in the affirmative, while the shrewd little man who was questioning me sat twiddling a pen with his thin fingers.

"And she told you of Marie Bracq? In what circumstances?"

"Well," I said. "It is a long story. Before I tell you, I would like to ask you one question, m'sieur. Have you received from Scotland Yard the description of a man named Digby Kemsley—Sir Digby Kemsley—who is wanted for murder?"

The dry little official with the parchment face repeated the name, then consulting a book at his elbow, replied:

"Yes. We have circulated the description and photograph. It is believed by your police that his real name is Cane."

"He has been in Brussels during the past few days to my own certain knowledge," I said.

"In Brussels," echoed the man seated in the writing chair. "Where?"

"Here, in your city. And I expect he is here now."

"And you know him?" asked the *Chef du Sureté*, his eyes betraying slight excitement.

"Quite well. He was my friend."

"I see he is accused of murdering a woman, name unknown, in his apartment," remarked the official.

"The name is now known—it has been discovered by me, m'sieur. The name of the dead girl is Marie Bracq."

The little man half rose from his chair and stared at me.

"Is this the truth, m'sieur?" he cried. "Is this man named Kemsley, or Cane, accused of the assassination of Marie Bracq?"

"Yes," I replied.

"But this is most astounding," the Belgian functionary declared excitedly. "Marie Bracq dead! Ah! it cannot be possible, m'sieur! You do not know what this information means to us—what an enormous sensation it will cause if the press scents the truth. Tell me quickly—tell me all you know," he urged, at the same time taking up the telephone receiver from his table and then listening for a second, said in a quick, impetuous voice, "I want Inspector Frémy at once!"

XXV

Frémy, of the Sureté

After a few moments a short, stout, clean-shaven man with a round, pleasant face, and dressed in black, entered and bowed to his chief. He carried his soft felt hat and cane in his hand, and seated himself at the invitation of Van Huffel.

"This is Inspector Frémy—Monsieur Edouard Royle, of Londres," exclaimed the *Chef du Sureté*, introducing us.

The detective, the most famous police officer in Belgium, who had been for years under Monsieur Hennion, in Paris, and had now transferred his services to Belgium, bowed and looked at me with his small, inquisitive eyes.

"Monsieur Frémy. This gentleman has called with regard to the case of Marie Bracq," said Van Huffel in French.

The detective was quickly interested.

"She is dead—been assassinated in London," his chief went on.

Frémy stared at the speaker in surprise, and the two men exchanged strange glances.

"Monsieur tells me that the man, Sir Digby Kemsley, wanted by Scotland Yard, is accused of the murder of Marie Bracq—and, further," added Van Huffel, "the accused has been here in Brussels quite recently."

"In Brussels?" echoed the round-faced man.

"Yes," I said. "He has letters addressed to the Poste Restante in the name of Bryant." And I spelt it as the detective carefully wrote down the name.

"He will not be difficult to find if he is still in Brussels," declared the inspector. "We had an inquiry from Scotland Yard asking if we had any report concerning Marie Bracq only this morning," he added.

"It was sent to you by my friend, Inspector Edwards, and whom I am assisting in this inquiry," I explained.

"You said that Marie Bracq was a friend of a lady friend of yours, M'sieur Royle," continued the *Chef du Sureté*. "Will you do us the favour and tell us all you know concerning the tragedy—how the young lady lost her life?"

"Ah! m'sieur," I replied, "I fear I cannot do that. How she was killed is still a mystery. Only within the past few hours have I been able to establish the dead girl's identity, and only then after narrowly escaping falling the victim of a most dastardly plot."

"Perhaps you will be good enough to make a statement of all you know, M'sieur Royle," urged the grey-haired little man; "and if we can be of any service in bringing the culprit to justice, you may rely upon us."

"But first, m'sieur, allow me to put observation upon the Poste Restante?" asked Frémy, rising and going to the telephone, where he got on to one of his subordinates, and gave him instructions in Flemish, a language I do not understand.

Then, when he returned to his chair, I began to briefly relate what I knew concerning Sir Digby, and what had occurred, as far as I knew, on that fatal night of the sixth of January.

I, of course, made no mention of the black suspicion cast upon the woman I loved, nor of the delivery of Digby's letter, my meeting with the woman Petre and its exciting results.

Yet had I not met that woman I should still have been in ignorance of the identity of the dead girl, and, besides, I would not have met the sallow-faced Ali, or been aware of his methods—those methods so strangely similar to that adopted when Sir Digby Kemsley lost his life in Peru.

The two police functionaries listened very attentively to my story without uttering a word.

I had spoken of the woman Petre as being an accomplice of the man who was a fugitive, whereupon Frémy asked:

"Do you suppose that the woman is with him?"

"She has, I believe, left England, and, therefore, in all probability, is with him."

"Are there any others of the gang—for there is, of course, a gang? Such people never act singly."

"Two other men, as far as I know. One, a young man, who acts as servant, and the other, a tall, copper-faced man with sleek black hair—probably a Peruvian native. They call him Ali, and he pretends he is a Hindu."

"A Hindu!" gasped the detective. "Why, I saw one talking to a rather stout Englishwoman at the Gare du Nord yesterday evening, just before the Orient Express left for the East!" He gave a quick description of both the man and the woman, and I at once said:

"Yes, that was certainly Ali, and the woman was Mrs. Petre!"

"They probably left by the Orient Express!" he cried, starting up, and crossing to his chief's table snatched up the orange-coloured official time table.

"Ah! yes," he exclaimed, after searching a few moments. "The Orient Express will reach Wels, in Austria, at 2.17, no time for a telegram to get through. No. The next stop is Vienna—the Westbahnhof—at 6. I will wire to the Commissary of Police to board the train, and if they are in it, to detain them."

"Excellent," remarked his chief, and, ringing a bell, a clerk appeared and took down the official telegram, giving the description of the woman and her accomplice.

"I suppose the fugitive Englishman is not with them?" suggested the *Chef du Sureté*.

"I did not see him at the station—or, at least, I did not recognise anyone answering to the description," replied the inspector; "but we may as well add his description in the telegram and ask for an immediate reply."

Thereupon the official description of Digby, as supplied to the Belgian police by Scotland Yard, was translated into French and placed in the message.

After the clerk had left with it, Frémy, standing near the window, exclaimed:

"Dieu! Had I but known who they were last night! But we may still get them. I will see the employée at the Poste Restante. This Monsieur Bryant, if he receives letters, may have given an address for them to be forwarded."

After a slight pause, during which time the two functionaries conversed in Flemish, I turned to Van Huffel, and said:

"I have related all I know, m'sieur; therefore, I beg of you to tell me something concerning the young person Marie Bracq. Was she a lady?"

"A lady!" he echoed with a laugh. "Most certainly—the daughter of one of the princely houses of Europe."

"What?" I gasped. "Tell me all about her!"

But the dry-as-dust little man shook his grey head and replied:

"I fear, m'sieur, in my position, I am not permitted to reveal secrets entrusted to me. And her identity is a secret—a great secret."

"But I have discovered her identity where our English police had failed!" I protested. "Besides, am I not assisting you?"

"Very greatly, and we are greatly indebted to you, M'sieur Royle," he replied, with exquisite politeness; "but it is not within my province as

Chef du Sureté to tell you facts which have been revealed to me under pledge of secrecy."

"Perhaps M'sieur Frémy may be able to tell me some facts," I suggested. "Remember, I am greatly interested in the mysterious affair."

"From mere curiosity—eh?" asked Van Huffel with a smile.

"No, m'sieur," was my earnest reply. "Because the arrest and condemnation of the assassin of Marie Bracq means all the world to me."

"How?"

I hesitated for some moments, then, hoping to enlist his sympathy, I told him the truth.

"Upon the lady who is my promised wife rests a grave suspicion," I said, in a low, hard voice. "I decline to believe ill of her, or to think that she could be guilty of a crime, or—"

"Of the assassination of Marie Bracq?" interrupted Van Huffel. "Do you suspect that? Is there any question as to the guilt of the man Kemsley?" he asked quickly.

"No one has any suspicion of the lady in question," I said. "Only—only from certain facts within my knowledge and certain words which she herself has uttered, a terrible and horrible thought has seized me."

"That Marie Bracq was killed by her hand—eh? Ah, m'sieur, I quite understand," he said. "And you are seeking the truth—in order to clear the woman you love?"

"Exactly. That is the truth. That is why I am devoting all my time—all that I possess in order to solve the mystery and get at the actual truth."

Frémy glanced at his chief, then at me.

"Bien, m'sieur," exclaimed Van Huffel. "But there is no great necessity for you to know the actual identity of Marie Bracq. So long as you are able to remove the stigma from the lady in question, who is to be your wife, and to whom you are undoubtedly devoted, what matters whether the dead girl was the daughter of a prince or of a rag-picker? We will assist you in every degree in our power," he went on. "M'sieur Frémy will question the postal clerk, watch will be kept at the Poste Restante, at each of the railway stations, and in various other quarters, so that if any of the gang are in the city they cannot leave it without detection—"

"Except by automobile," I interrupted.

"Ah! I see m'sieur possesses forethought," he said with a smile. "Of course, they can easily hire an automobile and run to Namur, Ghent, or Antwerp—or even to one or other of the frontiers. But M'sieur

Frémy is in touch with all persons who have motor-cars for hire. If they attempted to leave by car when once their descriptions are circulated, we should know in half an hour, while to cross the frontier by car would be impossible." Then, turning to the inspector, he said, "You will see that precautions are immediately taken that if they are here they cannot leave."

"The matter is in my hands, m'sieur," answered the great detective simply.

"Then m'sieur refuses to satisfy me as to the exact identity of Marie Bracq?" I asked Van Huffel in my most persuasive tone.

"A thousand regrets, m'sieur, but as I have already explained, I am compelled to regard the secret entrusted to me."

"I take it that her real name is not Marie Bracq?" I said, looking him in the face.

"You are correct. It is not."

"Is she a Belgian subject?" I asked.

"No, m'sieur, the lady is not."

"You said that a great sensation would be caused if the press knew the truth?"

"Yes. I ask you to do me the favour, and promise me absolute secrecy in this matter. If we are to be successful in the arrest of these individuals, then the press must know nothing—not a syllable. Do I have your promise, M'sieur Royle?"

"If you wish," I answered.

"And we on our part will assist you to clear this lady who is to be your wife—but upon one condition."

"And that is what?" I asked.

"That you do not seek to inquire into the real identity of the poor young lady who has lost her life—the lady known to you and others as Marie Bracq," he said, looking straight into my eyes very seriously.

XXVI

Shows Expert Methods

It being the luncheon hour, Frémy and myself ate our meal at the highly popular restaurant, the Taverne Joseph, close to the Bourse, where the cooking is, perhaps, the best in Brussels and where the cosmopolitan, who knows where to eat, usually makes for when in the Belgian capital.

After our coffee, cigarettes, and a "triple-sec" each, we strolled round to the General Post Office. As we approached that long flight of granite steps I knew so well, a poor-looking, ill-dressed man with the pinch of poverty upon his face, and his coat buttoned tightly against the cold, edged up to my companion on the pavement and whispered a word, afterwards hurrying on.

"Our interesting friend has not been here yet," the detective remarked to me. "We will have a talk with the clerk at the Poste Restante."

Entering the great hall, busy as it is all day, we approached the window where letters were distributed from A to L, and where sat the same pleasant, fair-haired man sorting letters.

"Bon jour, m'sieur!" he exclaimed, when he caught sight of Frémy. "What weather, eh?"

The great detective returned his greetings, and then putting his head further into the window so that others should not overhear, said in French:

"I am looking for an individual, an Englishman, name of Bryant, and am keeping watch outside. He is wanted in England for a serious offence. Has he been here?"

"Bryant?" repeated the clerk thoughtfully.

"Yes," said Frémy, and then I spelt the name slowly.

The clerk reached his hand to the pigeon-hole wherein were letters for callers whose names began with B, and placing them against a little block of black wood on the counter before him, looked eagerly through while we watched intently.

Once or twice he stopped to scrutinise an address, but his fingers went on again through the letters to the end.

"Nothing," he remarked laconically, replacing the packet in the pigeon-hole. "But there has been correspondence for him. I recollect—a thin-faced man, with grey hair and clean shaven. Yes. I remember him distinctly. He always called just before the office was closed."

"When did he call last?" asked Frémy quickly.

"The night before last, I think," was the man's answer. "A lady was with him—a rather stout English lady."

We both started.

"Did the lady ask for any letters?"

"Yes. But I forget the name."

"Petre is her right name," I interrupted. Then I suggested to Frémy: "Ask the other clerk to look through the letter 'P.'"

"Non, m'sieur!" exclaimed the fair-haired employée. "The name she asked for was in my division. It was not P."

"Then she must have asked for a name that was not her own," I said.

"And it seems very much as though we have lost the gang by a few hours," Frémy said disappointedly. "My own opinion is that they left Brussels by the Orient Express last night. They did not call at the usual time yesterday."

"They may come this evening," I suggested.

"Certainly they may. We shall, of course, watch," he replied.

"When the man and woman called the day before yesterday," continued the employée, "there was a second man—a dark-faced Indian with them, I believe. He stood some distance away, and followed them out. It was his presence which attracted my attention and caused me to remember the incident."

Frémy exchanged looks with me. I knew he was cursing his fate which had allowed the precious trio to slip through his fingers.

Yet the thought was gratifying that when the express ran into the Great Westbahnhof at Vienna, the detectives would at once search it for the fugitives.

My companion had told me that by eight o'clock we would know the result of the enquiry, and I was anxious for that hour to arrive.

Already Frémy had ordered search to be made of arrivals at all hotels and pensions in the city for the name of Bryant, therefore, we could do nothing more than possess ourselves in patience. So we left the post office, his poverty-stricken assistant remaining on the watch, just as I had watched in the cold on the previous night.

With my companion I walked round to the big Café Metropole on the Boulevard, and over our "bocks," at a table where we could not be overheard, we discussed the situation.

That big café, one of the principal in Brussels, is usually deserted between the hours of three and four. At other times it is filled with business men discussing their affairs, or playing dominoes with that rattle which is characteristic of the foreign café.

"Why is it," I asked him, "that your chief absolutely refuses to betray the identity of the girl Marie Bracq?"

The round-faced man before me smiled thoughtfully as he idly puffed his cigarette. Then, shrugging his shoulders, he replied:

"Well, m'sieur, to tell the truth, there is a very curious complication. In connection with the affair there is a scandal which must never be allowed to get out to the public."

"Then you know the truth—eh?" I asked.

"A portion of it. Not all," he replied. "But I tell you that the news of the young lady's death has caused us the greatest amazement and surprise. We knew that she was missing, but never dreamed that she had been the victim of an assassin."

"But who are her friends?" I demanded.

"Unfortunately, I am not permitted to say," was his response. "When they know the terrible truth they may give us permission to reveal the truth to you. Till then, my duty is to preserve their secret."

"But I am all anxiety to know."

"I quite recognise that, M'sieur Royle," he said. "I know how I should feel were I in your position. But duty is duty, is it not?"

"I have assisted you, and I have given you a clue to the mystery," I protested.

"And we, on our part, will assist you to clear the stigma resting upon the lady who is your promised wife," he said. "Whatever I can do in that direction, m'sieur may rely upon me."

I was silent, for I saw that to attempt to probe further then the mystery of the actual identity of Marie Bracq was impossible. There seemed a conspiracy of silence against me.

But I would work myself. I would exert all the cunning and ingenuity I possessed—nay, I would spend every penny I had in the world—in order to clear my well-beloved of that terrible suspicion that by her hand this daughter of a princely house had fallen.

"Well," I asked at last. "What more can we do?"

"Ah!" sighed the stout man, blowing a cloud of cigarette smoke from his lips and drawing his glass. "What can we do? The Poste Restante is being watched, the records of all hotels and pensions for the past month are being inspected, and we have put a guard upon the Orient Express. No! We can do nothing," he said, "until we get a telegram from Vienna. Will you call at the Préfecture of Police at eight o'clock to-night? I will be there to see you."

I promised, then having paid the waiter, we strolled out of the café, and parted on the Boulevard, he going towards the Nord Station, while I went along in the opposite direction to the Grand.

For the appointed hour I waited in greatest anxiety. What if the trio had been arrested in Vienna?

That afternoon I wrote a long and encouraging letter to Phrida, telling her that I was exerting every effort on her behalf and urging her to keep a stout heart against her enemies, who now seemed to be in full flight.

At last, eight o'clock came, and I entered the small courtyard of the Préfecture of Police, where a uniformed official conducted me up to the room of Inspector Frémy.

The big, merry-faced man rose as I entered and placed his cigar in an ash tray.

"Bad luck, m'sieur!" he exclaimed in French. "They left Brussels in the Orient, as I suspected—all three of them. Here is the reply," and he handed me an official telegram in German, which translated into English read:

"To Préfet of Police, Brussels, from Préfet of Police, Vienna:
"In response to telegram of to-day's date, the three persons described left Brussels by Orient Express, travelled to Wels, and there left the train at 2.17 this afternoon. Telephonic inquiry of police at Wels results that they left at 4.10 by the express for Paris."

"I have already telegraphed to Paris," Frémy said. "But there is time, of course, to get across to Paris, and meet the express from Constantinople on its arrival there. Our friends evidently know their way about the Continent!"

"Shall we go to Paris," I suggested eagerly, anticipating in triumph their arrest as they alighted at the Gare de l'Est. I had travelled by the express from Vienna on one occasion about a year before, and remembered that it arrived in Paris about nine o'clock in the morning.

"With the permission of my chief I will willingly accompany you, m'sieur," replied the detective, and, leaving me, he was absent for five minutes or so, while I sat gazing around his bare, official-looking bureau, where upon the walls were many police notices and photographs of wanted persons, "rats d'hotel," and other malefactors. Brussels is one of the most important police centres in Europe, as well as being the centre of the political secret service of the Powers.

On his return he said:

"Bien, m'sieur. We leave the Midi Station at midnight and arrive in Paris at half-past five. I will engage sleeping berths, and I will telephone to my friend, Inspector Dricot, at the Préfecture, to send an agent of the brigade mobile to meet us. Non d'un chien! What a surprise it will be for the fugitives. But," he added, "they are clever and elusive. Fancy, in order to go from Brussels to Paris they travel right away into Austria, and with through tickets to Belgrade, too! Yes, they know the routes on the Continent—the routes used by the international thieves, I mean. The Wels route by which they travelled, is one of them."

Then I left him, promising to meet him at the station ten minutes before midnight. I had told Edwards I would notify him by wire any change of address, therefore, on leaving the Préfecture of Police, I went to the Grand and from there sent a telegram to him at Scotland Yard, telling him that I should call at the office of the inspector of police at the East railway station in Paris at ten on the following morning—if he had anything to communicate.

All through that night we travelled on in the close, stuffy *wagon-lit* by way of Mons to Paris arriving with some three hours and a half to spare, which we idled in one of the all-night cafés near the station, having been met by a little ferret-eyed Frenchman, named Jappé, who had been one of Frémy's subordinates when he was in the French service.

Just before nine o'clock, after our *café-au-lait* in the buffet, we walked out upon the long arrival platform where the Orient Express from its long journey from Constantinople was due.

It was a quarter of an hour late, but at length the luggage porters began to assemble, and with bated breath I watched the train of dusty sleeping-cars slowly draw into the terminus.

In a moment Frémy and his colleague were all eyes, while I stood near the engine waiting the result of their quest.

But in five minutes the truth was plain. Frémy was in conversation with one of the brown-uniformed conductors, who told him that the three passengers we sought did join at Wels, but had left again at Munich on the previous evening!

My heart sank. Our quest was in vain. They had again eluded us!

"I will go to Munich," Frémy said at once. "I may find trace of them yet."

"And I will accompany you!" I exclaimed eagerly. "They must not escape us."

But my plans were at once altered, and Frémy was compelled to leave for Germany alone, for at the police office at the station half an hour later I received a brief message from Edwards urging me to return to London immediately, and stating that an important discovery had been made.

So I drove across to the Gare du Nord, and left for London by the next train.

What, I wondered, had been discovered?

XXVII

EDWARDS BECOMES MORE PUZZLED

A t half-past seven on that same evening, Edwards, in response to a telegram I sent him from Calais, called upon me in Albemarle Street.

He looked extremely grave when he entered my room. After Haines had taken his hat and coat and we were alone, he said in a low voice:

"Mr. Royle, I have a rather painful communication to make to you. I much regret it—but the truth must be faced."

"Well?" I asked, in quick apprehension; "what is it?"

"We have received from an anonymous correspondent—who turns out to be the woman Petre, whom you know—a letter making the gravest accusations against Miss Shand. She denounces her as the assassin of the girl Marie Bracq."

"It's a lie! a foul, abominable lie!" I cried angrily. "I told you that she would seek to condemn the woman I love."

"Yes, I recollect. But it is a clue which I am in duty bound to investigate."

"You have not been to Miss Shand—you have not yet questioned her?" I gasped anxiously.

"Not before I saw you," he replied. "I may as well tell you at once that I had some slight suspicion that the young lady in question was acquainted with your friend who posed as Sir Digby."

"How?" I asked.

He hesitated. "Well, I thought it most likely that as you and he were such great friends, you might have introduced them," he said, rather lamely.

"But surely you are not going to believe the words of this woman Petre?" I cried. "Listen, and I will tell you how she has already endeavoured to take my life, and thus leave Miss Shand at her mercy."

Then, as he sat listening, his feet stretched towards the fender, I related in detail the startling adventure which befel me at Colchester.

"Extraordinary, Mr. Royle!" he exclaimed, in blank surprise. "Why, in heaven's name, didn't you tell me this before! The snake! Why, that is exactly the method used by Cane to secure the death of the real Sir Digby!"

"What was the use of telling you?" I queried. "What is the use even now? The woman has fled and, at the same time, takes a dastardly revenge upon the woman I love."

"Tell me, Mr. Royle," said the inspector, who, in his dinner coat and black tie, presented the appearance of the West End club man rather than a police official. "Have you yourself any suspicion that Miss Shand has knowledge of the affair?"

His question non-plussed me for the moment.

"Ah! I see you hesitate!" he exclaimed, shrewdly. "You have a suspicion—now admit it."

He pressed me, and seeing that my demeanour had, alas! betrayed my thoughts, I was compelled to speak the truth.

"Yes," I said, in a low, strained voice. "To tell you the truth, Edwards, there are certain facts which I am utterly unable to understand—facts which Miss Shand has admitted to me. But I still refuse to believe that she is a murderess."

"Naturally," he remarked, and I thought I detected a slightly sarcastic curl of the lips. "But though Miss Shand is unaware of it, I have made certain secret inquiries—inquiries which have given astounding results," he said slowly. "I have, unknown to the young lady, secured some of her finger-prints, which, on comparison, have coincided exactly with those found upon the glass-topped table at Harrington Gardens, and also with those which you brought to me so mysteriously." And he added, "To be quite frank, it was that action of yours which first aroused my suspicion regarding Miss Shand. I saw that you suspected some one—that you were trying to prove to your own satisfaction that your theory was wrong."

I held my breath, cursing myself for such injudicious action.

"Again, this letter from the woman Petre has corroborated my apprehensions," he went on. "Miss Shand was a friend of the man who called himself Sir Digby. She met him clandestinely, unknown, to you—eh?" he asked.

"Please do not question me, Edwards," I implored. "This is all so extremely painful to me."

"I regret, but it is my duty, Mr. Royle," he replied in a tone of sympathy. "Is not my suggestion the true one?"

I admitted that it was.

Then, in quick, brief sentences I told him of my visit to the Préfecture of Police in Brussels and all that I had discovered regarding the fugitives, to which he listened most attentively.

WILLIAM LE QUEUX

"They have not replied to my inquiry concerning the dead girl Marie Bracq," he remarked presently.

"They know her," I replied. "Van Huffel, the *Chef du Sureté*, stood aghast when I told him that the man Kemsley was wanted by you on a charge of murdering her. He declared that the allegation utterly astounded him, and that the press must have no suspicion of the affair, as a great scandal would result."

"But who is the girl?" he inquired quickly.

"Van Huffel refused to satisfy my curiosity. He declared that her identity was a secret which he was not permitted to divulge, but he added when I pressed him, that she was a daughter of one of the princely houses of Europe!"

Edwards stared at me.

"I wonder what is her real name?" he said, reflectively. "Really, Mr. Royle, the affair grows more and more interesting and puzzling."

"It does," I said, and then I related in detail my fruitless journey to Paris, and how the three fugitives had alighted at Munich from the westbound express from the Near East, and disappeared.

"Frémy, whom I think you know, has gone after them," I added.

"If Frémy once gets on the scent he'll, no doubt, find them," remarked my companion. "He's one of the most astute and clever detectives in Europe. So, if the case is in his hands, I'm quite contented that all will be done to trace them."

For two hours we sat together, while I related what the girl at Melbourne House had told me, and, in fact, put before him practically all that I have recorded in the foregoing pages.

Then, at last, I stood before him boldly and asked:

"In face of all this, can you suspect Miss Shand? Is she not that man's victim?"

He did not speak for several moments; his gaze was fixed upon the fire.

"Well," he replied, stirring himself at last, "to tell you the truth, Mr. Royle, I'm just as puzzled as you are. She may be the victim of this man we know to be an unscrupulous adventurer, but, at the same time, her hand may have used that triangular-bladed knife which we have been unable to find."

The knife! I held my breath. Was it not lying openly upon that table in the corner of the drawing-room at Cromwell Road? Would not analysis reveal upon it a trace of human blood? Would not its possession in itself convict her?

"Then what is your intention?" I asked, at last.

"To see her and put a few questions, Mr. Royle," he answered slowly. "I know how much this must pain you, bearing in mind your deep affection for the young lady, but, unfortunately, it is my duty, and I cannot see how such a course can be avoided."

"No. I beg of you not to do this," I implored. "Keep what observation you like, but do not approach her—at least, not yet. In her present frame of mind, haunted by the shadow of the crime and hemmed in by suspicion of which she cannot clear herself, it would be fatal."

"Fatal! I don't understand you."

"Well—she would take her own life," I said in a low whisper.

"She has threatened—eh?" he asked.

I nodded in the affirmative.

"Then does not that, in itself, justify my decision to see and question her?"

"No, it does not!" I protested. "She is not guilty, but this terrible dread and anxiety is, I know, gradually unbalancing her brain. She is a girl of calm determination, and if she believed that you suspected her she would be driven by sheer terror to carry out her threat."

He smiled.

"Most women threaten suicide at one time or other of their lives. Their thoughts seem to revert to romance as soon as they find themselves in a corner. No," he added. "I never believe in threats of suicide in either man or woman. Life is always too precious for that, and especially if a woman loves, as she does."

"You don't know her."

"No, but I know women, Mr. Royle—I know all their idiosyncrasies as well as most men, I think," he said.

I begged him not to approach my well-beloved, but he was inexorable.

"I must see her—and I must know the truth," he declared decisively.

But I implored again of him, begging him to spare her—begged her life.

I had gripped him by the hand, and looking into his face I pointed out that I had done and was doing all I could to elucidate the mystery.

"At least," I cried, "you will wait until the fugitives are arrested!"

"There is only one—the impostor," he said. "There is no charge against the others."

"Then I will lay a charge to-night against the woman Petre and the

WILLIAM LE QUEUX

man Ali of attempting to kill me." I said. "The two names can then be added to the warrant."

"Very well," he said. "We'll go to the Yard, and I will take your information."

"And you will not approach Phrida until you hear something from Brussels—eh?" I asked persuasively. "In the meantime, I will do all I can. Leave Miss Shand to me."

"If I did it would be a grave dereliction of duty," he replied slowly.

"But is it a dereliction of duty to disregard allegations made by a woman who has fled in that man's company, and who is, we now know, his accomplice?" I protested. "Did not you yourself tell me that you, at Scotland Yard, always regarded lightly any anonymous communication?"

"As a rule we do. But past history shows that many have been genuine," he said. "Before the commission of nearly all the Jack the Ripper crimes there were anonymous letters, written in red ink. We have them now framed and hanging up in the Black Museum."

"But such letters are not denunciations. They were promises of a further sensation," I argued. "The triumphant and gleeful declarations of the mad but mysterious assassin. No. Promise me, Edwards, that you will postpone this projected step of yours, which can, in any case, even though my love be innocent, only result in dire disaster."

He saw how earnest was my appeal, and realised, I think, the extreme gravity of the situation, and how deeply it concerned me. He seemed, also, to recognise that in discovering the name of the victim and in going a second time to Brussels, I had been able to considerably advance the most difficult inquiry; therefore, after still another quarter of an hour of persuasion, I induced him to withhold.

"Very well," he replied, "though I can make no definite promise, Mr. Royle. I will not see the lady before I have again consulted with you. But," he added, "I must be frank with you. I shall continue my investigations in that quarter, and most probably watch will be kept upon her movements."

"And if she recognises that you suspect her?" I gasped.

"Ah!" he exclaimed, with a slight shrug of the shoulders. "I cannot accept any responsibility for that. How can I?"

XXVIII

Further Admissions

The secret of Digby Kemsley is still a secret, and will ever remain a secret."

I recollected Mrs. Petre uttering those words to me as that dark-faced villain Ali had forced my inert head down upon the table.

Well, that same night when I had begged of Edwards my love's life, I sat in his room at Scotland Yard and there made a formal declaration of what had happened to me on that well-remembered night outside Colchester. I formally demanded the arrest of the woman, of Ali, and of the young man-servant, all of whom had conspired to take my life.

The clerk calmly took down my statement, which Edwards read over to me, and I duly signed it.

Then, gripping his hand, I went forth into Parliament Street, and took a taxi to Cromwell Road.

I had not seen Phrida for several days, and she was delighted at my visit.

She presented a pale, frail, little figure in her simple gown of pale pink ninon, cut slightly open at the neck and girdled narrow with turquoise blue. Her skirt was narrow, as was the mode, and her long white arms were bare to the shoulders.

She had been curled up before the fire reading when I entered, but she jumped up with an expression of welcome upon her lips.

But not until her mother had bade me good-night and discreetly withdrew, did she refer to the subject which I knew obsessed her by night and by day.

"Well, Teddy," she asked, when I sat alone with her upon the pale green silk-covered couch, her little hand in mine, "Where have you been? Why have you remained silent?"

"I've been in Brussels," I replied, and then, quite frankly, I explained my quest after the impostor.

She sat looking straight before her, her eyes fixed like a person, in a dream. At last she spoke:

"I thought," she said in a strained voice, "that you would have shown greater respect for me than to do that—when you knew it would place you in such great peril!"

"I have acted in your own interests, dearest," I replied, placing my arm tenderly about her neck. "Ah! in what manner you will never know."

"My interests!" she echoed, in despair. "Have I not told you that on the day Digby Kemsley is arrested I intend to end my life," and as she drew a long breath, I saw in her eyes that haunted, terrified look which told me that she was driven to desperation.

"No, no," I urged, stroking her hair with tenderness. "I know all that you must suffer, Phrida, but I am your friend and your protector. I will never rest until I get at the truth."

"Ah! Revelation of the truth will, alas! prove my undoing!" she whispered, in a voice full of fear. "You don't know, dear, how your relentless chase of that man is placing me in danger."

"But he is an adventurer, an impostor—a fugitive from justice, and he merits punishment!" I cried.

"Ah! And if you say that," she cried, wildly starting to her feet. "So do I! So do I!"

"Come, calm yourself, dearest," I said, placing my hand upon her shoulder and forcing her back into her chair. "You are upset to-night," and I kissed her cold, white lips. "May I ring for Mallock? Wouldn't you like to go to your room?"

She drew a deep sigh, and with an effort repressed the tears welling in her deep-set, haunted eyes.

"Yes," she faltered in her emotion. "Perhaps I had better. I—I cannot bear this strain much longer. You told me that the police did not suspect me, but—but, now I know they do. A man has been watching outside the house all day for two days past. Yes," she sobbed, "they will come, come to arrest me, but they will only find that—that I've cheated them!"

"They will not come," I answered her. "I happen to know more than I can tell you, Phrida," I whispered. "You need have no fear of arrest."

"But that woman Petre! She may denounce me—she will, I know!"

"They take no notice of such allegations at Scotland Yard. They receive too much wild correspondence," I declared. "No, dearest, go to bed and rest—rest quite assured that at present you are in no peril, and, further, that every hour which elapses brings us nearer a solution of the tragic and tantalising problem. May I ring for Mallock?" I asked, again kissing her passionately upon those lips, hard and cold as marble, my heart full of sympathy for her in her tragic despair.

"Yes," she responded faintly in a voice so low that I could hardly catch it. So I crossed and rang the bell for her maid.

Then, when she had kissed me good-night, looking into my eyes with a strange expression of wistfulness, and left the room, I dashed across to that little table whereon the ivory-hilted knife was lying and seized the important piece of evidence, so that it might not fall into Edwards' hands.

I held it within my fingers, and taking it across to the fireplace, examined it in the strong light. The ivory was yellow and old, carved with the escutcheon bearing the three balls, the arms of the great House of Medici. The blade, about seven inches long, was keen, triangular, and, at the point, sharp as a needle. Into it the rust of centuries had eaten, though in parts it was quite bright, evidently due to recent cleaning.

I was examining it for any stains that might be upon it—stains of the life-blood of Marie Bracq. But I could find none. No. They had been carefully removed, yet chemical analysis would, without doubt, reveal inevitable traces of the ghastly truth.

I had my back to the door, and was still holding the deadly weapon in my hand, scrutinising it closely, when I heard a slight movement behind me, and turning, confronted Phrida, standing erect and rigid, like a statue.

Her face was white as death, her thin hands clenched, her haunted eyes fixed upon me.

"Ah! I see!" she cried hoarsely. "You know—eh? You *know*!"

"No. I do not *know*, Phrida," was my deep reply, as I snatched her hand and held it in my own. "I only surmise that this knife was used on that fatal night, because of the unusual shape of its blade—because of the medical evidence that by such a knife Marie Bracq was killed."

She drew a deep breath.

"And you are taking it as evidence—against me!"

"Evidence against you, darling!" I echoed in reproach. "Do you think that I, the man who loves you, is endeavouring to convict you of a crime? No. Leave matters to me. I am your friend—not your enemy!"

A silence fell between us. She neither answered nor did she move for some moments. Then she said in a deep wistful tone:

"Ah! if I could only believe that you are!"

"But I am," I declared vehemently. "I love you, Phrida, with all my soul, and I will never believe ill of you—never, never!"

"How can you do otherwise in these terrible circumstances?" she queried, with a strange contraction of her brows.

"I love you, and because I love you so dearly—because you are all the world to me," I said, pressing her to my heart, "I will never accept what an enemy may allege—never, until you are permitted to relate your own story."

I still held the weapon in my hand, and I saw that her eyes wandered to it.

"Ah! Teddy!" she cried, with sudden emotion. "How can I thank you sufficiently for those words? Take that horrible thing and hide it—hide it anywhere from my eyes, for sight of it brings all the past back to me. Yet—yet I was afraid," she went on, "I dare not hide it, lest any one should ask what had become of it, and thus suspicions might be aroused. Ah! every time I have come into this room it has haunted me—I seem to see that terrible scene before my eyes—how—how they—"

But she broke off short, and covering her face with both hands added, after a few seconds' silence:

"Ah! yes, take it away—never let me gaze upon it again. But I beg of you, dear, to—to preserve my secret—my terrible secret!"

And she burst into tears.

"Not a single word shall pass my lips, neither shall a single soul see this knife. I will take it and cast it away—better to the bottom of the Thames. To-night it shall be in a place where it can never be found. So go to your room, and rest assured that you, darling, have at least one friend—myself."

I felt her breast heave and fall as I held her in my strong embrace.

Then without words she raised her white, tear-stained face and kissed me long and fondly; afterwards she left me, and in silence tottered from the room, closing the door after her.

I still held the knife in my hand—the weapon by which the terrible deed had been perpetrated.

What could I think? What would you, my reader, have thought if the woman you love stood in the same position as Phrida Shand—which God forbid?

I stood reflecting, gazing upon the antique poignard. Then slowly and deliberately I made up my mind, and placing the unsheathed knife in my breast pocket I went out into the hall, put on my coat and hat, and left the house.

Half an hour later I halted casually upon Westminster Bridge, and when no one was near, cast the ancient "Misericordia" into the dark flowing waters of the river, knowing that Edwards and his inquisitive assistants could never recover it as evidence against my love.

Four days later I received a letter from Frémy, dated from the Hotel National at Strasbourg, stating that he had traced the fugitives from Munich to the latter city, but there he had lost all trace of them. He believed they had gone to Paris, and with his chief's permission he was leaving for the French capital that night.

Weeks passed—weeks of terror and apprehension for my love, and of keenest anxiety for myself.

The month of May went by, spring with all her beauties appeared in the parks and faded in the heat and dust, while the London season commenced. Men who were otherwise never seen in town, strolled up and down St. James's Street and Piccadilly, smart women rode in the Row in the morning and gave parties at night, while the usual crop of charitable functions, society scandals, Parliamentary debates, and puff-paragraphs in the papers about Lady Nobody's dances showed the gay world of London to be in full swing.

My mantelshelf was well decorated with cards of invitation, for, nowadays, the bachelor in London can have a really good time if he chooses, yet I accepted few, spending most of my days immersed in business—in order to occupy my thoughts—while my evenings I spent at Cromwell Road.

For weeks Phrida had not referred to the tragedy in any way, and I had been extremely careful to avoid the subject. Yet, from her pale, drawn countenance—so unlike her former self—I knew how recollection of it ever haunted her, and what dread terror had gripped her young heart.

Mrs. Shand, ignorant of the truth, had many times expressed to me confidentially, fear that her daughter was falling into a bad state of health; and, against Phrida's wishes, had called in the family doctor, who, likewise ignorant, had ordered her abroad.

"Get her out of the dullness of this road, Mrs. Shand," he had said. "She wants change and excitement. Take her to some gay place on the Continent—Dinard, Trouville, Aix-les-Bains, Ostend—some place where there is brightness and movement. A few weeks there will effect a great change in her, I'm certain."

But Phrida refused to leave London, though I begged her to follow the doctor's advice, and even offered to accompany them.

As far as I could gather, Van Huffel, in Brussels, had given up the search for the fugitives; though, the more I reflected upon his replies to my questions as to the real identity of Marie Bracq, the more remarkable they seemed.

Who was she? That was the great problem uppermost always in my mind. Phrida had declared that she only knew her by that name—that she knew nothing further concerning her. And so frankly had she said this, that I believed her.

Yet I argued that, if the death of Marie Bracq was of such serious moment as the *Chef du Sureté* had declared, then he surely would not allow the inquiry to drop without making the most strenuous efforts to arrest those suspected of the crime.

But were his suspicions, too, directed towards Phrida? Had he, I wondered, been in consultation with Edwards, and had the latter, in confidence, revealed to him his own theory?

I held my breath each time that idea crossed my mind—as it did so very often.

From Frémy I had had several letters dated from the Préfecture of Police, Brussels, but the tenor of all was the same—nothing to report.

One thing gratified me. Edwards had not approached my love, although I knew full well, just as Phrida did, that day after day observation was being kept upon the house in Cromwell Road, yet perhaps only because the detective's duty demanded it. At least I tried to think so.

Still the one fact remained that, after all our efforts—the efforts of Scotland Yard, of the Belgian police, and of my own eager inquiries—a solution of the problem was as far off as ever.

Somewhere there existed a secret—a secret that, as Phrida had declared to me, was inviolable.

Would it ever be revealed? Would the ghastly truth ever be laid bare?

The affair of Harrington Gardens was indeed a mystery of London—as absolute and perfect an enigma of crime as had ever been placed before that committee of experts at Scotland Yard—the Council of Seven.

Even they had failed to find a solution! How, then, could I ever hope to be successful?

When I thought of it, I paced my lonely room in a frenzy of despair.

XXIX

The Seller of Shawls

After much eloquent persuasion on my part, and much straight talking on the part of the spectacled family doctor, and of Mrs. Shand, Phrida at last, towards the last days of June, allowed us to take her to Dinard, where, at the Hotel Royal, we spent three pleasant weeks, making many automobile excursions to Trouville, to Dinan, and other places in the neighbourhood.

The season had scarcely commenced, nevertheless the weather was perfect, and gradually I had the satisfaction of seeing the colour return to the soft cheeks of my well-beloved.

Before leaving London I had, of course, seen Edwards, and, knowing that watch was being kept upon her, I accepted the responsibility of reporting daily upon my love's movements, she being still under suspicion.

"I ought not to do this, Mr. Royle," he had said, "but the circumstances are so unusual that I feel I may stretch a point in the young lady's favour without neglecting my duty. And after all," he added, "we have no direct evidence—at least not sufficient to justify an arrest."

"Why doesn't that woman Petre come forward and boldly make her statement personally?" I had queried.

"Well, she may know that you are still alive"—he laughed—"and if so—she's afraid to go further."

I questioned him regarding his inquiries concerning the actual identity of Marie Bracq, but he only raised his eyebrows and replied:

"My dear Mr. Royle, I know nothing more than you do. They no doubt possess some information in Brussels, but they are careful to keep it there."

And so I had accompanied Phrida and her mother, hoping that the change of air and scenery might cause her to forget the shadow of guilt which now seemed to rest upon her and to crush all life and hope from her young heart.

Tiring of Dinard, Mrs. Shand hired a big, grey touring-car, and together we went first through Brittany, then to Vannes, Nantes, and up to Tours, afterwards visiting the famous chateaux of Touraine,

Amboise Loches, and the rest, the weather being warm and delightful, and the journey one of the pleasantest and most picturesque in Europe.

When July came, Phrida appeared greatly improved in both health and spirits. Yet was it only pretence? Did she in the lonely watches of the night still suffer that mental torture which I knew, alas! she had suffered, for her own deep-set eyes, and pale, sunken cheeks had revealed to me the truth. Each time I sat down and wrote that confidential note to Edwards, I hated myself—that I was set to spy upon the woman I loved with all my heart and soul.

Would the truth never be told? Would the mystery of that tragic January night in South Kensington never be elucidated?

One evening in the busy but pleasant town of Tours, Mrs. Shand having complained of headache after a long, all-day excursion in the car, Phrida and I sauntered out after dinner, and after a brief walk sat down outside one of those big cafés where the tables are placed out beneath the leafy chestnut trees of the boulevard.

The night was hot and stifling, and as we sat there chatting over our coffee amid a crowd of people enjoying the air after the heat of the day, a dark-faced, narrow-eyed Oriental in a fez, with a number of Oriental rugs and cheap shawls, came and stood before us, in the manner of those itinerant vendors who haunt Continental cafés.

He said nothing, but, standing like a bronze statue, he looked hard at me and pointed solemnly at a quantity of lace which he held in his left hand.

"No, I want nothing," I replied in French, shaking my head.

"Ve-ry cheep, sare!" he exclaimed in broken English at last. "You no buy for laidee?" and he showed his white teeth with a pleasant grin.

I again replied in the negative, perhaps a little impatiently, when suddenly Phrida whispered to me:

"Why, we saw this same man in Dinard, and in another place—I forget where. He haunts us!"

"These men go from town to town," I explained. "They make a complete round of France."

Then I suddenly recollected that the man's face was familiar. I had seen him outside the Piccadilly Tube Station on the night of my tryst with Mrs. Petre!

"Yes, laidee!" exclaimed the man, who had overheard Phrida's words. "I see you Dinard—Hotel Royal—eh?" he said with a smile. "Will you buy my lace—seelk lace; ve-ry cheep?"

"I know it's cheap," I laughed; "but we don't want it."

Nevertheless, he placed it upon the little marble-topped table for our inspection, and then bending, he whispered into my ear a question:

"Mee-ster Royle you—eh?"

"Yes," I said, starting.

"I want see you, to-night, alone. Say no-ting to laidee till I see you—outside your hotel eleven o'clock, sare—eh?"

I sat staring at him in blank surprise, but in a low voice I consented.

Then, very cleverly he asked in his normal voice, looking at me with his narrow eyes, with dark brows meeting:

"You no buy at that price—eh? Ah!" and he sighed as he gathered up his wares: "Cheep, laidee—very goot and cheep!"

And bowing, he slung them upon the heavy pile already on his shoulder and stalked away.

"What did he say?" Phrida asked when he had gone.

"Oh, only wanted me to buy the lot for five francs!" I replied, for he had enjoined secrecy, and I knew not but he might be an emissary of Frémy or of Edwards. Therefore I deemed it best for the time to evade her question.

Still, both excited and puzzled, I eagerly kept the appointment.

When I emerged from the hotel on the stroke of eleven I saw the man without his pile of merchandise standing in the shadow beneath a tree, on the opposite side of the boulevard, awaiting me.

Quickly I crossed to him, and asked:

"Well, what do you want with me?"

"Ah, Mee-ster Royle! I have watched you and the young laidee a long time. You travel so quickly, and I go by train from town to town—slowly."

"Yes, but why?" I asked, as we strolled together under the trees.

"I want to tell you some-zing, mee-ster. I no Arabe—I Senos, from Huacho."

"From Huacho!" I gasped quickly.

"Yees. My dead master he English—Sir Digby Kemsley!"

"Sir Digby!" I cried. "And you were his servant. You knew this man Cane—why, you were the man who heard your master curse the man who placed the deadly reptile against his face. You made a statement to the police, did you not?" I asked frantically.

"Yees, Mee-ster Royle—I did! I know a lot," he replied in his slow way, stalking along in the short breeches, red velvet jacket, and fez of an Oriental.

"You will tell me, Senos?" I said. "You will tell me everything?" I urged. "Tell me all that you know!"

He grinned in triumph, saying:

"I know a lot—I know all. Cane killed my master—killed him with the snake—he and Luis together. I know—I saw. But the Englishman is always great, and his word believed by the commissary of police—not the word of Senos. Oh, no! but I have followed; I have watched. I have been beside Cane night and day when he never dream I was near. I tell the young lady all the truth, and—ah!—she tell him after I beg her to be silent."

"But where is Cane now?" I asked eagerly. "Do you know?"

"The 'Red' Englishman—he with Madame Petre and Luis—he call himself Ali, the Indian."

"Where? Can you take me to them?" I asked. "You know there is a warrant out for their arrest?"

"I know—but—"

"But what?" I cried.

"No, not yet. I wait," he laughed. "I know every-ting. He kill my master; I kill him. My master be very good master."

"Yes, I know he was," I said.

"That man Cane—very bad man. Your poor young laidee—ah? She not know me. I know her. You no say you see me—eh? I tell every-ting later. You go Ostend; I meet you. Then we see them."

"At Ostend!" I cried. "Are they there?"

"You go Ostend to-morrow. Tell me your hotel. Senos come—eh? Senos see them with you. Oh! Oh!" he said in his quaint way, grinning from ear to ear.

I looked at the curious figure beside me. He was the actual man who had heard the dying cries of Sir Digby Kemsley.

"But, tell me," I urged, "have you been in London? Do you know that a young lady died in Cane's apartment—was killed there?"

"Senos knows," he laughed grimly. "Senos has not left him—ah, no! He kill my master. I never leave him till I crush him—never!"

"Then you know, of what occurred at Harrington Gardens?" I repeated.

"Yes, Senos know. He tell in Ostend when we meet," he replied. "You go to-morrow, eh?" and he looked at me anxiously with those dark, rather blood-shot eyes of his.

"I will go to-morrow," I answered without hesitation; and, taking out my wallet I gave him three notes of a hundred francs each, saying:

"This will pay your fare. I will go straight to the Grand Hotel, on the Digue. You will meet me there."

"And the laidee—eh? She must be there too."

"Yes, Miss Shand will be with me," I said.

"Good, sare—very good!" he replied, thrusting the notes into the inner pocket of his red velvet jacket. "I get other clothes—these only to sell things," and he smiled.

I tried to induce him to tell me more, but he refused, saying:

"At Ostend Senos show you. He tell you all he know—he tell the truth about the 'Red' Englishman."

And presently, after he had refused the drink I offered him, the Peruvian, who was earning his living as an Arab of North Africa, bowed with politeness and left me, saying:

"I meet you, Mee-ster Royle, at Grand Hotel in Ostend. But be careful neither of you seen. They are sharp, clever, alert—oh, ve-ry! We leave to-morrow—eh? Good!"

And a moment later the quaint figure was lost in the darkness.

An hour later, though past midnight, I despatched two long telegrams—one to Frémy in Brussels, and the other to Edwards in London.

Then, two days later, by dint of an excuse that I had urgent business in Ostend, I found myself with Phrida and Mrs. Shand, duly installed, in rooms overlooking the long, sunny Digue, one of the finest sea-promenades in Europe.

Ostend had begun her season, the racing season had commenced, and all the hotels had put on coats of new, white paint, and opened their doors, while in the huge Kursaal they played childish games of chance now that M. Marquet was no longer king—yet the magnificent orchestra was worth a journey to listen to.

On the afternoon of our arrival, all was gay and bright; outside the blue sea, the crowd of well-dressed promenaders, and the golden sands where the bathing was so merry and so chic.

But I had no eyes for the beauties or gaiety of the place. I sat closeted in my room with two friends, Frémy and Edwards, whom I introduced and who quickly fraternised.

A long explanatory letter I had written to Brussels had reached Frémy before his departure from the capital.

"Excellent," he was saying, his round, clean-shaven face beaming. "This Peruvian evidently knows where they are, and like all natives,

wants to make a *coup-de-theatre*. I've brought two reliable men with me from Brussels, and we ought—if they are really here—to make a good capture."

"Miss Shand knows nothing, you say?" Edwards remarked, seated on the edge of my bed.

"No. This man Senos was very decided upon the point."

"He has reasons, no doubt," remarked the detective.

"It is just four o'clock," I remarked. "He has given me a rendezvous at the Café de la Règence, a little place at the corner of the Place d'Armes. I went round to find it as soon as I arrived. We're due there in a quarter of an hour."

"Then let us go, messieurs," Frémy suggested.

"And what about Miss Shand?" I asked.

The two detectives held a brief discussion. Then Edwards, addressing me, said:

"I really think that she ought to be present, Mr. Royle. Would you bring her? Prepare her for a scene—as there no doubt will be—and then follow us."

"But Senos will not speak without I am present," I said.

"Then go along to Miss Shand, give her my official compliments and ask her to accompany us upon our expedition," he replied.

And upon his suggestion I at once acted.

Truly those moments were breathless and exciting. I could hear my own heart beat as I went along the hotel corridor to knock at the door of her room.

XXX

Face to Face

We had, all four of us, ranged ourselves up under the wall of a big white house in the Chausee de Nieuport, which formed the south side of the racecourse, and where, between us and the sea, rose the colossal Royal Palace Hotel, when Frémy advanced to the big varnished oak door, built wide for the entrance of automobiles, and rang the electric bell.

In response there came out a sedate, white-whiskered man-servant in black coat and striped yellow waistcoat, the novel Belgium livery, but in an instant he was pinioned by the two detectives from Brussels, and the way opened for us.

"No harm, old one!" cried the detectives in French, after the man had admitted his master was at home. "We are police-agents, and doing our duty. We don't want you, only we don't intend you to cry out, that's all. Keep a still tongue, old one, and you're all right!" they laughed as they kept grip of him. The Continental detective is always humorous in the exercise of his duty. I once witnessed in Italy a man arrested for murder. He had on a thin light suit, and having been to bed in it, the back was terribly pleated and creased. "Hulloa!" cried the detective, "so it is you. Come along, old dried fig!" I was compelled to laugh, for the culprit's thin, brown coat had all the creases of a Christmas fig.

The house we rushed in was a big, luxurious one, with a wide passage running through to the Garage, and on the left a big, wide marble staircase with windows of stained glass and statues of dancing girls of the art nouveau.

Frémy, leaving his assistants below with the man-servant, and crying to Edwards to look out for anybody trying to escape, sprang up the marble steps three at a time, followed by the narrow-eyed Peruvian, while Phrida, clinging to my arm, held her breath in quick apprehension. She was full of fear and amazement.

I had had much difficulty in persuading her to accompany us, for she seemed in terror of denunciation. Indeed, not until I told her that Edwards had demanded her presence, had she consented.

On the first landing, a big, thick-carpeted place with a number of long, white doors leading into various apartments, Frémy halted and raised his finger in silence to us.

He stood glancing from door to door, wondering which to enter.

Then suddenly he stood and gave a yell as though of fearful pain.

In an instant there was a quick movement in a room on the right, the door opened and the woman Petre came forth in alarm.

Next second, however, finding herself face to face with me, she halted upon the threshold and fell back against the lintel of the door while we rushed in to encounter the man I had known as Digby, standing defiant, with arms folded and brows knit.

"Well," he demanded of me angrily. "What do you want here?"

"I've brought a friend of yours to see you, Mr. Cane," I said quietly, and Edwards stepped aside from the door to admit the Peruvian Senos.

The effect was instant and indeed dramatic. His face fell, his eyes glared, his teeth set, and his nails dug themselves into his palms.

"Mee-ster Cane," laughed the dark-faced native, in triumph. "You no like see Senos—eh? No, no. He know too much—eh? He watch you always after he see you with laidee in Marseilles—he see you in London—ha! ha! Senos know every-ting. You kill my master, and you—"

"It's a lie!" cried the man accused. "This fellow made the same statement at Huacho, and it was disproved."

"Then you admit you are not Sir Digby Kemsley?" exclaimed Edwards quickly. "You are Herbert Cane, and I have a warrant for your arrest for murder."

"Ah!" he laughed with an air of forced gaiety. "That is amusing!"

"I'm very glad you think so, my dear sir," remarked the detective, glancing round to where the woman Petre had been placed in an armchair quite unconscious.

Phrida was clinging to my arm, but uttered no word. I felt her fingers trembling as she gripped me.

"I suppose you believe this native—eh?" asked the accused with sarcasm. "He tried to blackmail me in Peru, and because I refused to be bled he made a statement that I had killed my friend."

"Ah!" exclaimed the native. "Senos knows—he see with his own eyes. He see Luis and you with snake in a box. Luis could charm snakes by music. Senos watch you both that night!"

"Oh! tell what infernal lies you like," cried Cane in angry disgust.

"You, the 'Red' Englishman, are well known in Peru, and so is your friend—the woman there, who help you in all your bad schemes," said

Senos, indicating the inanimate form of Mrs. Petre. "You introduced her to my master, but he no like her—he snub her—so you send her to Lima to wait for you—till you kill him, and get the paper—eh? I saw you steal paper—big blue paper with big seals—from master's despatch-box after snake bite him."

"Paper!" echoed Edwards. "What paper?"

"Perhaps I can explain something," Frémy interrupted in French. "I learnt some strange facts only three days ago which throw a great deal of light on this case."

"I don't want to listen to all these romances," laughed Cane defiantly. He was an astute and polished adventurer, one of the cleverest and most elusive in Europe, and he had all the adventurer's nonchalance and impudence. At this moment he was living in that fine house he had taken furnished for the summer and passing as Mr. Charles K. Munday, banker, of Chicago. Certainly he had so altered his personal appearance that at first I scarcely recognised him as the elegant, refined man whom I had so foolishly trusted as a friend.

"But now you are under arrest, mon cher ami, you will be compelled to listen to a good many unpleasant reminders," Frémy remarked with a broad grin of triumph upon his round, clean-shaven face.

"If you arrest me, then you must arrest that woman there, Phrida Shand, for the murder of Marie Bracq in my flat in London. She was jealous of her—and killed her with a knife she brought with her for the purpose," Cane said with a laugh. "If I must suffer—then so must she! She killed the girl. She can't deny it!"

"Phrida!" I gasped, turning to my love, who still clung to me convulsively. "You hear what this man says—this vile charge he brings against you—a charge of murder! Say that it is not the truth," I implored. "Tell me that he lies!"

Her big eyes were fixed upon mine, her countenance blanched to the lips, and her breath came and went in short, quick gasps.

At last her lips moved, as we all gazed at her. Her voice was only a hoarse, broken whisper.

"I—I can't!" she replied, and fell back into my arms in a swoon.

"You see!" laughed the accused man. "You, Royle, are so clever that you only bring grief and disaster upon yourself. I prevented Mrs. Petre from telling the truth because I thought you had decided to drop the affair."

"What?" I cried. "When your accomplice—that woman Petre—

made a dastardly attempt upon my life at your instigation, and left me for dead. Drop the affair—never! You are an assassin, and you shall suffer the penalty."

"And so will Phrida Shand. She deceived you finely—eh? I admire her cleverness," he laughed "She was a thorough Sport, she—"

"Enough!" commanded Edwards roughly. "I give you into the custody of Inspector Frémy, of the Belgian Sureté, on a charge of murder committed within the Republic of Peru."

"And I also arrest the prisoner," added Frémy, "for offences committed in London and within the Grand Duchy of Luxemburg."

The man, pale and haggard-eyed notwithstanding his bravado, started visibly at the famous detective's words, while at that moment the two men from Brussels appeared in the room, having released the white-whiskered man-servant, who stood aghast and astounded on the threshold. I supported my love, now quite unconscious, in my strong arms, and was trying to restore her, in which I was immediately aided by one of the detectives.

The scene was an intensely dramatic one—truly an unusual scene to take place in the house of the sedate old Baron Terwindt, ancient Ministre de la Justice of Belgium.

I was bending over my love and dashing water into her face when we were all suddenly startled by a loud explosion, and then we saw in Cane's hand a smoking revolver.

He had fired at me—and, fortunately, missed me.

In a second, however, the officers fell upon him, and after a brief but desperate struggle, in which a table and chairs were overturned, the weapon was wrenched from his grasp.

"Eh! bien," exclaimed Frémy, when the weapon had been secured from the accused. "As you will have some unpleasant things to hear, you may as well listen to some of them now. You have denied your guilt. Well, I will tell Inspector Edwards what I have discovered concerning you and your cunning and dastardly treatment of the girl known as Marie Bracq."

"I don't want to hear, I tell you!" he shouted in English. "If I'm arrested, take me away, put me into prison and send me over to England, where I shall get a fair trial."

"But you shall hear," replied the big-faced official. "There is plenty of time to take you to Brussels, you know. Listen. The man Senos has alleged that you stole from the man you murdered a blue paper—

bearing a number of seals. He is perfectly right. You sold that paper on the eighth of January last for a quarter of a million francs. Ah! my dear friend, you cannot deny that. The purchaser will give evidence—and what then?"

Cane stood silent. His teeth were set, his gaze fixed, his grey brows contracted.

The game was up, and he knew it. Yet his marvellously active mind was already seeking a way out. He was amazingly resourceful, as later on was shown, when the details of his astounding career came to be revealed.

"Now the true facts are these—and perhaps mademoiselle and the man Senos will be able to supplement them—his Highness the Grand Duke of Luxemburg, about two years ago, granted to an American named Cassell a valuable concession for a strategic railway to run across his country from Echternach, on the eastern, or German, frontier of the Grand Duchy, to Arlon on the Belgian frontier, the Government of the latter State agreeing at the same time to continue the line direct to Sedan, and thus create a main route from Coblenz, on the Rhine, to Paris—a line which Germany had long wanted for military purposes, as it would be of incalculable value in the event of further hostilities with France. This concession, for which the American paid to the Grand Duke a considerable sum, was afterwards purchased by Sir Digby Kemsley—with his Highness's full sanction, he knowing him to be a great English railroad engineer. Meanwhile, as time went on, the Grand Duke was approached by the French Government with a view to rescinding the concession, as it was realised what superiority such a line would give Germany in the event of the massing of her troops in Eastern France. At first the Grand Duke refused to listen, but both Russia and Austria presented their protests, and his Highness found himself in a dilemma. All this was known to you, m'sieur Cane, through one Ludwig Mayer, a German secret agent, who inadvertently spoke about it while you were on a brief visit to Paris. You then resolved to return at once to Peru, make the acquaintance of Sir Digby Kemsley, and obtain the concession. You went, you were fortunate, inasmuch as he was injured and helpless, and you deliberately killed him, and securing the document, sailed for Europe, assuming the identity of the actual purchaser of the concession. Oh, yes!" he laughed, "you were exceedingly cunning and clever, for you did not at once deal with it. No, you went to Luxemburg. You made certain observations and inquiries. You stayed at the Hotel Brasseur for a week, and then, you were afraid to approach the Grand Duke with an offer to sell back the stolen concession, but—well, by that time you had resolved upon a very pretty and romantic plan of action," and he paused for a moment and gazed around at us.

"Then robbery was the motive of the crime in Peru!" I exclaimed.

"Certainly," Frémy replied. "But I will now relate how I came into the inquiry. In the last days of January, I was called in secret to Luxemburg by the Grand Duke, who, when we sat alone together, informed me that his only daughter Stephanie, aged twenty-one, who was a rather erratic young lady, and fond of travelling incognito, had disappeared. The last heard of her was three weeks before—in Paris—where she had, on her return from Egypt, been staying a couple of days at the Hotel Maurice with her aunt, the Grand Duchess of Baden, but she had packed her things and left, and nothing more had been heard of her. Search in her room, however, had revealed two letters, signed 'Phrida,' and addressed to a certain Marie Bracq."

"Why, I never wrote to her in my life!" my love declared, for she had now regained her senses.

"His Highness further revealed to me the fact that his daughter had, while in Egypt, made the acquaintance at the Hotel Savoy on the Island of Elephantine, of the great English railroad engineer, Sir Digby Kemsley, who had purchased a railway concession he had given, and which he was exceedingly anxious to re-purchase and thus continue on friendly terms with France. His daughter, on her return to Luxemburg, and before going to Paris, had mentioned her acquaintance with Sir Digby, and that he held the concession. Therefore, through her intermediary, Sir Digby—who was, of course, none other than this assassin, Cane—went again to Luxemburg and parted with the important document for a quarter of a million francs. That was on the eighth of January."

"After the affair at Harrington Gardens," Edwards remarked.

"Yes; after the murder of Marie Bracq, he lost no time in disposing of the concession."

"It's a lie!" cried the accused. "That girl there killed her. I didn't—she was jealous of her!"

My love shrank at the man's words, yet still clinging to me, her beautiful countenance pale as death, her lips half parted, her eyes staring straight in front of her.

"Phrida," I said in a low voice, full of sympathy, "you hear what this man has alleged? Now that the truth is being told, will you, too, not speak? Speak!" I cried in my despair, "speak, dearest, I beg of you!"

"No," she sighed. "You—you would turn from me—you would hate me!"

And at her words Cane burst into a peal of harsh, triumphant laughter.

XXXI

SHOWS THE TRUTH-TELLER

S peak, laidee," urged the Peruvian. "Speak—tell truth. Senos know—
he know!"

But my love was still obdurate.

"I prefer to face death," she whispered, "than to reveal the bitter truth
to you, dear."

What could I do? The others heard her words, and Cane was full of
triumph.

"I think, Miss Shand, that you should now tell whatever you know
of this complicated affair. The truth will certainly have to be threshed
out in a criminal court."

But she made no answer, standing there, swaying slightly, with her
white face devoid of expression.

"Let Senos tell you some-tings," urged the narrow-eyed native.
"When that man kill my master he fly to Lisbon. There Mrs. Petre meet
him and go London. There he become Sir Digby Kemsley, and I see
him often, often, because I crossed as stoker on same boat. He go to
Luxemburg. I follow. One day he see Grand Duke's daughter—pretty
young laidee—and somebody tell him she go to Egypt. She go, and
he follow. I wait in Marseilles. I sell my rugs, wait three, four weeks
and meet each steamer from Alexandria. At last he come with three
laidees, and go to the Louvre et Paix, where I sell my rugs outside the
café. I see he always with her—walking, driving, laughing. I want to
tell her the truth—that the man is not my master, but his assassin. Ah!
but no opportunity. They go to Paris. Then she and the laidees go to
Luxemburg, and he to London. I follow her, and stay in Luxemburg
to sell my shawls, and to see her. She drive out of the palace every day.
Once I try and speak to her, but police arrest me and keep me prison
two days—ugh! After a week she with another laidee go to Paris; then
she alone go to Carlton Hotel in London. I watch there and see Cane
call on her. He no see me—ah, no! I often watch him to his home in
Harrington Gardens; often see him with that woman Petre, and once I
saw Luis with them. I have much patience till one day the young lady
leave the hotel herself and walk along Pall Mall. I follow and stop her.

She very afraid of dark man, but I tell her no be afraid of Senos. Quick, in few words, I tell her that her friend not my master, Sir Digby—only the man who killed him. She dumbstruck. Tells me I am a liar, she will not believe. I repeat what I said, and she declares I will have to prove what I say. I tell her I am ready, and she askes me to meet her at same place and same time to-morrow. She greatly excited, and we part. Senos laughs, for he has saved young laidee—daughter of a king—from that man."

"What? You actually told her Highness!" cried Frémy in surprise.

"I told her how my master had been killed by that man—with the snake—and I warned her to avoid him. But she hesitated to believe Senos," was the native's reply. "Of course, she not know me. That was date six January. I remember it, for that night, poor young laidee—she die. She killed!"

"What?" Edwards cried, staring at the speaker. "She was killed, you say?"

"Yes," Frémy interrupted, "Marie Bracq was the name assumed by her Highness, the daughter of the Grand Duke. She loved freedom from all the trammels of court life, and as I have told you, went about Europe with her maid as her companion, travelling in different names. Mademoiselle Marie Bracq was one that it seems she used, only we did not discover this until after her death, and after his Highness had paid the quarter of a million francs to regain the concession he had granted—money which, I believe, the French Government really supplied from their secret service fund."

"Then it was the daughter of the Grand Duke who fell a victim in Cane's flat?" I gasped in utter surprise at this latest revelation.

"Yes, m'sieur," replied Frémy. "You will recollect, when you told us at the Préfecture of the name of the victim, how dumbfounded we were."

"Ah, yes, I recollect!" I said. "I remember how your chief point-blank refused to betray the confidence reposed in him."

And to all this the assassin of Sir Digby Kemsley listened without a word, save to point to my love, and declare:

"There stands the woman who killed Marie Bracq. Arrest her!"

Phrida stood rigid, motionless as a statue.

"Yes," she exclaimed at last, with all her courage, "I—I will speak. I—I'll tell you everything. I will confess, for I cannot bear this longer. And yet, dearest," she cried, turning her face to me and looking straight into my eyes, "I love you, though I now know that after I have spoken—

WILLIAM LE QUEUX

after I have told the truth—you will despise and hate me! Ah, God alone knows how I have suffered! how I have prayed for deliverance from this. But it cannot be. I have sinned, I suppose, and I must bear just punishment."

There was silence.

We all looked at her, though the woman Petre was still lying in her chair unconscious, and upon the assassin's lips was a grim smile.

"You recollect," Phrida said, turning to me, "you remember the day when you introduced that man to me. Well, from that hour I knew no peace. He wrote to me, asking me to meet him, as he had something to tell me concerning my future. Well, I foolishly met him one afternoon in Rumpelmeyer's, in St. James's Street, when he told me that he had purchased a very important German patent for the manufacture of certain chemicals which would revolutionise prices, and would bring upon your firm inevitable ruin, as you pursued the old-fashioned methods. But, being your friend, and respecting us both, he had decided not to go further with the new process, and though he had given a large sum of money for it, he would, in our mutual interests, not allow it to be developed. Naturally, in my innocence I thanked him, and from that moment, professing great friendliness towards you, we became friends. Sometimes I met him at the houses of friends, but he always impressed upon me the necessity of keeping our acquaintance a secret."

And she paused, placing her hand upon her heart as though to stay its throbbing.

"One afternoon," she resumed, "the day of the tragedy, I received a telegram urging me to meet him without fail at five o'clock at Rumpelmeyer's. This I did, when he imparted to me a secret—that you, dear, were in the habit of meeting, at his flat, a foreign woman named Marie Bracq, daughter of a hair-dresser in the Edgware Road; that you, whom I loved, were infatuated with her, and—and that—"

"The liar!" I cried.

"He told me many things which naturally excited me, and which, loving you as I did, drove me to madness. I refused at first to heed his words, for somehow I mistrusted him—I know not why! But he offered to give me proof. If I went that night, or early in the morning, to Harrington Gardens, I would find her there, and I might question her. Imagine my state of mind after what he had revealed to me. I promised I would come there in secret, and I went home, my mind full of the lies and suspicion which he had, I now see, so cleverly suggested. I didn't then know him to be an assassin, but, mistrusting him as I did, I took for my own protection the old knife from the table in the drawing-room, and concealed it inside my blouse. At one o'clock next morning I crept out of the house noiselessly, and walked to Harrington Gardens, where I opened the outer door with the latch-key he had given me. On ascending to his flat I heard voices—I heard your voice, dear—therefore I descended into the dark and waited—waited until you came down the stairs and left. I saw you, and I was mad—mad! Then I went up, and he admitted me. The trap was already laid for me. I crossed that threshold to my doom!"

"How?" I asked in my despair. "Tell me all, Phrida,—everything!"

But at this point the Peruvian, Senos, interrupted, saying:

"Let me speak, sare. I tell you," he cried quickly.

"When I speak to the lady in Pall Mall I follow her. She go that afternoon to Harrington Gardens, but there see Mrs. Petre, whom she already know. Mrs. Petre find her excited, and after questioning her, induce her to tell her what I say—that Cane he kill my master. Then Mrs. Petre say, Sir Digby away in the country—not return to London—at Paddington—till one o'clock in the morning. I listen to it all, for Senos friend of the hall-porter—eh? So young laidee she says she come late in the night—half-past one or two o'clock—and ask himself the truth. But Cane in his room all the time, of course."

"Well, Phrida?" I asked quickly. "Tell us what happened on that night when you entered."

"Yes," cried Cane sarcastically, "Lie to them—they'll believe you, of course!"

"When I entered that man took me into the sitting-room, and I sat down. Naturally I was very upset. Mrs. Petre, whom I had met before, was there, and after he had told me many things about your relations with the daughter of a hair-dresser—things which maddened me—Mrs. Petre admitted her from the adjoining room. I was mad with jealousy, loving you as I did. What happened between us I do not know. I—I only fear that—that I took the knife from my breast and, in a frenzy of madness—killed her!" And she covered her face with her hands.

"Exactly!" cried Cane. "I'm glad you have the moral courage to admit it."

"But describe exactly what occurred—as far as you know," Edwards said, pressing her.

"I know that I was in a frenzy of passion, and hysterical, perhaps," she said at last. "I recollect Mrs. Petre saying that I looked very unwell, and fetching me some smelling-salts from the next room. I smelt them, but the odour was faint and strange, and a few moments later I—well, I knew no more."

"And then—afterwards?" I asked very gravely.

"When, later on I came to my senses," she said in slow, hard tones, as though reflecting, "I found the girl whom I believed to be my rival in your affections lying on the ground. In her breast was the knife. Ah, shall I ever forget that moment when I realised what I had done! Cane was bending over me, urging me to remain calm. He told me that my rival was dead—that I had killed her and that she would not further interfere with my future. I—I saw him bend over the body, withdraw the knife, and wipe it upon his handkerchief, while that woman, his accomplice, looked on. Then he gave me back the knife, which instinctively I concealed, and bade me go quickly and noiselessly back home, promising secrecy, and declaring that both he and Mrs. Petre would say nothing—that my terrible secret was safe in their hands. I believed them, and I crept down the stairs out into the road, and walked home to Cromwell Road. I replaced the knife in the drawing-room, and I believed them until—until I knew that you guessed my secret! Then came that woman's betrayal, and I knew that my doom was sealed," she added, her chin sinking upon her breast.

"You see," laughed Cane defiantly, "that the girl admits her guilt. She was jealous of Marie Bracq, and in a frenzy of passion struck her down. Mrs. Petre was there and witnessed it. She will describe it all to you, no doubt, when she recovers."

"And what she will say is one big lie," declared Senos, coming forward again. "We all know Mrs. Petre," he laughed in his high-pitched voice; "she is your tool—she and Luis. But he become a snake-charmer and give exhibitions at music-halls. He bit by one snake at Darlington, a month ago, and die quick. Ah, yes! Senos know! Snake bite him, because he brought snake and give him to that man to bite my poor master."

"Why will Mrs. Petre tell lies, Senos?" demanded Edwards who, with Frémy, was listening with the greatest interest and putting the threads of the tangled skein together in their proper sequence.

"Because I, Senos, was at Harrington Gardens that night. I knew that the laidee I had spoken to was going there, and I feared that someting might happen, for Cane a desperate man when charged with the truth."

"You were there!" I gasped. "What do you know?"

"Well, this," said the narrow-eyed man who had hunted down the assassin of his master. "I waited outside the house—waited some hours—when about eleven Cane he came down and unfastened the door and leave it a little open. I creep in, and soon after you, Mr. Royle, you come in. I wait and see you go upstairs. Then I creep up and get out of the window on the landing and on to the roof, where I see inside Cane's room—see all that goes on. My friend, the hall-porter, he tell me this sometime before, and I find the spot where, kneeling down, I see between the blinds. I see you talk with him and I see you go. Then I see Miss Shand—she come in and Mrs. Petre, and Cane talk to her. She very excited when she meet young laidee, and Mrs. Petre she give her bottle to smell. Then she faint off. The laidee, daughter of great Duke, she say something to Cane. He furious. She repeat what I say to her. Then Mrs. Petre, who had given Miss Shand the smelling-salts, find knife in her breast and secretly puts it into Cane's hand. In a moment Cane strikes the young lady with it—ah! full in the chest—and she sinks on the floor—dead! It went into her heart. Cane and the woman Petre talk in low whispers for few minutes, both very afraid. Then Miss Shand she wakes, opens her eyes, and sees the young laidee dead on the floor. She scream, but Mrs. Petre puts her hand over her mouth. Cane take out the knife, wipe it, and after telling her something, Miss Shand creep away. Oh, yes, Senos he see it all! Miss Shand quite innocent—she do nothing. Cane kill daughter of the great Duke—he with his own hand—he kill her. Senos saw him—with his own eyes!"

"Ah!" I cried, rushing towards the native, and gripping both his brown hands. "Thank you, Senos, for those words. You have saved the woman I love, for you are an eye-witness to that man's crime which with such subtle ingenuity he has endeavoured to fasten upon her, and would have succeeded had it not been for your dogged perseverance and astuteness."

"He kill my master," replied the Peruvian simply. "I watch him and convict him. He bad assassin, gentlemens—very bad man!"

XXXII

Is the Conclusion

D o you really believe that man?" asked Cane, turning to us quite coolly, a sarcastic smile upon his lips.

He was a marvellous actor, for he now betrayed not the slightest confusion. He even laughed at the allegations made against him. His bold defiance utterly amazed us. Yet we knew now how resourceful and how utterly unscrupulous he was.

"Yes, I do!" was the officer's reply. "You murdered her Highness, fearing that she should go to her father and expose you before you could have time to dispose of your stolen concession to him. Had she gone to him, the police would hunt you down as Sir Digby's assassin. But by closing her lips you hoped to be able to sell back the concession and still preserve your guilty secret."

"Of course," remarked Frémy, "the whole affair is now quite plain. Poor Miss Shand was drawn into the net in order to become this scoundrel's victim. He intended from the first to make use of her in some way, and did so at last by making her believe she had killed her alleged rival in Mr. Royle's affection. Truly this man is a clever and unscrupulous scoundrel, for he succeeded in obtaining a quarter of a million francs from a reigning sovereign for a document, to obtain which he had committed a foul and dastardly crime!"

"A lie—lies, all of it!" shouted the accused angrily, his face as white as paper.

"Oh, do not trouble," laughed Frémy, speaking in French. "You will have an opportunity to make your defence before the judge—you and your ingenious accomplice, Mrs. Petre."

"We want her in England for the attempted murder of Mr. Royle," Edwards remarked. "I'll apply for her extradition to-morrow. Your chief will, no doubt, decide to keep Cane here—at least, for the present. We shall want him for the murder of the Englishman, Sir Digby Kemsley."

"You may want me," laughed the culprit with an air of supreme defiance, "but you'll never have me! Oh, no, no! I'll remain over here, and leave you wanting me."

"Prisoner, what is the use of these denials and this defiance?" asked Frémy severely in French, advancing towards him. "You are in my custody—and under the law of the Kingdom of Belgium I arrest you for the murder of Sir Digby Kemsley, in Peru, and for the murder of Stephanie, daughter of his Highness the Grand Duke of Luxemburg." Then, turning to his two subordinates, he added briefly: "Put the handcuffs on him! He may give trouble!"

"Handcuffs! Ha, ha!" cried Senos the Peruvian, laughing and snapping his brown fingers in the prisoner's face. "It is my triumph now. Senos has avenged the death of his poor, good master!"

"A moment," exclaimed the prisoner. "I may at least be permitted to secure my papers before I leave here, and hand them over to you? They will, perhaps, interest you," he said quite coolly. Then he took from his watch-chain a small key, and with it opened a little cupboard in the wall, from whence he took a small, square deed-box of japanned tin, which he placed upon the table before us.

With another and smaller key, and with a slight grin upon his face, he opened the lid, but a cry of dismay escaped us, for next second we saw that he held in his hand a small, black object, sinuous and writhing—a small, thin, but highly venomous black snake!

It was over in an instant, ere we could realise the truth. Upon his white wrist I saw a tiny bead of blood, where the reptile had struck and bitten him, and as he flung it back into the box and banged down the lid he turned upon us in defiance, and said:

"Now take me! I am ready," he cried, uttering a peal of fiendish laughter. "Carry me where you will, for in a few moments I shall be dead. Ah! yes, my good friends! I have played the great game—and lost. Yet I've cheated you all, as I always declared that I would."

The two men sprang forward to slip the metal gyves upon his wrists, but Frémy, noticing the instant change in the assassin's countenance, motioned them off.

The culprit's face grew ashen grey, his thin jaws were fixed. He tried to utter some further words, but no sound came from him, only a low gurgle.

We stood by and watched. He placed both his palms to his brow and stood for a few seconds in the centre of the room. Then a paroxysm of pain seemed to double him completely up, and he fell to the carpet writhing in most fearful agony. It was horrible to witness, and Phrida, with a cry, turned away.

Then suddenly he lay stiff, and stretched his limbs to such an

WILLIAM LE QUEUX

extent that we could hear the bones crack. His back became arched, and then he expired with horrible convulsions, which held his limbs stiffened and extended to their utmost limits—truly, the most awful and agonising of deaths, and a torture in the last moments that must have been excruciating—a punishment worse, indeed, than any that man-made law might allow.

As Herbert Cane paid the penalty of his crimes the woman Petre at last recovered consciousness.

I saw the look of abject terror upon her face as her eyes fell upon the man lying dead upon the carpet before us.

She realised the terrible truth at once, and giving vent to a loud, hysterical scream, rose and threw herself on her knees beside the man whose wide-open eyes, staring into space, were fast glazing in death.

Edwards bent, and asked in a low voice whether I wished to give her into custody for the attempt upon me.

But I replied in the negative.

"The assassin has received his just punishment and must answer to his Maker," I replied. "That is enough. This scene will assuredly be a lesson to her."

"She falsely accused Miss Shand, remember," he said. "She knew all the time that Cane struck the poor girl down."

"No," I replied. "Now that the stigma has been removed from the one I love, I will be generous. I will prefer no charge against her."

"Ah! dearest," cried Phrida, "I am glad of that. Let us forgive, and endeavour, if possible, to forget these dark, black days and weeks when both our lives were blighted, and the future seemed so hopeless and full of tragedy."

"Yes," I said, "let us go forth and forget."

And with a last glance at the dead man, with the woman with dishevelled hair kneeling in despair at his side, I took the arm of my beloved, and kissing her before them all, led her out, away from the scene so full of bitterness and horror.

To further prolong the relation of this tragic chapter of my life's history would serve no purpose.

What more need I tell you than to say Mrs. Petre disappeared entirely, apparently thankful to escape, and that at St. Mary Abbots, in Kensington, a month ago, Phrida and I became man and wife, both Edwards and Frémy being present.

As I pen these final lines I am sitting upon the balcony of the great Winter Palace Hotel, in Luxor, within sight of the colossal ruins of Karnak, for we are spending a delightful honeymoon in Upper Egypt, that region where the sun always shines and rain never falls. Phrida, in her thin white cotton gown and white sun helmet, though it is January, is seated beside me, her little hand in mine. Below us, in the great garden, rise the high, feathery palms, above a riot of roses and poinsettias, magnolias, and other sweet-smelling flowers.

It is the silent, breathless hour of the desert sunset. Before us, away beyond the little strip of vegetation watered by the broad, ever-flowing Nile, the clear, pale green sky is aflame with crimson, a sunset mystic and wonderful, such as one only sees in Egypt, that golden land of the long-forgotten.

From somewhere behind comes up the long-drawn nasal song of an Arab boatman—that quaint, plaintive, sing-song rhythm accompanied by a tom-tom, which encourages the rowers to bend at their oars, while away still further behind across the river, lays the desolate ruins of the once-powerful Thebes, and that weird, arid wilderness which is so impressive—the Valley of the Tombs of the Kings.

Phrida has been reading what I have here written, and as I kiss her sweet lips, she looks lovingly into my eyes and says:

"It is enough, dearest. Say that you and I are happy—ah! so supremely happy at last, in each other's love. No pair in the whole world could trust each other as we have done. I know that I was guilty of a very grave fault—the fault of concealing my friendship with that man from you. But I foolishly thought I was acting in your interests—that being your friend, he was mine also. I never dreamed that such a refined face could hide so black and vile a heart."

"But I have forgiven all, darling," I hasten to reassure her! "I know now what a clever and ingenious scoundrel that man was, and how full of resource and amazing cunning. You were his victim, just as I was myself—just as were the others. No," I add, "life, love, and happiness are before us. So let us learn to forget."

And as our lips meet once again in a long, fond, passionate caress, I lay down my pen in order to press her more closely to my breast.

She is mine—my own beloved—mine for now and evermore.

THE END

A Note About the Author

William Le Queux (1864–1927) was an Anglo-French journalist, novelist, and radio broadcaster. Born in London to a French father and English mother, Le Queux studied art in Paris and embarked on a walking tour of Europe before finding work as a reporter for various French newspapers. Towards the end of the 1880s, he returned to London where he edited *Gossip* and *Piccadilly* before being hired as a reporter for *The Globe* in 1891. After several unhappy years, he left journalism to pursue his creative interests. Le Queux made a name for himself as a leading writer of popular fiction with such espionage thrillers as *The Great War in England in 1897* (1894) and *The Invasion of 1910* (1906). In addition to his writing, Le Queux was a notable pioneer of early aviation and radio communication, interests he maintained while publishing around 150 novels over his decades long career.

A Note from the Publisher

Spanning many genres, from non-fiction essays to literature classics to children's books and lyric poetry, Mint Edition books showcase the master works of our time in a modern new package. The text is freshly typeset, is clean and easy to read, and features a new note about the author in each volume. Many books also include exclusive new introductory material. Every book boasts a striking new cover, which makes it as appropriate for collecting as it is for gift giving. Mint Edition books are only printed when a reader orders them, so natural resources are not wasted. We're proud that our books are never manufactured in excess and exist only in the exact quantity they need to be read and enjoyed.

Discover more of your favorite classics with Bookfinity™.

- Track your reading with custom book lists.
- Get great book recommendations for your personalized Reader Type.
- Add reviews for your favorite books.
- AND MUCH MORE!

Visit **bookfinity.com** and take the fun Reader Type quiz to get started.

Enjoy our classic and modern companion pairings!

Bookfinity is a registered trademark of Ingram Book Group LLC. © 2023 Bookfinity. All rights reserved.